MURDER AT THE WILLOWS

A gripping cozy crime mystery full of twists

JANE ADAMS

A Rina Martin Mystery Book 8

Joffe Books, London
www.joffebooks.com

First published in Great Britain in 2023

Cover art by Dee Dee Book Covers

ISBN: 978-1-80405-716-2

PROLOGUE

June 1980

When the police arrived, the house had been unnaturally silent. They knew, from the neighbour who had summoned them, that there were children in the house. Children and the mother and the young man who had been lodging with them.

"Three children, including the little baby. The chap they're looking after, William, he's a bit . . . slow, you know, but seems harmless enough."

The officer had heard the weight of implication in the word 'seems'.

"The husband?"

"Well, I thought he was at work till I heard the shouting and the screaming and the breaking glass," she said. "I'm sure I heard his voice."

The two officers sent in the panda car had assumed they were going to a domestic. They'd arrived, they hoped to a situation already calmed down, planned to say a few words about disturbing the peace and leave. Now, approaching the silent house, through the small gate in the tall privet hedge they realise that their assumptions were probably going to

1

be wrong. The first sign of trouble was the small, red, transistor radio smashed on the garden path close by the gate. It looked as though someone had hurled it through an upstairs window. That, presumably, accounted for the breaking glass.

Not a sound came from the large, impressive but slightly run-down house. Then as they came through the gate and rounded the high and overgrown privet they saw the man. He was seated on the highest of the three steps that led up to the open front door, sitting incongruously between two large blue hydrangeas in massive terracotta pots.

He was covered in blood and a knife, long and broad and also heavily bloodied, lay at his feet. Blood, visible through the open door, also covered the hall floor behind him.

He looked up as the officers, more than a little afraid, approached cautiously.

But the man did not move. He was crying, tears pouring down the bloodied face and on to his reddened hands. "It's all my fault," he said. "I'm so sorry. It's all my fault."

CHAPTER 1

Present day

It was so good to be back, Rina Martin thought. She had been away filming the Christmas Special of *Lydia Marchant Investigates* and could not help but feel that having a Christmas Special on the back of two successful new series was a real marker of the series having re-established itself. Lydia Marchant, the first time round, had run for close on fifteen years and was still unfolding its mysteries on one channel or another most days of the week. Rina had thought she had retired after that, buying her beloved Peverill Lodge, a tall Victorian boarding house in Frantham on Sea and filling it with much loved permanent lodgers. She had been perfectly happy in her retirement but was ecstatic at the relaunch and very happy to be working again.

Today, however, was a day for walking on the beach, eating ice cream and catching up with friends.

Charmouth beach was a stony affair but good for fossils. Since Rina had moved to the Jurassic coast she had taken to collecting specimens of the local, long extinct wildlife. Her own much-loved beach at Frantham seemed to have missed out of the bounty of Lyme Bay and Charmouth, being a mix of sand and quite ordinary pebbles. The small town lay low between tall headlands and Rina suspected that the Jurassic strata dived deeper beneath the surface at Frantham, destined to be lost to the casual fossil hunter.

So today Charmouth was the beach of choice and Tim and Joy her chosen companions. Tim had spent several years living at Peverill Lodge — though he was younger than the rest of the inhabitants by many decades. Joy, his fiancée, had dropped precipitously into their lives when her father had been killed by business rivals (Mr Duggan was in *that* kind of business) and Joy had been kidnapped. It had been several weeks since Rina had seen these two young people that she regarded as the children she had never had.

"Ice cream," Joy said with a smile, handing Rina a cone. "Complete with flake and raspberry sauce." Joy, Rina noted, had opted for the same.

"Tim's being all grown up," Joy continued. "Decided he just wanted a choc ice."

"Is that grown up?" Tim queried. "It's still ice cream." He sighed, a contented sound, Rina thought.

"So, what have the pair of you been up to?"

They walked slowly along the beach, pausing to pick up bits of ammonite and the ferritic pebbles that so fascinated Tim. "Do you think," Tim asked, "I could actually smelt some of these and cast them into a wand?"

Rina laughed; it was the sort of question a child might ask. But as Tim was a professional magician it did make a kind of sense.

"Could you polish it?" Joy asked. "It might be a bit bland, otherwise. And wouldn't it be a bit heavy? I can just imagine you tapping something with it and forgetting you'd got an iron wand and splat! Scrambled eggs, or worse, a scrambled rabbit or a brained dove."

"Have you started incorporating animals into your act?" Rina asked. "I thought you'd given up on the rabbits when you stopped doing kids parties."

She heard Joy giggle and Tim shuddered at the memory. He'd never really been cut out to be a children's entertainer but when he was trying to get his career started would take what work he could get. He'd finally given up on the magical clown act following a dramatic choking incident . . .

"Never again, Rina," he said. "No rabbits, no doves, no kids and definitely no clown wigs."

Rina recalled the ceremonial burning of the clown nose and bright orange wig after Tim's last children's party. It had, she thought, been a relief to all concerned when Tim had stopped doing those gigs.

"Is it true there's going to be a special screening of your Christmas episode at the Palisades?" Joy asked.

"And where did you hear that?" Rina pretended to look askance, then smiled. "It's still supposed to be under wraps."

"Oh, Rina. You know Frantham, you know how people gossip. So, is it?"

"It's yet to be signed off, but yes. That's the plan."

Tim licked the rest of the ice cream from his fingers and then accepted the wet wipe Rina handed to him.

"You are such a child," she said.

"Well, I think it's very exciting," Joy said. "And then Tim's creating something really spectacular for Christmas and New Year, aren't you?"

"Apparently," Tim agreed. He didn't look too confident about that and Rina decided it might be time to change the subject.

"So, the only people I've not caught up with are George and Ursula. How are they?"

"Suffering through the last of their A-level exams," Joy said. "Can you believe they'll both be eighteen in a few weeks? We've got all sorts of birthday stuff planned—"

"Whether they like it or not," Tim added. "No, I think they're both OK. Just drowning in schoolwork and jobs and finding it all a bit hard at the moment. Ursula's got her uni place sorted, depending on results, of course, but we all know she'll walk her exams, so . . . she's staying local, which is good. At least she'll have less problems about where to live."

5

"Couldn't she move into student accommodation?" Rina asked.

"That would be OK, but most of it is only available in term time. She can hardly go home for the holidays, can she? She could come and stay with us or I know she could stay with you, but now she's got a place to stay, she wants to hang on to it."

"I can understand that," Rina said. George and Ursula had been in care since their early teens. They had left the children's home for what the council called transitional accommodation the year before. As Rina understood it, they could stay there until they were twenty-one, by which time Ursula should have graduated. What was supposed to happen then was anybody's guess.

George, not being so academically inclined, had opted for an apprenticeship. More studying, but also paid work . . . Rina could not help but worry about the two of them, though she knew that she and Tim and Joy and her precious friends at Peverill Lodge would help out in any way they could.

Rina bit through the last piece of her ice cream cone and threw the final, soggy end to a passing seagull. "Now," she said. "Let's see what the beach has to offer in the way of fossils today."

CHAPTER 2

Twenty months ago

Though the Covid restrictions on numbers of guests at funerals had eased, Sarah was grateful for the reticence still felt by many of their older neighbours and the perfect excuse this gave her for not even attempting to have a wake in her mother's memory. The neighbours had been nice. The day she had come back from the hospital, clutching the little bag of her mother's belongings they had come out on to the front doorstep and asked if there was anything they could do. Later on, Carol had come round and brought her a casserole so she wouldn't have to cook. Sarah thanked her and was also acutely aware that this small act of kindness would not have happened had her mother still been alive. Neither would it have been accepted; Constance ate only the food her daughter had prepared and would not even countenance an occasional meal out. The restrictions during lockdown and just after had just cemented her suspicions of the outside world and Sarah had to fight really hard just to convince her mother she really did have to go back to work. That they needed the money.

They did, but more than that, Sarah needed the few hours, four days a week, when she could be out of the house.

Everyone had seemed intent on being kind. There'd been sympathy cards pushed through the door and phone calls but truthfully, Sarah thought, what could anyone say?

Or, at least, what could anyone say that was in the least bit truthful. Constance Fredericks, nee Tatum, Sarah's mother, had been a horrible woman and what those neighbours really wanted to say was probably good riddance. To tell Sarah she was free now, that she would not have to be domineered and bullied, and that she could now have a life of her own.

Whatever that was supposed to mean.

Was she sorry that the restrictions meant she could not be at her mother's bedside when she had died? Honestly, she didn't know the answer to that one. All she could say with certainty was that those final days in the house on her own had felt so horribly uncomfortable she could hardly bear it. She felt haunted by the presence of the woman who was no longer there. The woman who had dominated Sarah's life for all of her forty years, telling her what to wear and what to think and what to do, resenting even the time Sarah was at work. She had long since learned not to talk about work once she'd got home. She never went to office parties or met colleagues socially. She was never even late home.

Those few days with her mother absent and in hospital she had come to realise that even the house dominated her. Her mother's presence permeated the walls, poured out through the taps, scented the air — talcum and sour breath and the perfume she had used since she was seventeen, worn like a badge because it was the first nice thing she'd been able to buy for herself.

And underlying it all, that unceasing anger, that resolute bitterness she felt at life having cheated her, and Sarah the living symbol of all of that.

Despite everything, a few people had come to the funeral anyway and afterwards offered words of sympathy and condolence and she had returned to the house with a sense of profound relief. The sight of her mother's coffin rolling slowly through the looped-back curtains and into the flames, Sarah supposed had been . . . had been what? Stunning. Ecstatic. Devastating? All she could think was that her mother always told her that fire was cleansing. That the flames drove out the evil.

Sarah had the scars that proved the power of her mother's conviction on that score.

She stood now in the centre of the small kitchen wondering if she had the energy to make herself a cup of tea when the doorbell rang.

Who the hell was that? Please, not Carol with another casserole. She didn't object to the gift of a meal, just the need to make conversation that accompanied it.

Sighing, she went to the door. Opened it. Stared hard at the man standing outside.

"Hello Sarah," Clive Tatum said.

She hadn't wanted to let him in — technically she supposed it might be allowed but she was so unused to anyone coming into her mother's domain that it felt wrong even now she was gone. But Clive, her mother's cousin and a man whose journalistic career had made him immune to the discomfort of others, was inside the house and inspecting the living room almost before she realised it.

"You shouldn't be here. What are you doing here? Mother would never allow . . ."

"Allow me over the threshold? No, I don't suppose she would. But then, I'd not want to be here if the old harridan was still around." He smiled at Sarah. It was an insincere curving of the lips, she thought, not a genuine expression.

"It can't have been easy, putting up with her all these years."

"What would you know about it?" she replied, defensively.

"Oh, you're forgetting. I knew her a long time ago. My little cousin, as was. I can't imagine she'd have changed all that much."

He cocked his head on one side reminding Sarah of a large, grey muzzled dog. Though, she thought, dogs generally had more integrity.

"Such a pretty thing, she was. Knew it, of course, and no one could blame her for making full use of that. Not knowing what she'd gone through as a youngster. But you'd think that would have made her a better parent, somehow, when it came to be her turn."

"You know nothing about that."

"Don't I?"

He was looking at her in that appraising manner she had noted from the moment she had opened the door. Comparing her, no doubt, to the image he carried of her mother — small, curvaceous, blonde and very pretty. Sarah knew herself to be plain. Square, was what her mother always told her. Square jaw, a squared-off body. Solidly built. Not fat but just very sturdy, like a carthorse.

She watched as he switched his attention from her and let his gaze travel around the room. The small desk with the laptop, the filing cabinet, the photographs, the books, the Murano glass in gaudy colours on the sideboard, the photographs from when her mother had been a young woman. She knew instinctively what he was seeing. There was nothing of Sarah in this room. Very little of her in the rest of the house either. Only in her own bedroom were a few personal possessions hidden beneath the bed. When Sarah had been a child even that had not been a safe hiding place but as her mother had aged, growing old before her time and then growing ill, at least according to her own reckoning, and then becoming ill in a real, diagnosable way, she had ceased to be able to search her daughter's room for signs of disobedience.

Other small, precious items; birthday and Christmas gifts from work colleagues or little things she had managed to buy for herself by sneaking tiny sums from the housekeeping, like the nail polish she had bought and never dared to use. The lipstick she had purchased one lunchtime because it had been on sale and the colour reminded her of the scented pink roses in a garden she passed on her way home. These were hidden in her locker at work.

It occurred to Sarah for the first time that she could bring these things home now. That she could—

For a moment she had almost forgotten about her visitor. He had been watching her, she realised, as though reading her thoughts.

"It must have been hard, growing up among ghosts," he said quietly. "Time to exorcise them, perhaps."

She looked at him in surprise at the sympathy in his tone. But his eyes were not sympathetic, they were acquisitive, covetous. "What would you know about that?" she asked again. "And look, I don't understand what's brought you here. You couldn't stand my mother so I don't think you've come to offer your condolences?"

He laughed at that. "No, indeed. But now she's gone I have come to ask you for something. Something that might benefit the both of us," he said. "I'll pay, of course. No doubt you could do with the money."

"Pay? Pay for what?"

"Information, my dear. What else. I've followed your mother's efforts over the years. To get compensation, to get her side of the story told. I offered to do that for her. Did she ever tell you that? But no, that would have been to surrender control. But I told her, if she wanted her side of the story to come out, to be told properly then she ought to trust me." He smiled at her again but it didn't touch his eyes. "But maybe you have more sense. Potentially there's money in this story, Sarah. Maybe you and I could—"

"Please Clive, don't. Whatever it is you want, I can't help. I won't. You might not understand this but the last thing I need right now is to have to rake over all that stuff. She's gone now. I just want a little bit of peace. An ordinary life, the sort that other people have."

Her legs felt weak as though Clive's presence, the things he was interested in had suddenly returned to weigh her down. Just for a brief time she had allowed herself to hope that her mother's dictatorial influence was really over and she could have a separate existence of her own. It was as though he had come to tell her that was an impossible hope, that she was still inexorably tied to her mother's needs and wishes and prohibitions.

"Please leave me alone, Clive. I want nothing to do with this."

"You don't even know what I want."

He sighed. "Believe me, my dear cousin, we can none of us just walk away from these things. You either lay the ghosts by exposing them to the light, or they'll pursue you for the rest of your life. Come on, Sarah, you know that as well as I do."

"No," she said. "I don't know that." She sat down in one of the green moquette armchairs her mother had liked so much and shook her head. "Look, Clive, I think you should go. You might want to muckrake, all I want is a bit of peace. I want to . . . to have a bit of a holiday. To be able to go out and know I don't have to be back at a particular time. To go with my friends to the pub after work, to—"

"Do you really have friends, Sarah?" he cut in. "Did she let you have friends? Do you really know them or are they just work colleagues who invite you to go out with them just to be polite?"

Sarah felt like she'd been slapped. Hard. He was right, of course and that was why his words fell so heavy and so hard. But they could be her friends now, couldn't they?

With a massive effort she got up and walked to the front door, trying not to show him how much her limbs were shaking or how hard she was finding it to speak. "Go now, please. Clive, I'd just like you to leave now."

He smiled at her, totally unfazed. Shrugged as though it really didn't matter to him. "A shame to take that attitude," he said, "when both of us could benefit."

Sarah didn't look at him as he brushed by her and stepped out through the front door. She closed it quietly behind him, leaned against it, exhaustion flooding her body.

Her mother would be furious, Sarah thought dimly. Furious with her cousin, Clive, for coming into her house.

More furious still at her daughter for letting him in and if she'd even suspected that Sarah might have been tempted by his vague offer . . .

Fire cleanses, Sarah thought. That's what she'd say. Fire keeps the evil thoughts at bay. It's what bad children deserve.

Slowly, Sarah got to her feet, went through to the kitchen and turned on the gas.

CHAPTER 3

Cal Hammond got out of the car and walked across the loose gravel of the drive, and then on to the ancient brick path that led around to the back of the house. He remembered how it had been, the first time they had seen this place and how he had known this would be their home. He had been ten years old had lived with Jean only for a short time. They were, he remembered, still getting used to one another and his grief for his parents was still raw and painful.

It had been a bright day, but frosty, winter bright, not this soft, late spring sunshine. The garden glistened with silvered spider webs and the remnants of summer flowers that no one had bothered to cut back, the low sun turning the overgrown and untidy plot into some kind of wonderland. They had both looked at the winter wonderland of a garden and known that this would be home.

He took the steps, two at a time, and entered the space above the garage that had become her studio. Windows with a view of the garden and the fields beyond, skylights in the roof. Cal recalled the times they had lain there on the floor, gazing up at the stars. Lately, Jean had complained that she was now too stiff and old to lie on the floor so he had brought her a lightweight recliner chair to use on stargazing evenings.

He'd had Sandy, her gardener come handyman, put locking castors on it so she could move it around. Spotting it now he realised with a pang that he had no idea if the chair ever got used. Work and home with his partner, Etta, took him away for far too long and far too often, though when he and Jean had spoken the evening before she had said how much she was looking forward to his visit.

"Jean?" he called her name as though she might be somewhere out of sight, despite the fact that the entire room could be taken in at a glance.

He took a moment to admire the finished piece sitting on the easel. The three women, he assumed was some variation on the maiden, mother, crone tradition, their bodies turning in some complex dance, the touches of gold leaf on the clothing and the hint of wings that reminded him of renaissance angels. This was a commission, a wedding gift, he remembered and hoped that the women it was intended for would love it as much as he did. But then, he was a sucker for Jean's work.

He was a sucker for Jean, really.

So, where the hell was she?

He went back down the stairs and into the garden. Down at the bottom end, close to the old tree and the tyre swing left from when he was just a kid, he saw her. She was sitting with her back to the tree resting against a cushion, legs outstretched, hands in her lap.

For a moment he thought she must have fallen asleep.

"Jean?" he touched her hand and then her cheek. "Jean? No, no, no!"

The hand and the cheek were still warm and the eyes were half closed and almost he could convince himself that there was nothing wrong. Almost . . .

He called her name again, shouted it, felt frantically for a pulse but the realistic part of his brain screamed with the horror of it. Jean was dead. She was gone.

CHAPTER 4

In the days that followed Jean's death Cal found it very difficult to remember what had happened next. He had found Jean mid-afternoon and the next clear memory he had was from around 9 o'clock that evening when Etta, had virtually forced him to eat something. He could not remember getting home and even now could not recall what he had eaten, just the act of sitting down and Etta putting the tray on his lap and threatening to spoon-feed him if he didn't do it on his own.

But the intervening time remained fragmentary, small episodes in sharp relief while the rest remained blurred and faded. He knew that he had called the police and also asked for an ambulance, even though he knew it was a pointless thing to do. He must have remembered at some point that Jean had seen her doctor only a couple of days previously and checked the list next to the phone for his number. He knew he had done this because Dr Carter arrived just as the ambulance was leaving, without Jean on board, and another doctor that the GP introduced as the police surgeon was kneeling beside Jean's body.

He remembered Dr Carter squatting down beside this stranger and talking to him and then going across and talking to the two police officers who were standing by the car. Then the male officer left, with the car, and the woman remained behind.

"My name is Yolanda," she told him.

"Yolanda." It was strange, he supposed, but Cal could remember exactly what he was thinking at that moment; that Yolanda was an unusual name, that he had never met a Yolanda before and that this small fair-haired woman did not look like a Yolanda. She looked like a Sarah, or a Nora or even a Ruby. His mind had seemed to play with these possibilities and he realised abruptly and uncomfortably that he was staring at her.

"Perhaps you should sit down," she said and then hesitated as though she wasn't quite sure where he should sit, given that she wasn't certain what was going on and that this might not, after all, be an ordinary, sudden death. That this peaceful garden might be a crime scene. Or at least that's what he'd thought the hesitation was all about. Cal had realised that the idea was forming in his mind that Jean had not died naturally, that something looked wrong, but he could not figure out what it was.

In the end she led him to a low retaining wall and he perched in among the rosemary and lavender, breathing the familiar scents and unable to take his eyes from the place where Jean sat, her back against the tree with a cushion behind her and another beneath, and her feet stretched straight. She had slumped a little as though she had fallen asleep and it was still hard for him to accept that this woman who had been at the centre of his life since he was ten years old really was gone.

The next fragment was the police surgeon getting to his feet and then the GP coming across to Cal and asking quietly if he was OK, which had seemed like such a stupid question then and an even stupider one in retrospect, but he must have nodded or said yes or something. And then Dr Carter speaking to this Yolanda and telling her that as far as he was concerned it was a natural death, that he had warned Jean only the day before that her heart was getting weaker, that she was simply wearing out.

Cal remembered that she had told him as much on the telephone when he had called to find out how this routine consultation had gone. Dr Carter had sent her to the hospital a few weeks previously but they had both known that her angina was much worse, and that, as Jean had put it "at ninety-five, I suppose the mechanism is bound to be a bit rusty". He remembered the feeling of shock when she had mentioned her age; Jean never talked about her age even though she enthusiastically celebrated her birthdays. It was, she said, only a number and what mattered was that she'd made it through another fruitful year. She had always declared that she would be working until the very end; that they would have to pry the paintbrush out of her hands.

And that had almost been the case. She must have just finished the painting then come out into the garden, sat down and died.

"She's holding something in her hand," Cal said to Yolanda. "I didn't like to . . . but."

"You want me to take a look?" Yolanda asked.

Cal remembered that she been perceptibly uncomfortable at this and glanced at Dr Carter and then the two of them left him and went back to the body and he saw Dr Carter gently lift Jean's hand and extract whatever was inside. He saw Yolanda take a bag out of her pocket and put whatever it was into the clear plastic packet and then they both came over to him again. Yolanda showed him the crushed flowers and leaves and he wondered briefly why she had placed them in what was he presumed an evidence bag.

"She must've been deadheading," Dr Carter said. "Had one of her funny turns and sat down."

A funny turn, the way Jean always described her dizzy spells. POTS was the technical term. Positional Orthostatic Tachycardia Syndrome.

"Why the evidence bag?" Cal was aware that his voice was croaky and his throat was dry.

Yolanda flushed pink as though suddenly embarrassed at what she had done. "Just habit, I guess. Sorry. I didn't mean to upset you."

"You said it was natural causes." Cal looked more closely at Dr Carter and the man just nodded.

"We knew her heart would fail, we knew this day would come. That she survived this long is remarkable."

"She'd just finished the last commission," Cal said. "It's beautiful."

He remembered then that a van had arrived, a scientific support vehicle and two people got out, a man and a young woman. Dr Carter and Yolanda spoke to them and then the man in the van returned to the vehicle and the young woman was talking on her mobile. And then there was another visitor, a very young girl in a small car and she looked shocked and horrified. Someone told him she had come for a drawing lesson and Cal had been surprised because he hadn't thought Jean did any teaching these days. And then he was told the mortuary ambulance was on its way but that it might take a while and then, blessings of blessings, Etta. She had taken his arm and got him into the car and spoken to the people milling around and then she had driven him home.

And so, he had eaten and he had felt better and she had given him tea and he'd felt his thoughts begin to settle, become less fragmentary. And it was at that point he realised what it was that had bothered him.

"Where was her stick?" he'd asked.

"Her stick? You mean her walking stick?"

He nodded. "She was sitting under the willow tree, but she didn't have her walking stick. How did she get to the willow tree without her walking stick?"

Etta frowned. "You know as well as I do that sometimes she would get an idea into her head and wouldn't think about what she needed or whether she should be doing it or not. You know how hard it was getting her to use the perching stool in the studio. She was convinced she could stand for just as long as she had been able to when she was twenty. If she spotted something in the garden that needed doing, then—"

"She always needed her stick in the garden. On uneven ground."

"You know that and I know that, so did Jean, that didn't mean she always used it."

He nodded, knowing that Etta was right but also knowing that since Etta had last seen Jean, she had become far frailer. He could not believe that she had walked all that way down the garden without her walking stick.

As though following his thoughts Etta said, "It's possible she dropped it, if she suddenly felt ill and dizzy and just managed to get to the tree. She loved to sit there you know that."

"She was sitting on a cushion, and there was one behind her."

Etta shrugged. "I'm not sure I understand what your point is. We bought her those waterproof ones to put on the bench seat so it didn't matter if she left them outside, you remember? We picked them up when we got her those two folding chairs. Maybe she had someone put them under the tree for her."

"Maybe," Cal agreed. He asked himself why would he want to think that Jean's death had been anything more than a sudden heart attack, something for which, as Dr Carter had reminded him, they had prepared themselves after her two serious attacks in previous years. Did she have her medication with her? Most likely it was in her cardigan pocket, she was at least pretty good at remembering that. He decided that it was almost easier to believe someone had *taken* Jean's life than that the end had come from something as banal and ordinary as an ageing heart. Perhaps he thought, that was all it was, this feeling of something wrong, something off. He'd realised he was too exhausted to deal with any more thinking that night and told himself he would talk to the police officers and the doctors and anyone else who might be able to shed light.

"Will there be a post-mortem?" Etta asked.

"Dr Carter said probably not. Or if there is it would just be a cursory one to make sure it was her heart. I've got to admit

I don't like the idea of Jean being cut up. She's been under medical supervision all this time, she only saw him yesterday for one of her regular check-ups and so I don't think it will be necessary. The police only came because I called them. If I'd just phoned Dr Carter he would probably have signed the certificate and called the undertaker or whatever they do and that would have been that." He realised he had only a vague idea of what the process was. Jean's death had been sudden, but expected, so he supposed it was not a suspicious death in any kind of legal way. It was only shocking because despite all the contrary evidence he had somehow expected her to go on forever.

* * *

Sarah had put her mother's house on the market as soon as possible after the funeral. She was thankful that the house had been left to her in the end — her mother had threatened to cut her out of her will often enough — but had not been prepared for the clause in the will that stated any profit from the house was to be used to pursue Connie's war of attrition through the courts.

Sarah could have cried. If she had hoped the money from the house could have provided her with a fresh start then her mother had so obviously been determined to scupper that.

She found herself a bedsit in what seemed to be a respectable, converted house and the day after she moved in went to a solicitor that a work colleague had recommended to ask for some advice. She left all of her mother's paperwork with him and two weeks later returned to find a very puzzled man and a very large bill for time taken to wade through the paperwork.

"I'm confused," he said, "as to what Mrs Fredericks was hoping to gain or to prove."

"She wanted compensation," Sarah told him.

"For what exactly?"

"For the death of her brother and also for breach of promise. The man she said was my father made no provision for us. Her brother had been murdered and she held this same man responsible." Sarah shrugged helplessly. "Truthfully, I'm not sure I know what she wanted anymore."

The solicitor regarded her with professional sympathy. Sarah compared his expression with the one she recalled on Clive Tatum's face and wondered if it was any more genuine. She itched to punch the man in the face, to go on punching until the expression — any expression — was wiped permanently away.

But that would get her nowhere, would it. With effort she held the impulse in check and asked what he advised.

"Well, the man concerned is dead. He, you'll pardon me for saying, was vehement in his rejection of your mother's claims and as far as I can tell there was nothing left in his estate that she might have claimed in compensation, even if she could have proved any kind of foundation for making one."

"So —"

"So, I can file some more paperwork, request more information from prison records and from the family but I doubt we'll turn up anything new."

Sarah's heart sank. "So, you get paid for doing something which is ultimately a waste of time," she said.

"I can't deny that, no. But there is one small glimmer of hope," he added. Fortunately, for his own peace of mind, he had no idea how close he had come to Sarah deciding it might be worth punching him in the face anyway.

"What's that?" she asked wearily. Keeping her temper in check was becoming harder and harder these days. Even the cleansing of the fire was unable to help.

"Well, I've spoken to colleagues and we all agree that as there's no one to challenge this will — apart from yourself."

"No one," Sarah agreed.

"And as the wording here and there is ambiguous. I'm guessing your mother constructed this herself?"

Again, Sarah nodded.

"Then we are justified not only in not pursuing avenues that have already been exhausted and thus wasting money, but also there's some wriggle room, as it were, allowing you to draw down expenses to support your efforts."

"How does that help me?"

"Well, to put it simply, so long as you are going by the letter of the will and allowing us to pursue these claims, even in a very limited way, then so long as you add your own voice to the project, in the form of a letter of support, for instance, then you are in a position to claim expenses for those supportive actions."

Sarah looked at him in confusion. Decided that this time the sympathy and concern was probably almost genuine — albeit tempered by the man's enjoyment of his own cleverness.

"What I'm saying," he told her, "is that so long as we keep a trickle of money going into the fulfilment of your mother's wishes, you can claim expenses against that. And there is nothing to stop those expenses being greater than the amount we spend in pursuit of the claim."

Sarah took this in. "You can do that?"

He shrugged. "It's irregular, but as there are no other persons impacted who might object, I'm sure we can come to some arrangement."

He had asked for some additional information and once she returned to the flat Sarah sorted through the rest of her mother's paperwork to find the missing pieces from the earlier legal processes. How much of their money had gone into this wild goose chase? Sarah wondered. What kind of life could they have had if Constance had given up these stupid ideas? If Constance had not been the woman she had become.

She had, Sarah thought, kept every tiny bit of ephemera from that earlier time. Clippings from various newspapers, relating to the lives and doings of the famous people she claimed she'd once known. Artists, actors, writers . . . all people with better lives that Constance had or that she'd allowed her daughter to hope for.

But now at least there might be a bit of extra money coming her way, Sarah thought and the irony of it was that her mother's refusal to allow anyone else to draft her will; her mother's arrogance, might have gifted that to her.

CHAPTER 5

It had been a lovely service, Rina Martin thought. Not like some where it was obvious the celebrant had never met the deceased and been briefed by relatives who had also probably not seen the dead person in years. The vicar had been a personal friend, had known Jean Hammond all the time she had lived in that rambling old place a couple of miles outside Frantham. Everyone who'd spoken their piece had related personal memories or performed music she had loved or — and this was the first time Rina had witnessed this happening in church — had simply raised a glass to their lost friend, usually accompanied by some elaborate toast. One had stood out for her, the wish that Jean's journey should be a joyful one. Rina had liked that.

Rina was well versed in Jean's predilection for a well-turned toast and by the end of the service the church had echoed with the laughter of more people than fire regulations would have usually permitted in the ageing building.

She stood now, gossiping to mutual friends in the bright June sunshine. Jean, much to Rina's surprise had been laid to rest in a corner of the churchyard. Few burials took place there these days and Rina had assumed it was fully occupied. Had the vicar moved a wall or something to fit her in, she wondered absently. Ursula would be sorry to have missed the funeral, Rina thought. She had not even been consciously aware that her young friend knew Jean until after her death but this was exam season and Ursula would at this very moment be halfway through a physics paper.

The crowd was thinning now, most people drifting off to the wake in the upper room of the local pub. Aware of someone coming to stand close by, she glanced up to see Cal smiling at her.

"It was a lovely service," she said.

"It was, wasn't it? I can't believe she isn't here to enjoy it. Jean hated to miss a party."

"She did indeed." Rina fell into step beside him. "And how are you," she said. "Apart from that being a damned fool of a question."

"I don't know how I am," Cal admitted. "I just thought she'd go on forever, you know?"

"I know. It's hard to imagine people like Jean ever popping their clogs, as she would have said." Rina paused, turning to look properly at him. "You still feel there's something wrong about all this, don't you?"

He sighed. "Look, I know I've no reason to. Her heart had been bad for years and you know Jean, she never would slow down or make allowances. She was always headlong into everything. I suppose I should be relieved she survived as long as she did; I mean she wasn't young when I went to live with her . . . and she kept going right to the end, you know. She finished her last commission just before she died. She was working to the last moment."

"Which would have pleased her immensely."

Calvin nodded. "And I couldn't have asked for a better parent."

"You were what, nine, ten, when you went to live with her?"

"Ten, yes. She lived in this funny little flat in the attic of a big Victorian place with most of the space turned into her studio. She decided on that first night that we should move, that I needed a place with a garden and a swing." He laughed. "I

25

think she was the one who wanted the swing. She knew nothing about kids, but you know Jean. Once she'd decided to commit there was no stopping her . . . and boy, did she commit to me."

Rina took his arm and squeezed it gently. If she was being honest — and Rina was always honest, at least with herself — she had always found Jean Hammond just a bit full on. She had liked her a good deal, but an hour or so in her company left even Rina exhausted; and most people described Rina as indefatigable. But Rina had known Jean to be a good woman, with a warm heart and a fine, strong sense of justice. And she had taken Calvin into her home and her heart and raised the boy with love. Cal was now a fine young man of thirty-four with a long-term partner and a good career. And if something was bothering him, then Rina, antenna in full twitch mode, felt she ought to find out what it was.

"So," she asked as they stood outside the pub, preparing to join the wake, the very un-funerary sound of raucous laughter escaping through the open window of the upper room. "What's got that brain of yours in a tizz?"

He laughed softly at her use of a Jean expression. "In a tizz indeed," he admitted, "and Rina, it's probably absolutely nothing at all."

"But?"

"But when I found her, she was sitting under that big tree at the bottom of the garden. So, she must have walked all the way across the lawn to get there."

Rina waited, a small part of her brain already guessing what it was he was going to say.

"Well, she *could* manage in the studio and even round the house, where it was all level, but I'm sure . . . well as sure as I could be, knowing Jean . . . that she never went outside without her stick. Not since she had that fall last year."

"And when you found her, her stick —"

"Was nowhere to be seen. And that wasn't the only thing. It was the way she was sitting, cushions underneath her, and behind her. Now she might just about have managed to cross the lawn without her stick but not carrying something."

"Cushions are not heavy," Rina pointed out.

"No, but . . . Etta thinks that she probably got someone to put them out there for her earlier. She loved sitting under that tree, but these days she usually sat in a chair. If she'd taken the folding chair, I could have understood it, she often hobbled around using that like a walking stick. We'd got her these two bright pink things made out of lightweight aluminium and she could manage those. She never could get the damn things folded up again, but she could take one outside and sit down."

He raised his hands as though defeated. Rina was aware that Etta was looking out through the pub doorway and calling his name, Calvin being the host of this already enthusiastic party. "We should go in," she said. "Look, I still have my friend in the police force, I could ask a few questions."

"I did that already, and the police told me that I was bothering myself about nothing. They were very nice about it, said it was not unusual for relatives to be overly anxious when a loved one was found dead, but—"

"But they told you there was nothing to investigate."

"Actually, I felt quite patronised," Calvin admitted. "And everything they said was totally reasonable. Her GP had been seeing her regularly and we knew it was only a matter of time. I am making a fuss, I know I am and it's probably because it never really occurred to me that Jean would die, ridiculous as that might seem considering her age and her health."

They both turned towards the door and moments later he was engulfed by other well-wishers, and making his way up the stairs. Rina followed more slowly, wondering if there really was anything for Calvin to have made a fuss about, any real reason for his brain to be in a tizz. She would of course talk to Mac, DI McGregor to give him his proper title, Sebastian if you really wanted to annoy him. It wasn't something that had crossed Mac's desk, Rina was pretty sure of that, but he was never averse to asking a few questions on her behalf and if she could set Cal's mind a rest that would be something.

CHAPTER 6

Rina did not get the opportunity to question Mac about anything for the next few days. It was Sunday teatime, when he and his partner Miriam came to join the family for cake and crustless sandwiches that she finally managed to grab him for five minutes while everyone else was busy loading the table with fancies.

"I thought George and Ursula might be here," Mac said, referring to the two young friends that Rina had taken under her wing.

"Gone to the cinema," Rina said. "One of those Marvel Universe film things. I don't think George was too keen but Ursula seems to a taste for them."

"The twins have been busy baking today," Mac observed referring to Steven and Matthew Montmorency. Usually referred to as twins, on account of their years as a twin double act, they could not in fact have looked more different. Steven was shorter, a little plump around the middle and definitely thinning in the hair department — a fact that no one ever mentioned. Matthew was tall with a mane of thick grey hair. Two of the other members of Rina's little household, the Peters sisters, Bethany and Eliza, who had also been a double act in their younger days, flitted around tweaking the table arrangement much to Matthew's annoyance.

"Tim and Joy will be popping in later," Rina said.

"He's not working tonight?" Tim had a regular gig at the local hotel, his brand of close-up magic and the occasional big illusion proving quite a draw for the newly renovated art deco Palisades.

"No, they've got some charity event going on up there. A 1920s themed dinner and dance I believe, so Tim gets the night off."

"It will be good to see him," Mac said.

Miriam drifted over to join them. "I think I'm in the way," she said. "I did offer to help, but you know what they're like, if it's not exactly the way they want it then it isn't right." She smiled fondly at the Montmorency twins. It had taken a little while, Rina remembered, from Mac to risk bringing his young lady to face the full impact of the Martin household. They had all been performers for most of their lives and they could be somewhat dramatic even now, but Miriam had taken it all in her stride.

"There's something I'd like to ask you both," Rina said wondering suddenly if a CSI had been called to the Jean Hammond death. She knew that, although the police had been called, this had all turned very routine and once her doctor had been spoken to any query the police may have had seemed to have been abandoned. But it was possible that procedure, once set in motion, had required a scenes of crime officer to take a look.

"Jean Hammond," she said. "Do either of you know anything about her death?"

Mac looked puzzled but Miriam said, "That was the artist wasn't it, Willow Tree House or something like that?"

"The Willows," Rina told her.

"Ah," Mac said. "So not one of mine, I don't need to be worried about having forgotten a dead body."

"I thought it was ruled natural causes," Miriam went on. "Agreed the scene did look quite odd, but from what I've heard about it she was quite an eccentric woman."

"Was it you that went out there?" Rina asked.

"As it happened, so it was. There she was, seated beneath this beautiful big willow tree, sat upright, feet straight out and back against the trunk of the tree. It was not the kind of thing you come across every day. Most sudden deaths are an old person slumped on the floor, usually between the bed and the wall, and tangled up in blankets. And usually just very sad."

"And did this one strike you as sad?"

"Oh yes, it's always sad. The end of life, the implications for the family. But it's always a relief too when it is *just* a sudden death. We only get called out when it has an odd look to it or the person hasn't seen the doctor recently or, as in this case, the relative who found her called the nines and the process just got set in motion. We often get called out to sudden deaths just in case there are suspicious circumstances. It's shocking how many we go to where no one has seen the dead person in days or even weeks, not even their doctor. When no one seems to have missed them. That happened so many times during the pandemic, and it's not improved much since. People seem to have isolated themselves so much more."

Rina nodded. "And there was no sense this death was unusual?"

Mac and Miriam exchanged a glance and then looked sharply at Rina. "Any reason we should think that?" Mac asked her.

"Well probably not, but Calvin is convinced that things aren't quite right. When she was found she didn't have a stick with her, and she was propped up on those cushions and he is certain she couldn't have organised that on her own."

"Did she always use a stick?" Miriam asked.

"Apparently, she was more surefooted on flat surfaces, so in her studio she could get around without it. But if she went out into the garden, she would generally have had a stick with her."

"And Calvin is the son?" Mac wanted to know.

"Well, as good as. His parents died when he was ten, I don't know the details but it was in a car crash. Jean was a close family friend and, apparently, she had been appointed Cal's guardian in their will. She was no spring chicken then, but she took him in and she seems to have done a very good job of raising him. Cal was absolutely devoted to her. He is now in his thirties, so she's been parent to him for most of his life and I know he was terribly shocked, even though he knew her health wasn't good."

"She was a very old lady," Miriam commented. "And didn't she have a heart condition or something?"

"Yes, she did. As I say, he just can't get used to the idea that Jean isn't here anymore. He'd not lived with her for the past few years, he went off to university and then got a flat in Exeter and now he lives with his partner, Etta, and his job is there, so obviously he wasn't over as often as he used to be. It's quite possible he either over or under-estimated her health and her ability to get around."

"Her studio was upstairs over the garage," Miriam remembered. "So, she must have been fairly good on her feet. She could manage the flight of stairs. Isn't the house a converted coach house or something? It was certainly rather lovely."

"It is rather lovely," Rina agreed. "Though when Jean moved there it was in a right state. She bought it very cheaply and then slowly got it done up. I think for the first year they both lived in a caravan in the garden. I didn't know her back then, though as it turns out we did have acquaintances in common. I got to know her properly six or seven years ago. She did quite a lot of charity work, volunteered for this and that. She held some event, I forget exactly what it was in aid of, on the lawn at The Willows. Some kind of art auction, lots of local artists contributing stuff to . . . I think it was the lifeboats but I can't remember exactly."

"Was she a friend of yours then?" Mac queried. "I don't remember you talking about her."

"No not really. We ran across one another from time to time, she was always fun but to be honest she was a little bit heavy going too, very intense. She was involved when we were trying to get money for the church roof, and then in the exhibition we put on at the airfield, you know just after the De Freitases bought it, when they were doing all the renovations. So, I suppose I'd run across her three or four times a year and we'd usually sit down and have a chat and coffee or a drink or whatever but no, I wouldn't say she was a close friend, just that we had a lot of common interests. Cal does something at a law firm, pretty junior, but he's a nice young man and, when I saw him at the funeral, I said I'd just take advantage of knowing you and ask." Rina smiled. "After all, what are pet policeman for."

"Right now they are for sharing tea and cake," Matthew told her sternly, the table evidently now set to his satisfaction. The rule being that nothing business-like should be discussed at mealtimes, and this feeling a little too close to business, the conversation was abandoned. Miriam took her usual seat between the Peters sisters and prepared for girly chat, Mac took his place between Rina and Matthew and prepared for the usual interrogation about how his week had been and what he thought about whatever it was that Steven and Matthew had been reading in the papers.

Tim and Joy turned up about half an hour later and more tea was made, more cake served. Standing beside Joy always made Tim look even taller than he was, Mac thought. Tim was a little over six feet tall, still as gangly as a teenager, and Joy was petite and slim with a mass of red hair. They had met under strange circumstances; Joy had been kidnapped then rescued, then brought to Rina to be looked after. Tim had fallen for her hook, line and sinker, Mac remembered, and from the way he was looking at her now that hadn't changed one iota.

As usually happened when everyone was present, Joy swapped places with Mac, taking the seat next to Matthew and preparing for a long chat while Mac went and plonked himself down beside Tim.

"And how has your week been?" Tim asked.

"Somewhat eventful," Matthew replied. "Though there seem to have been no murders so at least that's something. A spate of robberies though, haven't there Sebastian?" Matthew was the only one who used Mac's given name; even his mother had given up the effort, but it did tend to make Mac wince every time he heard it.

Tim grinned at him, but at that moment Joy said something that captured Matthew's attention and he and Steven turned their full consideration to her.

"So, what else has been going on?" Tim asked.

"Oh, nothing much, Rina wondering if there was a murder we'd missed, but apart from that . . ."

"Oh, do tell."

"You remember that artist that died a little while ago. Jean Hammond?"

"Indeed, I do. She must have been over ninety, but her work was still as fresh as it had been when she was in her twenties. I think there's going to be a retrospective soon, one of the big galleries in London."

"So, she was well known then?"

"Yes, later in her career she was connected somehow with the Brotherhood of Ruralists, artists like Peter Blake and David Inshaw. Apparently, there were quite a few woman artists associated, despite the name. But I'm not sure Jean Hammond was part of any particular school for long because she went too much her own way. Most of her work was inspired by folklore and magic and, like the Ruralists, nature and our response to it. She's often referred to as a feminist artist and not just feminism, she took up issues that were often quite controversial at the time. She was promoting gay rights, for instance, long before it was even legal, I suppose on the one hand she didn't do herself any favours, a lot of people wouldn't exhibit her in the early days, but more recently she'd been seen as something of an icon and her work was making big money."

"You know quite a lot about her."

"James up at the Palisades, he bought a couple of her early pieces last year so I got interested. From what James said only the really early stuff was in any way affordable. They have a sort of Art Deco look, a bit like that de Lempicka woman, though her later stuff was more naturalistic. I expect even the early work will have gone up in value now," he added, a little wryly. "Anyway, I thought she just had a heart attack or something? She was getting on a bit."

"Well, yes," Mac agreed, "but her adopted son has been worried that things were not quite right. It's probably nothing, but I'll ask around just to satisfy Rina's curiosity." And her sense of justice, he could have added.

"Very wise," Tim agreed. "Otherwise, she'd be forced to go poking around on her own and we both know where that might lead to."

CHAPTER 7

When Sarah had sold her mother's house, she had rented
a small lock-up for all the boxes and files she did not have
room for in her little flat and which she didn't have the mental energy to cope with either. She had sold the house for
cash to a developer who wanted the place for rental and she
had managed to get a small but welcome extra payment for
the white goods and furniture she had been relieved to leave
behind. A local charity shop had provided almost all of the
furnishings for her new place, her one luxury being a brand-
new bed with a deep red headboard and drawers beneath for
storage.

Over the next weeks, and partly at the urging of her new
legal advisor, she had brought the boxes and the files one by
one to the flat and sorted through them. Anything that might
have a legal complexion went to her solicitor. Anything that
could be got rid of went into the recycling or into the bin.
Some of that was fished out again the following day after
nightmares that recalled her mother's displeasure. Much of
it went back into storage where at least it was out of sight.

It all took so much damned time, Sarah thought as she
tackled the latest of her mother's possessions — even if the
boxes contained something pertaining to herself, Sarah could

never own any of this. It was burdensome and frightening and she hated it all.

Sarah tipped the box on its side and emptied the contents on to the rug and then stared hard at it. It didn't take much working out, what the box contained. She recognised her own childish handwriting and that of her mother's. The plain brown exercise books, the envelopes, the lists, the reprimands . . . always written so she could reflect on what she might have done before receiving punishment for her sin or crime.

Sarah raked through the remnants of childhood, trying hard to fight down the rising panic — like a tight hand had clamped in her chest, stopping her lungs from drawing breath. She closed her eyes and then with a massive act of will she opened them again.

"Right, you can do this. That can go in the bin and that can go into the recycling and that . . ." She paused, her hand coming to rest on a small white envelope, the words 'return to sender' printed neatly on the front. Several more, held together by an elastic band lay beneath it.

She didn't have to open the letter to know what it contained.

For several years when Sarah had been small, from about five years old until she was perhaps eight, her mother had insisted she write these letters and draw pictures for the father who was 'away'. In prison, though she would never say that, not even in the privacy of their home. At school she would make Christmas cards for her mother and another for 'daddy', glittering both with equal, carefully measured amounts of silver and gold. She told him about her largely imagined life and her trips to the park and to the shops and to fictional birthday parties and visits to the zoo. Somehow Sarah had always hoped that these fictions would somehow transmute themselves into real experiences if she wrote them well enough. If she put enough effort and passion into the making of these false memories.

In the end the unreal had become so real in her own head that even her teachers believed the stories of the lions she had seen and the visits to see Santa at the big department store in Exeter whose name she could not recall . . . she had never even been to Exeter. Their belief reinforced by the smiling mother who made a point of turning up at parents' evenings — events Sarah dreaded probably more than anything else — but the smile always faded before they left the school. Her efforts were never good enough, no matter how hard she tried.

And he had opened none of the letters. This mythical father, less real to her than the lions and Father Christmas. She knew the lions existed because she had seen them on TV and Father Christmas visited their school at the end of term. Her father just returned her letters and her pictures and little gifts, never having even looked inside. Her mother had kept the unopened letters, inferring that they had not been opened because Sarah was in some way undeserving of her father's attention. That this lack of love on his part was all her fault.

Impatiently, Sarah bundled everything back into the box and shoved the box into the cupboard beside the front door with the vacuum cleaner and the mop. Truth be told, she didn't even know if what her mother told her was true. If this man really was her father.

And then he had died and her mother's rage had cranked up a notch and Father Christmas and even the lions seemed to lose their hold on reality. They belonged in a world where her mother was not. A world Sarah would never occupy again. A world where everyone had a better life than she did, even those who had done nothing to deserve it, like the models and artists and actors and writers in her mother's cuttings book and photo albums. Those people she had once claimed to know and whose public stories she glued to the pages as though taking ownership of some part of them.

"This is the life we should have had," she would tell Sarah. "Stolen from us by that coward of a man and by all the rest of them that let us down."

* * *

37

It was several days later before Mac had opportunity to ask anyone about the Hammond death. This came when he had reason to visit divisional headquarters for a meeting and happened to run into a young constable that he knew had attended the scene.

Yolanda had always been a little wary of him; the first case she had worked on with Mac had involved walking long distances through fields of cows in unsuitable shoes. To say that they had not necessarily made the best of impressions on one another was probably true, but in the last couple of years Yolanda had, in Mac's opinion, settled into her role in a much more satisfactory fashion. He wasn't sure what she thought of him.

She had been walking down the corridor on her way to a meeting, carrying a stack of papers. She paused and thought about his question, "Yes, I was there, the old lady that died in her garden? That's a good way to go out, don't you think, sitting in the sun, propped up with cushions, leaning against your favourite tree."

"I can think of worse ways," Mac admitted and Yolanda rewarded him with a big smile. "But did you notice anything odd about it? Apart from the inevitable oddity of, as you say, a deceased old lady sitting beneath a tree propped up with cushions."

Her eyes narrowed and she peered at him closely. "What makes you ask that? It was ruled a natural death. Admittedly looked a bit out of the ordinary, but . . ."

"Anything in particular," he persisted.

Yolanda fidgeted with the papers she was carrying and then set them down on a convenient table and leaned against the wall with her arms folded. She seemed to be buying herself some time before she replied.

"Look," she said finally, "it just looked a little off, you know. But I couldn't exactly tell you why. You know Miriam was the CSI on call for that one? She was only there briefly, though. Everyone seemed satisfied there was nothing worth looking at. The police surgeon figured she'd only been gone a couple of hours and she certainly looked peaceful enough. Though it must have been a big shock for her son, when he found her."

Mac nodded. "And did Miriam have anything to add to what the doctor said?"

"No, I don't think so. There wasn't much for her to do and she went off on another call about half an hour later."

"But you felt things were off?"

She frowned, as though recalling the episode. "Once everyone else had buggered off, I was left in charge of waiting for the undertaker to come and get her. So, I was just looking around, as you do when you're bored and you got nothing useful to do. The son, Calvin, he'd said that there was something in the old lady's hand and he was bothered about it, so Dr Carter had taken it out of her hand and I'd put it in an evidence bag because I didn't know what else to do with it. Dr Carter said she'd probably been deadheading stuff in the garden and got taken ill. Sat down and that was that. But like I say, I'd got nothing better to do and I got kind of curious. I had a look at what had been in her hand, it was a bit of plant material, it looked like a bit of dried hydrangea flower, actually. My auntie has one outside her front door. Like Dr Carter said, it was as if she'd been gardening and she'd suddenly needed to sit down." She paused. "I think she might have intended to go back into her studio. She'd left her music on, playing on repeat. I switched it off after the doc had decided it was not suspicious."

"And it looked as though she'd simply set the cushions out and sat there," Mac asked.

"Well, yeah. She'd still got her painting clothes on so she must've been working in her studio, come downstairs, decided she wanted to be outside for a while and had a heart attack or whatever. At least that's what the police surgeon and her GP had speculated anyway. I mean there was nothing violent about it, she looked peaceful and quiet and calm, like she just sat down and died."

"And so?"

Yolanda looked slightly uncomfortable. "Like I said, I was bored, you know what it's like when you're left in charge of the scene and nobody thinks it's suspicious; you just have to look after things until somebody comes and relieves you."

Mac nodded. "And so?" he asked again.

"So, I took a picture of the flower on my phone, the one in the evidence bag that had been in her hand, and I went to see if I could find it in the garden. And, well I know I'm not much of a gardener, but I can compare one thing to another, and I know what a hydrangea looks like. I'll swear there isn't one in the garden."

Mac felt a sudden wriggle of unease and excitement in his gut. "You put this in your report?"

"Of course I did, and I told my boss, Dave Kendall. He made sure it was passed on, but then it was all ruled natural death, so . . . I just assumed I'd got it wrong and, well, it didn't really matter in the end, did it."

"Could it have been from a houseplant?"

"A hydrangea? You know even less about gardening than I do." Yolanda shrugged. "Wouldn't they be too big to be an indoor plant?" She shrugged, "I didn't see one, but I only went into the house to check all the doors were locked before I left. Somebody had sent her a bouquet of flowers and that was on the table in the hall, with a card beside it. Someone called Philip, if I remember right, and I did look because they sometimes get used in cut flower bouquets but there was nothing like it.

"She had all sorts in the garden, it's a gorgeous garden, have you seen it? And she had this area with herbs and stuff in it and," Yolanda paused, "A few with spiky leaves that maybe shouldn't have been there."

"Did she indeed," Mac said.

"But there was nothing quite the same as the flower in her hand. Believe me I looked, I had an hour or more to kill until the mortuary ambulance came and another half-hour until Kev came back for me. He'd been called to another shout. And she seemed like a nice old lady, but it's still kind of creepy you know, just me and her propped against the tree. I know Miriam was worried about leaving me there but I told her I'd be fine."

Mac nodded.

"Look, I've got to go. Have a word with DI Kendall, he knows all about it. I can send you a picture of the plant." She scooped up her paperwork.

"Do that," Mac told her.

"You think we missed something?"

"Almost certainly not, but," he remembered that the one thing he had commended Yolanda on when they had first met had been her powers of observation. That was the one thing that had made him think she might one day become a decent officer. "What do *you* think? Gut feeling?"

She hesitated, coloured slightly. "It felt off," she said. "Just little things. Like the way she was sitting, legs straight out and back against the tree. And the flower in her hand and . . . well you only had to look at her to see she was frail and there was a stick stand in the hall full of different walking sticks and they all looked used, you know, like she'd thought that if she *had* to use a stick she may as well have a choice. But she hadn't been using one that day, or at least I couldn't see one and, like I said, I was curious. Occupational hazard. I thought it was most likely she'd have dropped the stick wherever she was standing when she started to feel ill, if that's what happened, so I thought, you know, it was likely to be wherever she'd been when she picked that flower."

She shifted uneasily. "Like I said, I was bored and a bit, well, uncomfortable, if I'm honest."

"Understandable," Mac told her.

"Anyway, I really do have to go. I've got to take this lot into a meeting," she indicated the paperwork she was carrying.

"Thanks, Yolanda." He watched absently as she bustled away, thinking how much more confident she was now than she had been when they had first met.

And what she had to say was interesting, Mac thought. Worth pursuing? Nothing to be lost having closer look, was there?

CHAPTER 8

"You didn't tell me how you met Jean," Rina said. They were bumping along a narrow country lane — one very much in need of maintenance — in Ursula's little car. The ageing Fiat, an old-style Panda that Rina was amazed had passed its MOT, was small and cramped and the engine noisy enough to make the radio totally unusable. Rina felt like she was being shaken around in a baked bean can. Ursula had been working all hours she could, alongside her college work, just to afford her driving lessons. She was now doing the same just to pay for her insurance. I have to pass first time, Rina remembered her saying. She couldn't afford to keep taking lessons otherwise.

And she had. She had started her lessons the moment she had turned seventeen and passed on her first attempt. Rina totally understood her need for a car. Living in a rural area with pretty lousy public transport links and the need to work to supplement what was — in Rina's view — the very inadequate financial support Looked After Children got once they had left the care system.

Ursula and Rina both knew just how many kids ended up homeless within six months of leaving residential care and, although Rina would have stepped in long before it came to that for either Ursula or George, she also knew how important it was for both of them to prove that they were independent beings.

"Jean was one of my cleaning jobs," Ursula said. "I liked her a lot. She'd put a card in the post office advertising for help and didn't like any of the applicants. Mrs Trevelley, my 6 o'clock, Tuesday morning lady, knew Miss Hammond slightly and she recommended me."

"And how did the drawing lessons happen?"

Ursula looked slightly discomforted and Rina understood that she'd found a raw nerve — though she wasn't sure why. There was nothing wrong in wanting to be creative. "It must have been a real break from your studies and all that science and maths. Very refreshing, I'd have thought," she said cautiously.

She saw Ursula relax slightly and then nod. "Rina, sometimes it feels like all I do is work. George and I, we manage the occasional trip to the cinema and sometimes tea with all of you on a Sunday but apart from that it's all working towards exams and working to earn a bit of extra money just so I can run the car and make sure I can pay the electricity bill. It's the same for George. Soon as we turn eighteen and we can take on a tenancy agreement, we're thinking about finding a flat so we can at least share expenses." She shook her head. "But anyway, Jean. I was in the studio one day cleaning up and Jean was working. She was just so focused and so . . . I don't know, totally involved. And I just happened to say something really stupid like how it must feel really good to be making something that other people are going to love and she said if I really meant that, why wasn't I doing it."

Rina laughed. "That sounds like Jean."

"And suddenly it was all coming out. All of the frustration and the exhaustion and the . . . the feeling that I don't get to have choices, not if I want to have any kind of life. Like I've chosen my degree because everyone needs pharmacists, not because I want to do it. Like I chose my A levels because everyone told me I was good at maths and sciences so

I should focus on that because it improved my job prospects and because . . . because."

"You feel you have no safety net, no family to fall back on," Rina said quietly. "Ursula, you know that if there's ever anything you need. You or George. That as far as any of us are concerned, you are both family." She realised belatedly that she sounded slightly hurt and just a little put out and that she was in fact deeply jealous of Jean Hammond for having been on the receiving end of Ursula's outpouring. *Why couldn't you come to me?* she thought. I would have listened. I would have acted.

It seemed that Ursula knew exactly what she was thinking. "Sometimes it's easier to say these things to a stranger," she said. "Sometimes it's easier to admit things to someone who doesn't really matter. Rina, you've all been brilliant and I love you very much, you know that. You and Tim and everyone else, you are my true family, but I'm scared, Rina, scared that if I can't stand on my own two feet—"

"What are you afraid will happen?"

Ursula shrugged. "I don't know."

"You'll never end up like Grace or Brandon," Rina said gently, guessing that this was at the heart of Ursula's anxiety. Grace and Brandon had both been at Hill House, the children's home where Ursula and George had lived for several years. Both were a little older and both had fallen into very bad places when they had been thrust out into the world to fend for themselves. Grace had initially been in the same accommodation that Ursula and George now occupied. A block of tiny studio flats provided by a local charity for teenagers leaving the system. Much better than where many of them ended up. Brandon, Rina remembered, had ended up in a B&B through that first winter and found himself ousted when the tourist season started. He had sofa surfed for a while, got involved in drugs, and ended up on the streets before a place had been found for him in a hostel, miles away from anyone he knew.

Rina had gone with George and Ursula to Grace's funeral. She had drowned and although the coroner had ruled it an accidental death everyone had known just how unhappy Grace had been, and everyone who had known her wondered if the verdict was correct.

"Do you talk to George about this?" Rina asked gently.

"George knows. It doesn't need saying," Ursula's voice was uncharacteristically harsh. Then she relented, just a little. "We talk, we help one another, but sometimes it just feels like it's the last thing you want to talk about. When I'm with George I want to have fun, even if that's just going for a coffee."

Rina nodded. She wasn't certain about the status of their current relationship. There had been a time when Ursula and George had been best friends, then a spell when they had definitely been an item. That seemed to have come to an end when they had moved into separate little apartments and, both had seemed intent on proving . . . what? How independent they could be? How self-contained? They were, she was sure, still the best of friends, closer than some old married couples, but that seemed to be it, just now. Were they, Rina wondered, preparing for the separation that university would bring, even though Ursula was not going far away? Though she'd probably move into university accommodation, she would still be living nearby or would they actually find somewhere together, as Ursula had suggested. George had a job lined up and couldn't wait to get out of school. He'd had casual work at a small boatyard just along the coast for the past year and an opening had come up for an apprentice boat builder. He had applied and got it. Rina had no doubt that he would thrive, so was that part of the issue?

"You feel that George has been able to plan a future he actually wants," she said quietly. "And you can't help but be a bit jealous of that."

"Oh God, that sounds so bad, Rina."

"There's only you and me here, sweetheart, and I'm not about to judge you." She could see that Ursula was close to tears. "We're almost there," she added, trying to give Ursula time to gather herself. It distressed Rina to see her young friend suffering like this but she wasn't sure what she could do about it. If and when Ursula asked for help then it would be there, as expansive and unstinting as might be required, but she remembered all too vividly being Ursula's age and that overwhelming need she'd had to 'prove herself' whatever that had meant . . . It seemed this painful process was something youth had to endure.

Though one thing was perhaps different, Rina thought. She had first met Fred when she was Ursula's age. They had been friends at first and then a year after had been officially courting. A year after that, they married. Five years later and Fred was dead. But not gone, Rina thought, her fingers stroking the little watch he had given her for their first anniversary and which she still wore when she felt the occasion required a little extra strength.

She wasn't certain why today was one of those days.

Ursula slowed the car and pulled into the short gravel drive that led to Jean Hammond's house. Cal's vehicle was already there, as was a small blue van advertising the owner as a Gas Safe plumber. As they parked up, Cal opened the front door and waved.

"I've never been in through the front door," Ursula commented. "I always went round the side, through the kitchen."

"I don't think she used it much," Rina agreed.

They crunched across the gravel and Cal stood back to welcome them in.

"Problem?" Rina indicated the plumber's van.

"The pipe leading to the boiler has a leak," Cal said. "He's busy in the kitchen so I thought it was easier to let you in through the front. Then I had trouble finding the key. I eventually found it in the—"

"Tea caddy on the hall stand," Ursula said automatically. Rina was aware of Cal's quizzical look and that Ursula had noted it too and felt she had to explain. "I was here the day when she had that big sofa delivered. She opened the front door so they could get in through the front and straight into the living room."

"Ah, right." Cal seemed suddenly at a loss.

"We probably need to go into the studio anyway," said Rina. "Ursula's things are in one of the drawers in there. And you did promise me a look at the garden."

"Of course, "Cal said. "Sorry, I'm finding this a bit difficult. I came over this morning to sort some things out. I thought, right, Rina's coming over, it's a good time to kill two birds with one stone, get the rest of the stuff sorted out here . . . then I get here and there's a puddle on the kitchen floor and then I'm trying to find a plumber who can come out immediately and you can imagine how hard that one was."

Rina nodded. She laid a hand on Cal's arm. "It's a horrible job," she said gently, "having to go through personal things and tidy someone's life away. It feels like a betrayal, somehow. Like you're—"

"Tipping them in the bin with the rest of the rubbish," Ursula said.

They both turned to look at her and Ursula flushed bright red.

What's that about, Rina wondered but Cal nodded thoughtfully. "You've hit the nail on the head there," he said. "Truthfully, it's hard to know where to start. There's just so much stuff."

"If you need a hand," Rina offered. "I'd be glad to help."

They went back out of the front door and round the side of the house to where the stairs to the studio rose up against the end wall and entered through a door which had once been used for loading hay into the loft.

"This is a lovely room," Rina said honestly. "It's just so Jean."

"The essence of her," Cal agreed. "Do you know where your drawings will be?" he asked Ursula.

"Over in the big plan chest, third drawer down."

Cal looked startled. He laughed. "That used to be my drawer," he said. "When I lived here. I was never any good, but Jean said I should store my work properly and treat it with respect. That the effort still mattered even if I wasn't satisfied with the results." He seemed, Rina thought, caught between feeling hurt and impressed that this young blonde woman he didn't know had taken even a part of what he and Jean had once shared.

Rina noticed that he watched as Ursula crossed the room and opened the drawer. He seemed to be resisting the urge to follow her across the broad wooden boards, reclaimed, so Jean had once told her, from the demolition of a local farmhouse, to the two sizeable plan chests rescued when a local architect had closed down. Rina wondered absently how they had got them up here. Maybe they had used the block and tackle still in place above the door from when this had been a coach house and hay store.

Ursula had knelt beside the chest and had the drawer open. She withdrew two plain, large, card portfolios but seemed to be hesitating about something. On impulse, to distract Cal, Rina turned to the pin-boards that stretched along the opposite wall, between the broad windows let into the thick stone walls. "Was this what she was working on?" Rina asked.

Cal turned. "Yes. It was a commission. It's called *The Wedding Coat*. I don't know what the significance was. There was a time we'd have talked about it. I feel bad, Rina, like I hadn't made enough time for her lately."

"I'm sure she understood," Rina said gently. She looked closely at the working drawings on the wall and at the printouts of what had clearly been an almost finished piece. She remembered Jean telling her that sometimes seeing work at a different scale or simply printed out and pinned up with the preliminary drawings helped her to see any issues she'd not noticed. That it was like shifting perspectives.

"I wonder why it wasn't called *Three Women Dancing*," she said thinking that an image of three women seemed a little odd for a wedding gift. Behind her she heard Ursula closing the drawer and start back across the boarded floor but she was certain that just a moment before she had heard another drawer open and close. She would need to speak to Ursula later, Rina thought. Find out just what it was she hadn't told her about Jean Hammond.

CHAPTER 9

Rina scrolled through the photographs she had taken of Jean Hammond's garden and the jars of dried herbs and seeds stacked on narrow shelves in the little potting shed alongside small pots of ointments, tall bottles of flavoured oils and jars of pickles and chutneys and jams. There was even a small distillation unit sitting in the corner alongside packets of natural dyes and homemade inks. This was a side of Jean she had no idea even existed.

"She liked to experiment," Cal had said. "Was always into her herb teas."

To Rina's eye this was a step beyond the odd cup of Chamomile. Jean Hammond had been serious about this and, from the quick glance Rina had been able to get of the notebooks lying on the bench, had been knowledgeable too.

Cal, she thought, had been oddly dismissive of the whole set-up as though he was either genuinely not interested or was so used to seeing it that it no longer made an impression. Rina had the feeling — though maybe just in hindsight — that he hadn't wanted to hang around in the little shed and was now in fact quite impatient for Rina to go. Ursula had left for college and Cal had said he'd give Rina a lift home if she wanted to take a look around the garden.

They had wandered amiably enough for a time, but Cal had seemed distracted, she thought and, eventually, maybe just bored with her company and keen to be off. After all, he didn't know her that well and their whole acquaintance was predicated on their mutual connection to Jean.

The garden itself had been full of surprises. Colourful herbaceous borders and a formal potager — both now, three weeks after Jean's death, in desperate need of a weed and tidy. Rina had taken many photographs and she now sat happily ensconced with her computer, comparing online pictures with those she had on her phone.

Jean liked her herbs, culinary and medicinal. She had also created a veritable poison garden, Rina thought, though you'd not notice that at first, not the way the garden was laid out. Aconite sat with the last of the foxgloves, Jimson weed filled the gap against the wall, reaching up to where the wisteria had now finished flowering and a clematis with little nodding bells of yellow clambered through the stems.

She recognised laburnum, of course, and the red leaves and pompom flowers of false castor oil from which Ricin was derived and the laurel and monkshood, pennyroyal — an innocent looking mint that had been used as both contraceptive and abortifacient. From memory Rina thought it had been used widely in medieval cookery but the oil could be lethal. Foxgloves, different shades and stature, grew all over the garden. Both medicine and poison, Rina thought, though she loved them probably as much as Jean seemed to have done. And when you thought about it, the average garden and certainly the average kitchen or bathroom were repositories of poisons galore and the base materials for many an explosive concoction could be had from the local supermarket.

She drew from her bag the folded piece of paper she had taken from the studio when Cal had been momentarily diverted. It was a colour print of *The Wedding Coat* and looked, to Rina, to be of the picture in its final stages. It was an intriguing work, Rina thought. Three women dancing on a grassy lawn, dotted with daisies and self-heal and buttercups. It reminded her vaguely of Botticelli, romantic looking women, dancing in gardens of detailed and pedantically realised, identifiable plants.

But no, this was different. The women in Jean's picture were clearly modern, not idealised and, she realised, distinctive enough that they were probably portraits.

A thought struck her; was it possible, given the publicity surrounding Jean Hammond's death, that the last painting she had done would be posted somewhere online?

Slightly annoyed with herself that she had not thought of this before, Rina began her search and was delighted to find that *The Wedding Coat* was indeed available for viewing. It was on temporary loan to a London gallery before the final recipients moved it into their own home when they returned from their honeymoon. Reading about this, she got the impression that the gallery had approached the couple very much at the last minute, just after Jean's death had been reported. The curator was also keen to do a retrospective and it seemed that the Fellingdon gallery, in a previous incarnation and some decades before, had championed her work.

"So, we're cashing in on that are we," Rina muttered to herself.

In addition to this she found several other high-resolution images and was able to track the small changes Jean had made in the final stages of the picture. The three women, one older and two younger had their hands linked like children playing Ring of Roses. They were clearly happy, relaxed in each other's company and the whole picture had a joyful look to it. The older woman was grey-haired and had intense blue eyes that matched the forget-me-nots in the grass. There was no interest in seasonality, Rina noted; springtime plants that would have been finished by the time the summer plants were flowering sat side-by-side. The older woman's skin tone suggested someone perhaps from the Mediterranean rather than from northern Europe and the painting of her face was detailed enough that Rina could see the crows-feet at the corners of her eyes. The two younger women were different again. The one with short dark hair, who wore what Rina was assuming was the wedding coat, looked to Rina's eye to be in her mid-or even late forties whereas the pale skinned redhead, freckle faced with blue eyes darker than forget-me-nots, more heliotrope, Rina thought, looked to be in her twenties.

There was no sense that they were related, no similarity in the way they looked or even in the way they dressed. The oldest woman wore faded jeans and a white shirt and was barefoot. The youngest was in a summer dress. The colour picked up the blue of the faded denim and on her feet she wore what looked like bright red canvas shoes with white laces. The dark-haired woman wore a coat of almost black. It had a Victorian look to it, pinched in the waist with a flared skirt. It was long, reaching to her ankles, flipped out by the movement of the dance so that it showed the lining, a bright striped silk. The coat itself was heavily embroidered, and Rina zoomed the image so that she could see the flowers in more detail. She recognised daisies and buttercups, self-heal, wild roses, forget-me-nots, violets and poppies. The embroidery was so dense that the dark material showed through only in scant patches. There was something about the way that all the clothing moved that made her think that perhaps they had been captured from life. The blue dress billowed, the white shirt fell back from the wrist as the older woman raised her arm, the coat swirled. Beneath the coat the woman wore a bright red dress that also fell to her ankles and, if this was the bride, then she looked as happy as any bride-to-be ought to look. Was this what she was going to wear for her wedding day? Or did it have some other meaning. Or did the painting even depict the bride? Rina found that she really had to know, that she wanted to know more about the painting's owners but also about the women in this picture. Who were they? What did the painting mean?

She found her attention drawn back to the younger woman, focusing more closely on the dress.

She was pregnant, Rina observed. There was a sense that, despite there being no obvious sign of them being blood relatives, there were four generations in this painting, grandmother, daughter, grandchild and child as yet unborn. Dancing in a field of flowers.

Rina called up other images of Jean's work. This one was different. Though Jean had painted a lot of women and a lot of semi-mystical, hard to read pictures, there was something about the lightness, the joy and the sheer exuberance of this one that set it apart. Many of Jean's works had an air of melancholy about them, even of sadness or loss. There was a picture simply entitled *Robin* which depicted a young man standing on a cliff top, the ground around him dissolving into a mass of imagery that Rina could not begin to decipher, though much of it seemed to do with travel, perhaps? There were fragments of maps and railway lines that disappeared into the ground, a vintage car — or at least a part of one — all of which seemed at odds with the young man himself who had been described with almost stark clarity. It was obviously a portrait. Rina made a mental note to find out who this Robin was.

Then there was a woman and child standing, hand-in-hand, at the entrance to a clipped hedge maze. The child, her body turning away from the woman, looked excited, gazing into the entrance in a state of happy expectation. The woman was looking out at the viewer, her gaze challenging and direct. The whole thing was rendered in the same stark detail as the man on the cliff but there was an oddness about the perspective. The maze rose up behind them as though, Rina thought, it was seen from above and the perspective foreshortened in a way she couldn't quite get her head around. It was as though the artist was saying something about the solvability of the maze, if they just took time to look — except that the child was too small to see over the hedge and the woman had her back determinedly turned towards the solution.

"Turn around, you silly girl," Rina found herself saying out loud. She laughed; knowing Jean that was probably exactly the response she wanted from the viewer.

She went back to look at the image of the three women. Yes, she thought, the mood was definitely different. There seemed no undercurrents in this picture. It was an image of pure celebration. Of sheer and unadulterated joy.

Technically, the biggest change in the finished picture compared to the printout Rina had were the gilded elements that really did remind her of a Renaissance painting. There were touches of gold in the women's clothing, hints of wings, subtle and almost possible to ignore, but definitely there, as though the women themselves were becoming transcendent.

"You loved them," Rina murmured, coming to a sudden realisation. "Whoever they were, you knew them well and you loved them."

A knock on the door alerted her to the fact that it was teatime and she would have to stop her perusal and her investigation and rejoin her family. She knew that this was now a mystery she would find impossible to leave alone. Jean Hammond had captured her in a way that she had never done in life. Alive, Jean had been a woman that Rina was prepared to like as long as she only had to deal with her in small doses, but she had not known this side of Jean. The garden, these women, the herbs and potions — more and more she was beginning to realise that Cal had been uncomfortable that afternoon, that he had not really wanted her in the shed or asking questions. But asking questions about what? Rina wondered.

And what had young Ursula taken from the studio?

CHAPTER 10

The items Ursula had taken from the studio were currently causing her a lot of worry. She was only carrying out Jean's wishes, but the fact that she'd had to carry out Jean's wishes meant that something really was terribly wrong. Jean had been worried. Ursula had put it down to the fact that the elderly lady was occasionally getting a little absent-minded, sometimes overreacting to simple things, getting very upset when she lost an item for instance. In the year that Ursula had known her she had become acutely aware that Jean's memory was not always reliable, particularly over the recent weeks before her death. Jean had seemed suddenly cautious and troubled and this was totally out of character — or at least totally out of character for the woman Ursula had come to like very much despite her occasional abruptness and her sense that she was always right, no matter what.

Ursula thought that Rina and Jean were actually a pair of bookends, so similar were they in character, but she was totally aware that Rina would be deeply upset by that comparison. Rina always viewed Jean as a more awkward person to deal with, as overly intense and demanding and would have brooked no direct comparison at all.

Ursula's studio flat, what her aunt referred to quite correctly as a bedsit, was small. A single bed and small wardrobe took up all of one wall, the bedside table and chest of drawers butted up to the two-seat sofa, she had manoeuvred a second chest of drawers, rescued from a skip and painted, into place and this supported a small television and a Bluetooth speaker. A breakfast bar separated the kitchen area from the rest of the living space, a hob, a small oven, a run of workspace, cupboards above and below.

It was basic, the breakfast bar doubled up as a desk though a lot of the time she simply worked on her projects in the college library. She was also aware that the space was bare, compared to others in the building. There was little clutter and only a couple of photographs — of the Martin household, plus Mac and Miriam and one of herself and George. Even her books were out of sight, kept at the bottom of the wardrobe. Had anyone asked — though only George really got the opportunity as Ursula discouraged invasions of her space — she would not have been able to explain why she kept her room decoration so sparse. She had tried adding 'personal touches' as her key worker described them, but somehow nothing felt or looked quite right. Perhaps it was because she could not think of this place as anything approaching her permanent home.

Ursula leaned against the breakfast bar and stared at the portfolio and small package that now lay on her single bed and wondered what to do. A light knock on the door broke into her thoughts. She knew it would be George and for a moment she thought about pretending not to be there. George would ask the questions that Ursula was trying not to answer, would come up with solutions that she could come up with herself but didn't want to take up. Why didn't she want to, what was wrong with asking for help?

Sighing, she opened the door. George came through and bent to kiss her. She remembered the skinny, short, mop haired kid then a little shorter than herself that she had felt so sorry for on his first night at Hill House. This had been the children's home he had found himself deposited in when his mother had committed suicide and his sister had gone away, leaving George behind for reasons they had not immediately understood. A deep friendship had begun that first evening and progressed and grown until they had become 'a couple'. Lately, since moving into this apartment block, both had backed off a little. Inhabiting separate spaces and both wrapped up in exams and jobs and the sheer need to survive, their relationship had lapsed back into friendship rather than anything else and Ursula was relieved that George understood. She wasn't rejecting him, far from it, but there was just only so much she could cope with right now.

George had grown; no longer the undernourished, skinny, short-for-his-age child he had been, he was now, at seventeen, much taller than Ursula. The mop of hair hadn't changed though, bright red curls that never did anything they were told and which Ursula occasionally tried to tame with the aid of a pair of nail scissors.

Ursula went back to her position beside the breakfast bar and George joined her, taking her hand and staring at the bed. "Have you looked inside yet?"

She shook her head. "She just told me to make sure that if anything happened to her, I would get that envelope. At the time I just thought . . . I just thought, well she is getting old, and she's ill, she's bound to think about dying."

"Well, I suppose old people do," George agreed. "Either that or they refuse to think about it. So, what are you worried about now? You just did what she asked you to. Did she say who you were to give the envelope to?"

Ursula shook her head. "I know I'm being silly; if she'd just died in the hospital or something, I'd just feel differently about it. I'd have told Mr Hammond . . . Cal . . . that she asked me to collect the envelope and that would have been an end to it, but he was there today and I couldn't tell him."

"Why not?"

"I don't know," Ursula admitted. "I've never met Cal before, I mean I've heard all about him, Jean talked about him loads. But he sort of was not what I expected."

"In what way?"

She shrugged. She didn't know the answer to that either.

"OK then." George had his practical head on, she could tell by his tone. "We just open the envelope and then we decide what to do. And can I see your pictures?"

She laughed at the plaintive tone. "If you behave," she said.

Ursula sat on the bed with George beside her and pulled the big manila envelope on to her lap. She remembered the day that Jean had showed her this package in the second drawer down, the drawer above where Ursula kept her portfolios. If anything happens to me, she had said, please make sure you take this away and deal with it.

"Deal with it?" Ursula had said not really understanding.

"As a favour to me. You'll know what to do."

Ursula had agreed, not really knowing what she was agreeing to and the matter had been dropped. That had been just before Christmas, she remembered. Jean had not been well and was out of sorts since returning from a friend's funeral. She was worried, she said, about leaving everything in place should she not make it to the New Year but by January she was fit again, or as fit as she was going to get with her ongoing medical problems, and Ursula had forgotten about the envelope or at least put it to the back of her mind.

It was only in the last few weeks that it had been mentioned again. "Jean suddenly seemed worried," Ursula told George. "Like she was before Christmas and I asked her if she was feeling really unwell and had she seen the doctor, and just generally made a fuss of her. She kept saying she didn't like a fuss, but I know she did. We all need to be cared about and she was sad that she saw so little of Cal."

George nodded. "So, open it," he said. "I don't quite see what the problem is."

He sat back, half leaning against the wall. Ursula knew he was waiting for her to sort out what the problem was, for her to tell him. It was something they had always been very good at doing for each other, just waiting until the words came and then listening without comment until a comment was actually asked for.

Actually, though she didn't have to think too hard this time, she knew what was bothering her. "It was when I turned up that day, the day she died?"

He nodded.

"I told you I saw her, when I parked my car where I usually do, which is near the gates, so when I got out I looked across the garden. I couldn't understand what the police were doing there and then I saw the constable coming towards me and realised he was trying to stop me going into the garden. I looked through the gate and I saw her, sitting under the tree with her legs straight out in front of her. It looked wrong."

"You said she never sat like that; that it hurt her knees?"

"Jean never sat on the floor. There were seats all around the garden, and a couple of folding chairs she could take out. She never sat on the floor because she used to joke that she was like a toddler and couldn't get up without holding on to something. That she'd have to crawl across the carpet till she found something to pull herself up on, like a little kid learning to walk."

"Maybe you should have mentioned that to Mac," George said. "I know it wasn't his case, I know there wasn't a case, I know they said it was natural causes but—"

"I suppose it was, and she sat down in a hurry and didn't think about how she was going to get up again. And if that was just it, well that would just be it, but I knew she'd been scared. I know she was worried, George. I just don't know what about."

George reached across and took the envelope from her and she watched as he opened it and tipped the contents out on to the bed. It was an odd sort of envelope, Ursula thought. There was a little hole in the flap that a paper fastener poked through so the envelope could be closed or opened as many times as you liked to add things or take things out. One of the offices she cleaned at used them for their internal mail but she hadn't seen them anywhere else.

Together they stared at the objects on the bed. This was not, Ursula thought, what she had expected to be in that envelope, not at all.

CHAPTER 11

It hadn't taken much persuasion to get Joy to take her out to
Jean Hammond's place the following morning. She didn't
expect to meet Cal or anyone else there, but had an excuse in
hand, just in case, that she'd lost some keys and wondered if
she might have dropped them in the garden.

"How are Tim's rehearsals going?" Rina asked as they
got out of the car. They'd spent the journey catching up with
Joy's news and with what her mother, Bridie, was getting up
to. Fitch, technically a one-time employee of the family but
always a lot more than that had, as Joy put it, finally got his
act together and proposed.

Everyone was delighted, the wedding was being planned
and Joy was to be chief bridesmaid. It was, Rina thought,
likely to be as over the top as everything else Bridie did.

"Not as well as he'd hoped," Joy said cautiously, "but
you and I both know they never go as well as he hopes and
it always works out OK. I don't think it's the illusions themselves that are causing the problem as trying to fit everything
in with what Lily and James are hoping for. They wanted
Tim's magic to fit in with one of their themed weekends and
for the magic stuff to be sort of woven through it all, if you
see what I mean."

"I'm not really sure I do, what's the theme?"

"Well, I think that's the issue. They're planning another of their murder mystery events in the gap between Christmas and New Year, you know how well they go down, they're always booked up weeks in advance. This is going to be a big three-day thing, it's set in nineteenth-century London or nineteenth-century Frantham or somewhere nineteenth-century, anyway. Lily's got a bee in her bonnet about authentic costumes and everyone wearing crinolines or something and so the magic has to be in keeping with that but she keeps changing her mind as to exactly what she wants in terms of the story. Driving him daft, it is, but I'm sure they'll figure it out. I've learned it's best not to ask him too many questions at this stage."

Rina nodded wisely. "Because he might well feel the need to tell you at very great length."

Joy laughed. She took Rina's arm and studied the house intently. "It's rather lovely isn't it," Rina said. "I always rather fancied a place like this but it wouldn't do for our lot, too far away from the shops and the promenade and all of the things they like to do."

"Well Matthew has a driving licence, so does Steven. For that matter so does Bethany. And so do you. The answer might be to buy a little car. Though how much would a place like this be on the market for? That's assuming the son wants to sell."

"Cal's life is in Exeter, not here. He'll sell up."

They walked around the side of the house and through the small gate into the garden. "Wow," Joy said. "This is amazing." She reached into her pocket for her phone. "Let me get some pictures, lots of ideas for my garden."

Rina stood watching as Joy wandered around the flower beds. It was a beautiful house and a lovely garden and she had to admit she was sorely tempted. But a prospective if slightly impractical move wasn't what she was here for. She went up the stairs to the studio and tried the door and was somewhat surprised to find it open. She stood just inside the doorway waiting for her eyes to adjust to the relative gloom, realising that the last time she had been here light had flooded in through the skylight and through the windows along the long wall. Blinds had been drawn across both; thick, canvas, roller type blinds that she didn't even recall seeing before when she had been focusing on other things.

She looked for a light switch and flicked it on. The walls had been stripped bare, the easels gone, the shelves emptied of their paint and pots of brushes and all the artistic detritus that Jean had left behind. Only the heavy plan chests remained.

Rina frowned; she had not been expecting this. It had been only yesterday that she had been here with Cal and at that point he had been flummoxed by the task of packing Jean's life away. Maybe he'd decided he just had to get rid quickly and be done with it. Why, she asked herself, did that bother her so much?

She could hear Joy calling to her and then coming up the stairs. "Is this where she worked? Wow what a studio."

"You should have seen it before," Rina said, wishing she'd managed to take photos of this space when she had last been here. "It looks like Cal has started on his clear-up. Just about everything's gone."

"That's sad," Joy replied. Her attention was drawn to the plan chests. "How will they get those out?"

"I was wondering that." Rina went over to the sets of drawers and opened them one by one. Empty. "I expect even her working drawings would fetch a fair bit in the current market," she said. "I imagine Cal just felt they'd be safer elsewhere."

"So why not move them before? You said everything seemed to be here when you came over the other day. She'd already been gone three weeks or so by then."

It was a good point, Rina thought.

They went back down the stairs and through the veg garden to the shed where Jean had stored her herbs and remedies. Joy followed the path around the shed and into a sunny patch of garden that Rina had not visited. Rina heard her laugh. "Purely for medicinal use I guess," she said.

Curious, Rina followed her. The scent from the little cluster of spiky leaved plants was strong as Joy crushed a leaf between her fingers.

"She grew marijuana?" That, Rina figured, was why Cal had not been keen on her hanging around in the shed. She remembered the sudden change of mood and wondered if he'd been aware of Jean's crop. Maybe he'd just spotted it yesterday and been worried what Rina might think.

Joy was studying the plants thoughtfully. "Well," she said, "Jean Hammond grew just about everything else, so why not. Lots of medicinal uses and who's going to notice a few . . . irregular plants in among the herbaceous borders? Though if Cal was having a clear out, I'm surprised he missed these. Not the sort of thing your local estate agent is going to be pleased about when they arrange their viewings."

"Indeed not," Rina agreed. She examined the bed more closely. "Cannabis plants, tomatoes, nasturtiums, kale. And the little bench seat in the middle of it all."

"Rina, who did the garden for her?" Joy asked.

Rina blinked. It was an obvious question and one that she had not thought to ask. Yes, everyone knew that Jean Hammond still loved her garden, pottered around it is much as she could, but she could not possibly have been the one who managed it. The heavy digging involved in her veg beds or the weeding in the long borders, or the pruning of the fruit trees, would have been extensive. Rina could see it had all been well maintained, as had the hedges that surrounded the garden, mostly native plants and left to do pretty much what they wanted, but obviously kept within bounds so that they didn't overrun. Jean had once told her that the hedges had been planted for the wildlife and the garden was planted for herself and they all rubbed along very nicely together.

"A very good question," she said. "And one we need to find the answer to."

In the shed everything was still in place and Rina took more photographs so that she could research further into what the various herbs might be used for. On impulse she slipped Jean's notebooks into her capacious handbag. She was amused to find a jar labelled as 'Mary Jane' and Joy opened it and poked about inside.

"This looks to be parts from the whole plant," she said. "My guess is she's not using it for smoking or even to make resin, she's probably using it in an infusion for tea or possibly an extraction. She could make an alcohol extraction and use the drops. Or she could just infuse the whole lot in a jar of alcohol if she wanted to keep it simple." She pointed to a series of jars on the shelf filled with clear liquid and plant material next to a selection of fine sieves and a stack of folded muslin cloth.

"You seem very well-informed."

"Dad tried to keep us out of the business., He reckoned I hadn't got the head for it and Patrick as you know wanted to go his own way, but we still learned a lot as we went along. You pick things up. Anyway, don't forget, Gran and Grandad were legitimate pharmacists and they were also really interested in herbs. Gran had a still very much like that one and she taught me and Mum a lot about home remedies. It wasn't really Dad's thing," she added. "Not enough profit in creams and cures. I'm still finding my way when it comes to planting stuff, but when I was growing up I learned a lot about what to do with it when it had grown. All the hemp family is good for making ropes and fabric and paper, creams for arthritis and skin problems, and one of the traditional uses for cannabis tea is in childbirth. It's an anti-inflammatory and helps with pain relief. If she was in pain, it would have helped."

"And the monkshood?" Rina asked, pointing to another jar. "I can't see that being much help for her."

"Not unless she wanted to poison someone," Joy agreed. "Aconite is pretty powerful. Wasn't there a case a while ago when a woman poisoned her husband by mixing it in with his curry?"

"Now you mention it, that does sound familiar, yes."

They left the shed and walked back down the garden and Joy pointed to the willow tree. "Is that where she was found?"

Rina nodded.

"People are strange, aren't they?" Joy said.

"They are, but why do you say that now?"

"Well, from what I heard, they reckon she was in the garden deadheading, was taken ill and she wanted to sit down. Well, if that's the case, why choose the willow tree. Look, this garden is obviously arranged for somebody who can't walk very far but who likes to be out and about in it. There are seats everywhere. Two by that border, another on the edge of the lawn, two more benches near that old wall. If she was deadheading in any of the borders, she wouldn't have had to walk more than a few yards to get any of them. But the tree is right down at the bottom of the garden away from everything. It just seems a bit strange."

Twice in the past few minutes, Joy had taken her by surprise and asked obvious questions that Rina had just missed. *Must do better*, she told herself.

"Have you seen anything of Ursula and George lately?" Rina asked.

"Not for the past week or two. We WhatsApp most days but they're both up to their ears in exams and work, we plan to meet up end of next week. I said I'd take them out for a meal, celebrate the end of exams." Joy hesitated and then added, "I tend to nip round with groceries and stuff maybe a couple of times a month. I know they're both having a tough time."

"If they need help, they only have to ask, you know that."

"Of course, they do. Look, Ursula's been helping me with my studies. Going back to college has not been easy. I'm loving it, especially all the practical stuff, but the essays are a killer. I told Ursula, as she's helped me out with my essays, I can pay for her time by taking her some groceries, and often I order pizza and then we have some time to chat and watch a film or whatever. It's like I've got a younger brother and sister and they look up to me as a big sister, and that feels really good, you know. And it's easier to accept help from the big sister."

Rina nodded, appreciating that but still a little upset. "Well, if you can think of a way that I can help then let me know?"

"I will, I promise. But Rina, that wasn't just a casual question, that was a loaded one. So, what's your problem? Are you worried about them?"

"I'm not sure. You know that Ursula knew Jean Hammond?"

"I know she did some cleaning for her and I know she got on well with her. Miss Hammond gave her some free drawing lessons."

"Yes, I came over with Ursula to collect her portfolios. I have to say I was surprised, I knew nothing about it. But then, I don't see either of them as often as I did."

"They were just up the road before. Now they're twenty minutes away by car and I know that doesn't sound like much, but it adds up, with all the stuff they've got to deal with."

"I know, I do know. And I've been away filming and, oh, it's only natural that they should be busy and involved with other things and . . ."

"So, what's bothering you? Apart from the fact that you hoped you'd be the first line of defence when either Ursula or George was in trouble?"

The words were softened by a smile and a hug but Rina knew them to be spot on and that she was indeed smarting. She told Joy what had happened on the day they had come over, what Cal had said about the third drawer being his at one time and that she was certain Ursula had opened another and taken something out. That she had aided and abetted by keeping Cal's attention turned away, because she'd been sure there was something Ursula did not want Cal to see.

"I just had this feeling that Ursula was hesitating over something; was up to something. I don't mean underhanded, at least I wouldn't have thought so, but—"

"So, you acted on instinct and helped her do whatever it was and now you're miffed because you don't know what it was you were drawing the attention from."

Again, there was the hug and the smile and Rina had to laugh at herself. "You know me so well," she said. "But I am concerned too, Joy, and not just curious. It's not like Ursula to be in any way underhanded. It would have been easy for her to tell Cal that she had her portfolios in one drawer and some other possession in another. I don't think he'd have thought twice."

"And so, you think she might have taken something that wasn't strictly hers," Joy said.

Rina nodded.

"That seems like a fair assumption, but Rina, you know Ursula. She's honest as the day and protective of those she cares about. She cared about this Jean Hammond, I could tell that from the way she talked about her."

"She didn't mention her to me."

"And that hurt you? Rina, I don't even know that Ursula was aware you knew her. Why should she be? I've not heard you mention her before. It's not like she was a close friend, just someone you saw from time to time on some committee or other. Miss Hammond and her lessons were a private, personal, sensitive thing for Ursula. We all think of Ursula as the ultimate academic, the scientist, the kid who does what's expected of her. Yes, even you, Rina darling, we think we've got her sussed so I think it's hard for her to break our expectations. She didn't even tell George at first and she kept her drawings here, not in her flat. We all need to squirrel away some space for ourselves from time to time, Jean Hammond was just hers."

Rina nodded, accepting all of that but still concerned.

"So, will you ask her or should I," Joy said. "Or should we wait for her to come to us? She will, you know, if she can't sort whatever it is herself. Rina, you might not be Ursula's first line of defence these days, but you can be very certain that you're her back-up plan."

CHAPTER 12

When Joy and Rina arrived back at Peverill Lodge that evening they spotted Ursula's car parked just a little down the road.

"Well, well," Joy said. "Maybe you're going to find out what Ursula took without asking her."

Rina nodded but she could hear the slight anxiety in Joy's voice and knew that the young woman was thinking as she was that if Ursula had come over to see Rina then it was likely to have a problem dealt with.

They opened the door and stepped into the hall, the space filled with the scent of baking bread and rich tomato sauce, Matthew's go-to recipe when guests turned up unexpectedly. It's easy, he had once explained to Rina. It suits the vegetarians as is and can easily be turned into a Bolognese. Whatever the reasoning, it tasted good, Rina thought, recognising abruptly that she was really rather hungry.

Voices also drifted through into the hall, Steven and the Peters' sisters and Ursula and George. Matthew came out from the kitchen and smiled to see Joy and Rina. "Just in time," he said. "We have extra people for dinner and there'll be plenty if Tim or anyone else should happen to turn up. Fortunately, I also baked today. And I've put the kettle on."

"You are an absolute treasure," Rina told him. "How long have they been here?"

"About an hour. I think there's a little difficulty needs solving so Ursula has brought it home for us all to help."

He bustled back into the kitchen and Rina was aware of Joy giggling. "Of course, she has," Joy said. "How could you ever think otherwise Rina?"

Joy kicked off her shoes and tucked them underneath the hall table as she always did; in winter Rina kept a pair of slippers for her to change into when she arrived. She paused before following Joy, breathed deeply, gathering her thoughts and her resources and suddenly deeply and overwhelmingly grateful that she had these people around her even though some of them were undoubtedly eccentric. That this place had indeed become a family home.

Peverill Lodge had a small front room that Rina kept as her personal space and then a very large room which served as both dining room and sitting room. It had a big fireplace for the winter and large French doors which stood open most of the summer. When she went in everyone was already gathered around a small table set beside the French doors. The Peters sisters were twittering excitedly, Steven was speaking to Ursula in what looked to Rina to be a very serious and considered manner, but then that was typical Steven. He would have made a brilliant father, Rina thought, had circumstances been different. Over the years he had been very protective of these young people who had come so unexpectedly into their lives. George was standing a little to one side, looking serious, and Joy now had an arm around his shoulders and was listening to whatever it was he was saying.

The objects which were the focus for their attention were set on this table, lying on top of a manila envelope.

Tea and cake had already been consumed, Rina noted as Matthew bustled in with yet more.

"Jumpy as a little deer, the poor thing has been," he said confidingly. "Apparently she's been wanting to come and see us all since yesterday but what with college and work, this is the first opportunity they've had." He set his tray down on the sideboard and Rina assumed that Matthew must already have taken a good look at whatever Ursula had brought with her.

She went over to stand beside her young friend, aware that all eyes had now swivelled in her direction, the Peters sisters' wide with expectation, Steven with confidence that all would now be sorted satisfactorily and George and Ursula with a little more anxiety.

"This is what you took from the other drawer in the studio?" Rina asked, looking at Ursula.

Ursula nodded. "She asked me to. This was before Christmas when she was very poorly and she was seriously worried about not making it to New Year. Then she seemed to forget about everything until a few weeks before she died. She seemed worried about something for a while but when I arrived one day, it must've been a Tuesday . . . well she seemed genuinely upset and she reminded me about the envelope and she made me promise that if anything happened to her I would deal with it. She said I must take it away, look inside and that I would then know what to do."

"Well, I don't know what to do but we figured, George and me, that if Jean knew you then she might expect me to bring it here."

"We did wonder," Steven said, "and I think Ursula is right in her assumption, why Jean Hammond could not ask you directly. But Ursula very wisely suggested that had you been asked for help you would have felt compelled to try and find out what was going on. And that might not have been what Jean wanted at that point. Perhaps timing was important to her."

Matthew was busying himself topping up everybody's tea and coffee requirements. Matthew was at his happiest, Rina reflected, when he was feeding and watering people especially if he was feeling unsettled. She looked at the objects on the table then pulled up a chair and settled down to examine them more closely. "Well, let's get to the bottom of this shall we?"

CHAPTER 13

Mac stood at the entrance to the studio, studying the room as Rina had done the previous day. It seemed, according to Calvin Hammond, that Rina's conscience had got the better of her and she had phoned Cal to say that she had called round looking for some lost keys and had noticed the studio door was unlocked. She had during the course of their conversation mentioned that Cal must have cleared the studio out and apparently been sympathetic about how difficult that must have been. At which point alarm bells had rung because Jean Hammond's adopted son had no idea what Rina was talking about.

He had removed the commission, of course. First thing on the day after Jean's death, Etta had gone and collected it for him. But he hadn't touched anything else. Apparently, Cal Hammond hadn't yet felt prepared for that. And so the police had been called and now Mac was here, with Yolanda as it happened, and he was slightly irritated with Rina Martin because Mac knew her well enough that her phone call to Cal had not been to apologise for some minor trespass. It must have been because Rina had suddenly realised that it was likely some person other than Calvin had removed Jean Hammond's belongings.

Mac's irritation was due to the fact that, if she'd called him, he could have dealt with the matter sooner. Perhaps, if he was honest, it was also due to the fact that this whole situation had too many niggles in it. At the back of his mind he was quite prepared to find out that the death of the elderly artist was not so straightforward. And if that was the case then so much time been lost it was going to be very hard to get any kind of investigation on track.

So, he wasn't really annoyed with Rina, Mac acknowledged, so much as at the situation.

The young woman standing behind him began to fidget. Yolanda was no good at staying still. "Art thieves, you reckon?"

"Of course, that's possible. But the security on this place is rubbish, you'd have thought if anyone wanted to pinch a Jean Hammond painting they would have come in straight after her death was reported. It was common knowledge within hours and once you'd left the place was unguarded."

"I made sure everything was locked up tight."

"I'm sure you did, but what did that involve. Closing the padlock on the studio door? Shooting the bolts in the kitchen? Like I say, this place is a security nightmare."

Yolanda walked into the middle of the studio and turned in a slow circle. "Whoever it was, they've taken everything," she said. "Not even a stick of charcoal left."

Mac joined her. "What do you remember about this room?"

"Pity I didn't think to take photographs," Yolanda said. "I did take some of the garden, I thought there was no harm in that and I was trying to match that flower she had in her hand. But it wouldn't have felt right to have taken pictures of this place, this is where she painted, where she lived, it's all personal."

"You were tempted though?" Mac smiled at her.

"Oh sure, who wouldn't be? I'd never been in an artist's studio before, never mind a famous one. It was fascinating."

"So, describe it to me." He knew Yolanda's powers of observation were excellent, having worked with her previously. She noticed odd things that often proved useful.

"OK, wouldn't it be better to get the son to do that once he arrives."

"I can always ask him as well, compare notes. You're more likely to notice things that he wouldn't. This is a familiar place to him and, to a certain extent, we stop seeing familiar places."

Yolanda nodded and turned to face the door. "There were aprons on the coat hooks by the door. And a smock thing, covered in paint. Those shelves there, closest to the door, on the top shelf were lots of different solvents and things to mix paint with. Some were for cleaning brushes, there was something called a brush restorer in a little pot, there were different oils and waxes." She closed her eyes. "Poppy oil, linseed, turpentine, odourless thinners and various mixes with faded labels on. It looks like she must've been a bit of a magpie, or bit of a hoarder. On the shelf underneath there were loads of books about art, all lying on their sides because they wouldn't fit upright and the shelf was bowing — you can see that now."

Mac nodded; the shelf had indeed been distorted by objects that were much too heavy for its intended use.

"Then there were brushes and pallet knives on top of that built-in cupboard. Obviously, they couldn't take that away, whoever they were. Some of them were stored upright in pots and some are hanging from these little racks. It looked like they were in a particular order that she understood, but I've no idea what it might have been. The only kind of paintbrush I've ever used, since I left school, is for painting walls."

"Did you look in the cupboards?"

She looked slightly shocked and then shook her head. "No this was strictly standing in the middle of the room and looking. Look with your eyes and not with your hands, as my mum used to say. If I'm honest I was a bit overawed, especially by the painting on the big easel. That was gorgeous."

The sound of a car pulling up on the gravel interrupted them. Cal arriving, Mac assumed. "Write it down," he said. "Anything you can remember. Draw a map."

She gave him a quizzical look.

"It's just good practice," Mac told her.

* * *

By the time he had descended the metal stairs, Cal was coming round the side of the house, his steps swift and his face creased with concern. He brushed past Mac and raced upwards to the studio. Mac waited at the foot of the steps, hearing exclamations of horror and anger and Yolanda's more soothing tone.

Cal was back down only moments later. "They've stripped the place," he said. "Taken every damned thing. Taken the fucking lot."

"We should go into the house," Mac said. "See if there's anything missing there. Tell me, Mr Hammond, was there anything particularly unusual in the materials Miss Hammond used that would make them especially valuable? I can understand that thieves might take artworks, even rough drawings in the hope of selling them to collectors, but it seems odd to have taken paints and brushes and thinners. My colleague commented that they'd not even left a stick of charcoal behind."

"What? Oh, I don't know. How would I know what goes through people's minds when they do something like this?" He frowned, gestured towards the studio. "She was here the day Jean died."

"Yolanda . . . DC Connors, yes, she was. She stayed with you until your partner arrived to take you home and then stayed on until Miss Hammond's body was collected."

Cal blinked as though processing that. "On her own?" he asked. "That must have been . . . I wondered who'd locked up. When Etta came over the following day everything was locked and my neighbours had the keys."

Mac began to move towards the back door of the house. Cal followed his lead. "Do your neighbours routinely have keys? Or anyone else we should know about?"

"You're saying someone let themselves in with the key?"

"I'm saying we don't know. DC Connors remembered that the padlock wasn't a particularly heavy one, bolt croppers would have taken care of that. It's likely someone cut through and got in that way but, as it's missing, we just don't know."

"The thief took the padlock away? Isn't that odd?"

"Not if they were worried about fingerprints or tool marks, though most likely they wore gloves. This doesn't look like a random burglary. Not with the place being picked clean the way it has been. It's also possible that the thief simply put the padlock in a pocket without thinking about it. Shall we go in, Mr Hammond, the door to the kitchen is still fastened."

Cal hesitated, key in hand. "Shouldn't we wait until everything has been fingerprinted?"

"There's no one available until tomorrow morning," Mac explained. "Resources are a tad stretched." He didn't feel like explaining that a tidy break-in to an unoccupied house, would not come as high up the list of police priorities. Mac was fairly sanguine about this, he'd seen often enough the impact of such a robbery, of having your belongings pawed and thrown around the room, urinated on or worse, to feel that such incidents deserved any resources that could be thrown their way. Lord alone knew that was little enough, Mac thought. Whoever had broken into Jean Hammond's studio and left with all of her materials, sketches, and whatever else, had been organised and thorough and had probably taken their time over it. The Willows was set well back from the road and the high hedge in front practically guaranteed that any van parked up ready to receive the stolen goods would not be seen.

Sighing, Cal unlocked the door, trying not to touch anything, Mac noted, as he pushed it wide open.

Inside the kitchen everything looked clean and tidy. There was the slightly musty smell of a house locked up and unaired for a succession of summer days. The refrigerator hummed softly and Mac found himself hoping that Cal had emptied it after Jean Hammond's death.

"At least the boiler isn't leaking now," Cal said absently.

"The boiler?"

"Oh, I got here yesterday to meet Rina — Miss Martin—"

"I know Rina Martin."

"Oh, right, yes of course you do. She said she'd ask you if there were any doubts about Jean's death being just natural causes."

"She did ask me and I asked around those that had been here that day. There seemed to be no suspicious circumstances and as she'd seen the doctor in the previous forty-eight hours and been under his care for some time, it all seemed perfectly understandable."

"And now?"

"And now there's been a burglary," Mac said. "It happens more often than you might thing after someone dies. There's always someone ready to take advantage." He paused, allowed that thought to settle and then prompted Cal, "You were telling me about the leaky boiler?"

"Oh. Yes. I got here and there was water on the floor. Not much, just like a seep from the pipe. I called a plumber and they came straight out."

"That was lucky."

"That was persistence. The fifth so-called emergency plumber I phoned said he could fit me in as long as it was a quick job. He said he'd come and have a look but anything major and he'd need to come back later."

"But he fixed it."

"It's not leaking so he must have done." Cal sounded dismissive. "He was working on it when Rina and the girl arrived."

"Girl?"

"Ursula . . . something. She'd left some things here and Rina brought her to pick them up."

"We should check the rest of the house," Mac said, "and I'll need contact details for the plumber, just in case he spotted anyone hanging about."

Cal nodded but passed no further comment.

"You were telling me who might have keys," Mac went on as they passed from the kitchen into the flagstone hallway. It was, he thought, a little like stepping back in time. The hall betrayed signs of the original use and age of the building with heavy beams and a solid looking door; equally solid doors led off into living room and dining room. The upright columns of dark oak, originally holding the upper storey, had been cleverly integrated into the studding. The walls, though they looked solid and thick were, Mac realised, stud partitions, probably with insulation between, brought out to the thickness of the ancient uprights and used to subdivide the massive area. The carriage house would once have been a single, open space, presumably.

He asked Cal about how the building was originally used.

"Where the wide front door now hangs had originally been much wider, double doors," Cal replied. "The place had been part-converted before Jean bought it. Stone from another outbuilding was used to fill in part of the old archway where the carriages were brought in and the door came from a stable block that was in such a state they'd had to knock it down. The house was in a hell of state when we first moved and we lived in a caravan in the garden while she got it fixed up. She bought it at auction for a song and it was so bad it didn't even reach the reserve price, so she had the auctioneer approach the owner. Fortunately, they just wanted to get rid. I think they thought she was some naive idiot townie and that it would be back on the market within six months, but once Jean had set her mind to something, that was that."

He led the way into the living room and looked around. The TV and hi fi were still there, as was an extensive collection of vinyl and CDs, Mac noted. "Did she hang any of her own work in the house?" Mac asked.

"Not in here. All the pictures in here are from ex-students. Some going back to just after the war. Some of them are famous in their own right now, but everything seems to be here."

Mac would have liked a closer look but Cal was already heading across the hall to the dining room. Then he stopped abruptly.

"They're gone," he said. "Damn it, I should have taken them away. I just never thought. Fuck, fuck, fuck!"

Mac looked past the vast dining table and the antique dresser to the far wall where two paintings were clearly missing, delineated by where the pale green wallpaper was darker than the surrounding areas.

"Did you have the pictures insured?" Mac asked.

"I don't know," Cal told him. "I didn't live here, remember? I don't know what Jean did about insurance. But even if they were, even if the insurance pays out, what does that matter. They're gone, aren't they. No one can replace them."

* * *

It was almost 10 o'clock when Mac drove back into Frantham, but he wanted to check in with Rina before he finally went home. The theft of valuable artwork had put what was now an actual police investigation on to a different footing and brought a forensic team and other officers to Jean Hammond's coach house. When Mac had finally left, the scene had been handed over to a specialist SIO, one more experienced than Mac in the theft of artworks.

Now, he wanted to know, what was it that had finally prompted Rina to confess her visit to Cal Hammond.

The light was on in Rina's front room and she opened the door before he knocked. She must have been expecting him and listening out for his footsteps, Mac thought. From the hallway he could hear the television in the living room. He followed Rina into her small, private domain. No one, not even those she loved and lived with — not even Tim — came into this space without her say so. Mac settled in his usual seat by the fireplace. This time of year, the grate was filled with fresh flowers in a dark blue vase. He found he missed the cheer of the open fire.

She kept a kettle in her room and he was soon hugging a mug of strong coffee between both hands.

"Don't want you falling asleep on the way home," Rina said.

"I think we need a long talk before that, don't we?"

She nodded, produced a tin of homemade cookies and set them on the small table beside his chair. "So, what else was taken?" she asked.

"Two Jean Hammond originals that hung in the dining room."

"I know the ones. Anything else?"

"As yet we're not sure. Cal Hammond thinks the house has been searched, but a very tidy search."

"But they decided to take everything in the studio. Doesn't that strike you as odd?"

"Very," Mac agreed, helping himself to a cookie and taking a bite. "These are good."

"I'll tell Matthew you said so. It's a new recipe. So, they searched the house—"

"Took the paintings."

"Which were an easy find. Perhaps they were searching for something else too? They started on the studio and realised they had been there too long . . . that it would be easier to take everything away?"

"It's possible. It would help if we knew what they might have been looking for. Was it something small enough to have been hidden in a tube of paint? I mean that's the only reason I can think of that might have led them to strip the studio.

Rina nodded. "Well, perhaps I can help with that."

Mac frowned at his friend. "Rina, what—"

"Oh hush," she said. "For once I've not done anything you'd disapprove of. I don't think so anyway." He watched as she went to her bureau and withdrew a large brown envelope.

"You know that Ursula also knew Jean?"

"Cal mentioned her. You'd gone with her to collect some drawings?"

79

"Jean had been giving her lessons. Ursula also cleaned for her."

"Ursula can draw? Sorry, that sounds . . ." He wasn't sure how it sounded. Just a tad incredulous, maybe. "Is there anything that girl can't do?"

Quickly and concisely, Rina filled him in on her visit with Ursula and the suspicion that the girl had taken something more than her portfolios. Then her second visit with Joy, when they discovered that the studio had been raided.

"When we got back this afternoon George and Ursula were waiting for us. She had, as instructed by Jean, taken this envelope and opened it. Jean had told Ursula that once she'd seen the contents, she would know what to do about them. What she did was bring them to me."

Of course, she had, Mac thought. "And that's the envelope?"

Rina nodded. She placed a folding table between them and emptied the contents on to the surface. Mac stared. "Who's handled these?"

"Ursula and George. They tipped them out on to the table to show us, but George suggested that no one else should touch them in case there were fingerprints. Personally, I think it's a bit late for that but—"

Mac nodded. "The key looks like it might fit a locker or a padlock."

"I don't think I recognise anyone in the photograph either. It looks to have been taken a while ago. From the clothes I'd have said late 1970s."

"I'd agree."

"What was Ursula supposed to do with this though? What am I supposed to glean from it? No idea."

"It's not like you to be short on the ideas front." Mac smiled. "It would help if we knew what the key fitted."

"There looks to be a serial number on it and it looks pretty new. Maybe try the local banks first? See if she had a safety deposit box."

"I'll have to take these away, Rina. I'm assuming you've taken a copy of the photograph."

She tapped the mobile phone sitting on her chair arm. "You know me well."

"I should be warning you that these may be evidence—"

"Of what?"

"Hard to say. But if whoever took her possessions was looking for this envelope . . . I suppose she was still of sound mind?" he asked cautiously.

"Sharp as a tack last time I saw her, which admittedly was in February. Ursula said she was getting more forgetful and that she was definitely worried about something, as I told you earlier. She first talked to Ursula about taking the envelope late last year, then again a few weeks before she died."

"If she was so keen to entrust it to someone, why not have Ursula take it away then. Or give it to you?"

"The consensus about that seems to be that I might have interfered, poked my nose in," Rina said wryly. "As to why she didn't give it to Ursula, maybe she hoped that whatever action she wanted taking would in the end not be necessary."

That seemed like a reasonable assumption, Mac thought. Or at least one that would do for now. "So why not leave instructions. Some sort of clue."

Rina shrugged. "She seems to have had faith in Ursula making the right call," she said. "It's possible Ursula knows more about this than she realises. Right now, she's just upset and confused but with someone asking the right questions she might be able to tell us more."

"The right questions . . ." Mac said. "Well, if you or anyone else comes up with a list of those, be sure to let me know." He drained his coffee and stood. "I need to be going. It would be nice to get a few hours' sleep before tomorrow's briefing. I'm off to see Dave Kendall, and whoever else is going to be looking into what is now an art theft, in the morning."

"Give him my best," Rina told him.

Mac grinned at her. DI Dave Kendall was never quite sure what to make of Rina Martin. "I'll be sure to do that," he said.

* * *

81

When Mac had gone Rina picked up her phone and switched on her printer. She had bought one with a Bluetooth connection the previous year and it had definitely proved its worth. She printed the photograph and then stepped back as though to put some distance between herself and the contents of the envelope. She felt deeply resentful of Jean Hammond for having involved Ursula in whatever this was. She also felt very uneasy but wasn't at all sure why. She sensed that the answer to this lay in something she had already seen and this feeling drew Rina to look more closely at the photograph, a little impatient with herself.

Rina frowned. Then retrieved her phone from the chair arm and scrolled through the pictures she had taken of the original, zoomed in on some of the faces acknowledging that several looked vaguely familiar, though perhaps only in that way that pretty young people often looked like one another. Then she recognised Jean Hammond. Younger than when Rina had known her, of course but older than the rest of the group in the picture. She looked very glamorous and beautifully turned out in a simply cut, tailored dress. She must, Rina made a rough guesstimate, have been around fifty. She looked more closely at the rest of the group and . . . Rina almost dropped the phone as the significance of one face hit home. He was standing in the back row, not looking into the camera but at something that seemed to have attracted his attention across the room. And now that vision had resolved into recognition, she could not believe she had not seen it before.

Rina rarely swore but now she wanted to, and her hand shook.

Suddenly impatient with it and especially with her own shocked reaction, she picked up the photograph and shoved it into a desk drawer. This could wait until morning when hopefully she could snatch an hour with Joy and Tim. Perhaps they could bring some perspective to bear because right now Rina had none. She just felt angry with Jean Hammond, with the man in the picture, with the memories that surfaced, sudden and stabbingly sharp. Angry and oddly afraid that she had only ever seen the surface of this woman; only that part which she was happy to expose to the world.

What was she hiding, Rina wondered, and did Cal have any idea?

CHAPTER 14

The following morning Mac followed DI Kendall and Yolanda into the briefing room. A woman from the unit specialising in the investigation of high-level art and antiques thefts was waiting for them. She was plump and blonde, dressed in a smart suit, and exuded the kind of energy Mac usually associated with the likes of Rina Martin.

"DI Stella Fullhurst," she introduced herself, shaking hands with Mac and Yolanda and acknowledging Dave Kendall with a friendly smile. "So, we've got a bit of a mystery on our hands as well as a theft. Who put the list together, by the way?"

"Of the stuff in the studio? That would be me," Yolanda looked anxiously at the senior officer. It was odd to see her insecurities on display, Mac thought. She usually put on a very good show of being in total control.

"Did you take notes at the time?" Stella Fullhurst sounded intrigued.

"Um, no. I was just interested and to be honest I was a bit . . . bored. And, like I told DI McGregor, I'd never seen an artist's studio before. I didn't touch anything, I just looked"

"You remember a lot."

"I've got a head like a rag bag, my mum always says. Everything gets kept and nothing gets sorted. I mean—" As though she suddenly realised how off-hand that sounded, Yolanda blushed.

"From what I've seen you do a good job of sorting," Mac said quietly, earning himself a raised eyebrow from Kendall and a surprised look from Yolanda. He'd made no secret of the fact that he'd found Yolanda a waste of space when he'd first encountered her. But she'd matured. Or maybe he'd just been paying more attention recently.

"I didn't know what half the stuff was," she explained. "Waxes and varnishes and oils. I went home and looked up what they did. Some of them are really pricey. I'd no idea you could spend hundreds on a tube of paint or a bottle of cold pressed linseed oil."

Stella laughed. "She was an artist at the top of her game, she would have been thinking about the longevity of her work now. It has to be said that in her early days she used what she could afford and what happened to be available, just like most artists have to."

"So, it might be worth someone stealing her stuff just for what it is?" Yolanda asked. "I mean, to actually use?"

"I suppose that's possible," Stella sounded doubtful. "The drawings and half-finished work would certainly be worth something. The finished pictures are very valuable. The two from the house were valued at between twenty and thirty thousand each, but that valuation hasn't been uprated in the past decade, so it's well out. And now she's dead and there'll be no more Jean Hammonds, well."

"Nothing else was taken," Mac said. "There was a half decent hi fi and a good music collection. Some very nice pieces of jewellery just stuffed into a box in a dressing table drawer. She doesn't seem to have been someone who put a lot of thought into what things were worth."

"And nothing else was disturbed?"

"Well, the son can't be sure but he thinks some of her papers had been moved. She had a tiny office for her computer and paperwork, next to her bedroom, but he admits it was never the tidiest of places, so it was hard to tell."

"And he's no sense of what might have been shifted?"

"Not for certain, though he reckons however messy she was with everything else, she kept all her tax stuff in strict order on a top shelf. He speculated that someone had taken the records down and put them back in the wrong order, but—"

Stella nodded.

"Her studio wasn't like that," Yolanda put in. "It was dead clean and tidy enough that even my mum wouldn't be able to find fault."

Yolanda's mum seemed to figure heavily in the young woman's consciousness, Mac thought wryly.

"I always imagined an artist's studio would be messy. Paint splatters and mucky palettes everywhere and stuff."

"Some artists are messy," Stella told her.

"No, but you're right," Mac frowned. "I didn't see the studio intact, but even the shelves were clean. No solvent or oil spills, no paint marks. I'd make more mess painting a wall."

"You think it might have been cleaned after the theft?" Kendall asked. He'd been busying himself making tea and coffee and now set mugs down on the table.

"Forensics have found prints on the door, the drawers, random other places where you'd expect them to be, even the shelves, so I'm inclined to think not. However, it's something to keep in mind. Cal, the son, he mentioned one other thing that might have been examined by the thieves. Her collection of photo albums. He noticed one was in the wrong place. Apparently, they were also kept in strict date order."

"And have we got access to the paperwork from the office? Her computer?"

"Yes, and the photo albums, which will probably tell us nothing, but you never know. It's odd that the computer was still there."

"Was there a password?"

"No, she never bothered apparently, so it's possible if the thieves wanted something they just downloaded the information and left the computer there. All I can say is that it must have taken them some time to clear the studio and they'd have needed a van to take it all away."

"And that while they were completely happy to announce the theft of the contents of Miss Hammond's studio they seem to have been more cautious about revealing that they'd been into the house," Kendall commented.

"Though they took the paintings and maybe searched elsewhere," Stella objected.

"*Maybe* searched. Miss Hammond might just have put things back in the wrong place. She was an old lady, maybe the odd thing got away from her. If it hadn't been for Mrs Martin looking for her keys," Kendall paused and let that hang for a moment. He'd had enough experience of Rina, Mac thought, to know there had been no errant keys.

"But for Mrs Martin going over there, it might have been another week or more before the son realised anything was gone. And we don't know how likely he'd have been to go into the studio. He'd been content to leave everything there, even though he must have known that any of Jean Hammond's works would suddenly have gone up in value. Most people would have moved everything that might be worth anything as fast as possible."

Mac nodded. That had struck him as a little odd too. "Apparently the neighbour had a key to the kitchen door in case of emergency or for when Miss Hammond was away. But Cal could think of no one else that might have one. Even he didn't have a spare key for the studio but as we're assuming whoever our thieves were they simply bolt croppered the padlock, it's a moot point."

"And the neighbour's key is accounted for?"

"It is, yes." He paused, and produced a selection of photographs from the folder he had with him. "As you'll see, the front door has a very old lock with a very large key that lives in a tea caddy in the hall. It's a solid door and also has two massive bolts. Miss Hammond was used to coming and going via the kitchen door. She had her groceries delivered straight into the kitchen, the post was dropped off into a metal box by the door. The door itself is a standard, wooden, half glazed back door. There are bolts top and bottom which she apparently used at night and a standard Yale which she habitually kept on the latch in daytime. There's also, as you can see in the pictures, an ordinary roller catch that kept the door closed when the locks weren't in use, which was apparently most of the time. Miss Hammond's keys, including the spares, hung on a hook just behind the kitchen door so theoretically anyone coming to the house could have seen and taken them, got copies made."

"You have a list of people who might have had access." Stella asked.

"We've made a start on that," Mac said. "It's likely to be long. She wasn't much keen on going out shopping and preferred to have everything delivered. The computer seems to have been used for online shopping more than anything else. We've someone going through the emails and any documents, but there doesn't seem to be a lot of anything."

"Did she have a mobile phone?"

"She did, yes. Cal says that she was far from being a technophobe. She liked social media, belonged to several WhatsApp groups, though he was a bit vague as to who else was involved. Unfortunately, the phone seems to be missing."

"That was taken in the robbery?"

"Possibly. Equally possibly it was taken the day she died. No one was looking for a mobile phone that day, so . . . We do know that it doesn't seem to have been used since but the fact that it's missing adds to the puzzle."

"So . . ." Yolanda began.

She sounded cautious, Mac thought, as though she might feel she was speaking out of turn.

"Does the robbery and possibility that the phone might have been taken by someone who was there when she died. Does that change our minds about her death being a natural one? I mean, there was no post-mortem because the doctor had seen her and no suspicious circumstances apart from the way she was sitting and the flower. But now, with the thefts and the fact that her phone is missing, it's starting to look—"

"Flower?" Stella interrupted.

"A bit of plant clasped in her hand," Mac said. "It was assumed she'd been dead heading or something and had felt unwell. But as Yolanda discovered, the plant she was holding didn't look like anything she'd got in her garden."

He was aware that Stella Fullhurst was staring at him. "What is it?" he asked.

"What kind of plant was it?"

Yolanda produced her phone and scrolled through the gallery. How many pictures did she have on that phone, Mac wondered.

"It was this," Yolanda said, showing Stella the crushed and rather pathetic-looking specimen she had tucked into the evidence bag. "I think it's a hydrangea, but she didn't have anything like it in her garden or at least not that I could find. It's a funny thing as well. If she'd just picked it in the garden, you'd expect it to be green, or at any rate not so brown wouldn't you? This one looks like it's been dried and half crushed."

"That's because it had been," Stella said quietly.

There was a beat or two of silence as they all watched Stella absorbing this and then Mac asked, "You've seen something like this before?"

She nodded slowly. "You might want to think about getting an exhumation order."

CHAPTER 15

Rina had arrived at the cottage where Tim and Joy lived a little after 10 o'clock. Now that Tim had moved out of Peverill Lodge, there was no one resident with a car and Rina had to take a taxi. Opening the garden gate she thought of two things. The first was that she really must get a car of her own and perhaps have Matthew or Steven put on the insurance as second driver; and the second was that the bedroom curtains were closed and perhaps she should have phoned ahead. Tim would have been working late the night before so it was quite likely he was sleeping in or possible that her visit would be disturbing something more intimate than just sleep.

Usually, she thought, she would have phoned Joy to check it was all right to come over, even if just to confirm that they were at home, but her brain had been full of the problems posed by the envelope Ursula had brought to her and she was desperate to consult Tim. She acknowledged that all other thoughts had been wiped from her mind and that she was perhaps being very inconsiderate.

A third thought occurred to her, that she really should have asked the taxi to wait.

As she stood at the gate pondering her options the front door opened and Joy stood on the doorstep barefoot and in shorts and a T-shirt.

"I heard the gate and came to see who it was then I saw you through the window," Joy said. "Come on in. Is anything wrong?"

"Only that I promised you a long time ago that I wouldn't turn up unannounced and that's exactly what I've done. I used to hate it when people just turned up out of the blue."

Joy laughed. "Don't be daft," she said. "I've got the kettle on, and I'm just about to wake Tim. He didn't finish till two, so he's a bit knackered."

Rina made her way up the short garden path and into the cool, quarry tiled hall, then followed Joy into the kitchen just as the kettle switched off.

"I've been out in the garden since early this morning," Joy said. "No lectures today, just an essay to write later on, so I thought I'd do some digging. The veg patch is coming on nicely."

Rina looked out through the kitchen window. When they had first moved here the garden had been a wilderness. Joy had restored some of the order, but not too much. The two tall ash trees still stood at the bottom and Joy scrutinised them regularly for any signs of ash dieback. Native hedging surrounded most of the garden and though she had cut this back to stop it taking over it had been left thick enough to encourage the birds to nest and the berries to grow. She had a small greenhouse, the veg patch and what she grandly called the patio, broken slabs that she had rescued from the rest of the garden and cemented in crazy paving the like of which Rina hadn't seen since the seventies.

Joy brought tea mugs over to the table. "Grab the biscuit tin, I'll just go and wake his nibs. You'll have to give him a little while to return to the land of the living, but I'm sure you remember what he's like when he first wakes up."

Rina laughed. It had always taken Tim a while to get going first thing, or what passed for first thing where Tim was concerned.

She got the biscuit tin, settled herself at the table and thanked her lucky stars yet again for good friends that had become good family.

When Joy returned a few minutes later she took the chair opposite Rina and helped herself to a couple of biscuits. "So, this is about Ursula and Jean Hammond," she guessed.

Rina nodded. Quickly she updated Joy on the events of the previous day. That she had finally decided she should phone Cal and ask him about the studio. How it turned out that Cal had not been the one to empty the space and the police were now involved, that two paintings had been stolen and that she had handed the contents of the envelope over to Mac.

"Of course, you've kept a copy of the picture."

"Of course I have and there's lots to research to be getting on with and I'm curious about the photograph and the key and . . ."

"And?" Joy tipped her head on one side and regarded Rina thoughtfully. Rina felt as though she was stripped bare by the scrutiny. It was odd, she thought to be on the receiving end of this for once.

"And something feels off," Rina confessed. "Joy, you know I'm usually totally ready to dive in feet first but this worries me and I'm not sure why. It's just a feeling, a sense of unease and something is telling me to leave well alone."

Joy reached for another biscuit. "That's not like you at all," she said. "So, what's bothering you?"

Rina sipped her tea. From upstairs there were sounds of Tim moving about.

"You want to wait until he's down?" Joy asked.

There was no sense of judgement in the question or any indication that Joy would be put out by this. She knew how close Rina and Tim had been.

But Rina shook her head. "No, my dear, I trust your judgement just as much as I trust his. What's making me hesitate is that I don't quite know where to begin or how to explain this feeling. I thought it might be just because Jean was someone I liked, though she was never a close friend. To be honest she was always a little full on and I found her hard work. No doubt other people would say the same about me so you can imagine two of us in the same place, well . . ."

"Would have been formidable," Joy said. "Have you managed to identify anyone in the photograph?"

Rina reached into her handbag and removed her copy of the picture and placed it on the table.

"And there was no annotation on the back of the photograph, nothing to say who they were?" Joy asked.

"No, nothing like that and in fact the photograph Jean had wasn't the original. I think it was just a good copy. There was a watermark in the paper," she explained. "I looked it up and the paper is a modern, good quality inkjet paper, whereas the people are obviously dressed in 1970s' fashion so unless they were all in period dress for some kind of 1970s' commemorative, I'm assuming that Jean just made a copy of it."

"So, it's possible she downloaded it from a website somewhere? If it's possible to find the source of photographs, we could re-photograph it or scan it, upload it and see if we can backtrack. You want me to give it a go?"

Rina hesitated then said, "I think you've got enough on at the moment, my dear."

"Is that the real reason? What's actually bothering you? Rina darling, I know that look. Your brain's in investigating, so what's holding you back?"

Tim appeared at the kitchen door looking bleary eyed and sleep creased. He flopped down into another chair and Joy got up and fetched the teapot over to the table. "I'll put the kettle on again in a minute," she said. "Rina was about to tell me why she's worried about getting involved in this one."

Tim straightened up and turned his attention to his mentor. "When does Rina Martin not get involved?"

Rina sighed. "When she recognises someone in a photograph that she would rather not have recognised."

* * *

Stella Fullhurst called up the appropriate folders on her computer and summarised the previous deaths.

"The first was discovered on 26 November last year. A painter and printmaker by the name of Christopher Hayes. He was seventy-nine and lived alone and was found dead by his cleaning lady. He was already in very poor health, so initially nobody was particularly surprised. He had a care package which meant someone came in twice a day. Once to get him up and then to help him get into bed. The evening carer found him just before nine o'clock,. but time of death was uncertain. He felt the cold and the heating was on high so it was difficult to estimate. He was alive when the morning carer left and he spoke to a friend on the phone just after ten in the morning. A neighbour *thought* she had seen someone at his front door mid-morning, a woman, but she can't be certain of the day and there was no useful description."

She turned the laptop around so that they could see it. "As you can see from the crime scene photographs he was found lying on his bed, partly propped up against the pillows and the assumption was that he had felt ill and lay down and that was that. He had mesothelioma. Before he became a full-time artist he worked in an industry where he was exposed to asbestos and he'd been ill for quite some time. The one strange thing was that this man lived in a flat, didn't even have a window box and yet he was found with a flower clasped in his hand."

"So how did this come to your notice, in your department?" Kendall asked.

"A picture was stolen from his rooms." It was Yolanda who had spoken. She had been examining other crime scene photos in the same file and now she pointed at the wall. There was a gap evidenced by the patch of darker wallpaper.

Stella raised an eyebrow but nodded. "The painting in question had been a gift some years before, given by Jean Hammond. Early in her career she also did some teaching at St Martin's College and the Slade and later at Ruskin College and that's where she met Hayes."

"But was the painting valuable enough to kill for?" Yolanda asked.

"People have killed for small change," Mac said heavily. "But how much would it have been worth?"

"Three, four thousand maybe. Not vast amounts. It was an early work and not in the style or form that made her famous."

Stella turned her laptop around and a moment later showed them the image of a yellow horse on a blue ground. It was a small painting carefully mounted and in a broad, swept frame. It reminded Mac of something but he couldn't immediately place it.

"Before the Second World War," he said, "there was an artist, a German artist who did something like this?"

"You're probably thinking of the Expressionist, Franz Marc," Stella said. "He was popular around the end of the First World War but later the Expressionists fell foul of the Nazis who saw their art as degenerate. There's no doubt her painting was referencing Marc, though the style is different; very much hers. In fact, she mentioned Franz Marc's *Little Yellow Horse* in an interview she gave in 1957. Which was probably around the time she gave this painting to her friend Christopher Hayes. They shared a flat for a time along with another artist Philip Goodman who is still very much alive so far as we know."

"Philip Goodman," Yolanda said. "There were flowers in the hall at Jean Hammond's house with a card from Philip. Could they have been from him?"

"It's certainly possible and he is certainly someone we need to speak to if he was still in touch with Jean Hammond."

"And the second death?" Mac asked.

"Graham Jackson, died 23 March this year, aged thirty-two, worked as a backing musician for most of his adult life. I'm told he was reliable and flexible and always in work which is unusual in any of the creative industries. Found dead by his wife and young daughter when they returned from a shopping trip." Again, she called up a folder and turned the computer around so that they could see the screen.

"The wife worked as a teaching assistant. The family were doing OK but were certainly not rich. Two children.

Sally who was five when her father died and Frankie who was just eighteen months."

"What was taken?" Mac asked, certain now that something must have been.

"A small sketch of Graham Jackson's mother and this time a few items of jewellery that had also belonged to the mother and that Graham had given to his wife. Nothing was insured beyond a listing on the normal house insurance. They seemed unaware that either the jewellery or the drawing might be worth anything. They were just family pieces."

"And were they worth anything?" Yolanda asked. "And was he holding a flower in his hand? And has it been the same plant in all cases?"

She glanced at Mac as though suddenly aware that maybe he should be asking the questions. Mac just smiled at her, amused by her enthusiasm. "What Yolanda just asked," he said.

"Yes, they had a value. The jewellery, well the mother wore it on special occasions but everyone, including her, assumed the gems were pastes. The drawing was also by our old friend Jean Hammond who apparently knew the family back when the mother was in her early twenties. Fortunately, we do have a picture."

She called it up on screen. Mac peered at the delicate drawing of a young woman. She was pretty in a round faced, sparkly eyed kind of way and was clearly at ease with the artist. "Quite different from Jean Hammond's later work," he commented.

"It's also different from much of the work she was producing at this time. But Jean Hammond kept an extensive series of sketchbooks, she drew daily and she often drew friends and family as a kind of practice I suppose. The sketchbooks in their entirety sell quite well but the individual drawings only for a few hundred usually. They do come up from time to time because she was quite prolific. This is more finished than most and was clearly intended as some kind of study rather than just a quick sketch. To the family it was very precious and it seemed like an odd thing to steal."

"So how did you come to hear about it?" Mac asked.

"Well two things happened. Whoever took these items was in a bit of a hurry and they left an earring behind, one of the pair obviously. This is the other one."

She showed them an image of a very striking art deco earring with what looked like blue baguette stones dangling in a fringe from a chevron of black and white enamel. "We are fortunate in that one of the constables attending what was deemed a suspicious death linked to a burglary was on the ball. The family had been asked to see if anything more had been stolen when the wife noticed the picture was missing and of course the first thing she went to look for was the jewellery. This single earing was on the floor in the bedroom and the constable realised that it actually might be the real McCoy. The reason neither Graham Jackson nor his wife had thought that the pieces were anything more than pastes was because they couldn't see any hallmarks."

"Were they platinum?" Kendall asked.

"Right on the nose. So the constable was right and this was a very expensive piece and when the other one was offered for sale a few weeks later, along with some other pieces, it was flagged. The second thing that happened, quite separate to our investigation, was that a post-mortem was done on Graham Jackson and he was found to have a massive dose of morphine in his body which obviously begged the question; was this suicide or was it murder. Suicide was ruled out quite quickly. The dose was massive, death would have been too quick for him to have had time to dispose of morphine and syringe, so they were left with the conclusion this must have been murder.

"So, nothing to do with the plant material he was holding in his hand, and we've still not fully understood the significance of that. It could be that it's some kind of bizarre calling card but as yet we really don't know. To cut a long story short, because the Jean Hammond painting had been stolen from Christopher Hayes the theft of the Jean Hammond drawing also triggered some flags in the system.

Because that earlier robbery had also featured a dead body, Christopher Hayes' body was exhumed. The tox screen was inconclusive after several months in the ground, but a small mark was found at the nape of his neck which could have been the site of an injection.

"The plant in his hand, as Yolanda thought, is a common or garden blue hydrangea. The flower heads dry well and florists sometimes use them in arrangements. It's not toxic, it's not rare. What killed Graham Jackson was an overdose of morphine. A massive dose, administered via an injection in the back of his neck. There was also bruising on his neck as though someone had grasped him around the throat before injecting him. So, all things considered, it might not be a bad idea to get your body exhumed and examined."

"So, who would have access to that amount of morphine. A medical professional? A vet? Any thefts reported in the area?"

"All options looked at and nothing obvious emerging," Stella said.

"And have any other cases come up?" Kendall wanted to know.

"We don't think so but would never have made the connection between Graham Jackson and Christopher Hayes had it not been for the Jean Hammond association and the local police might well have missed that if it hadn't been for the copper who spotted that the jewellery was expensive and wondered if the drawing might be too. Then the fact that Graham Jackson was young and healthy. All of these factors led to a more detailed PM than would normally have been carried out."

"So, there may be other deaths that have gone unnoticed," Mac said. "Especially if the victim was old or in poor health."

Stella nodded. "Obviously, we're hoping not. Another interesting thing is, the earrings once belonged to Jean Hammond. We don't know about the other stolen pieces but we do know that these were a wedding gift to Graham

Jackson's mother. I believe she gave the groom a tie pin but the family don't seem to recall what happened to that. You know, Jean Hammond may have taken a while to make a name as an artist but she was from what had been a wealthy family and, although she shared a flat with other up-and-coming artists during the forties and fifties, what I didn't tell you was her family owned the block. It was pretty run down by then and a fair amount of the family money had been lost in death duties, but she was by no means a starving artist working in a garret. It also seems she had a few items of value left to give away as wedding presents. It's possible, of course, that she didn't know the value either. The earring does look a bit too flashy to be anything other than pretty costume jewellery."

"Did anyone contact Jean Hammond about the earrings and the drawing?" Yolanda asked.

"Yes, she was interviewed by the local force. Seems she knew Graham Jackson's father particularly. She recalled the mother but was slightly surprised she'd drawn a picture of her. She told the officer that she tended to draw anyone or anything that would sit still for long enough. And to be fair that's probably true and it was a long time ago. She wasn't certain about the earring and said the family were possibly mistaken though agreed it was the kind of thing she might have given as a wedding present. She might have had a point. Memories get conflated and confused over time," Stella shrugged.

"The other jewellery that was offered for sale," Yolanda asked. "Was that from the same robbery?"

Stella shook her head. "No, we've managed to track the owners of a pearl necklace with a diamond clasp and some rather nice rubies set into dress clips but so far as we can ascertain the jewellery had changed hands a couple of times before it was offered to a legitimate shop. The man that offered it said it had been sold to a pawnbroker who'd realised after that it might be dodgy and asked the man to get rid of it. Which might be true but, as he claims, he can't recall the name of the pawnbroker, who knows. The theft of the jewellery does set this incident apart from the other two — if we're including Jean Hammond. However, apart from the actual fact of the thefts and the deaths, everything is speculation thus far."

Mac was silent for a moment and then he withdrew the manila envelope from his document case and emptied the contents, now in evidence bags, on to the table.

"This came into my possession yesterday evening," he said. "It came from Jean Hammond's studio, a young woman who had drawing classes with her was asked by Jean to take this away if anything happened to her."

Briefly he explained who Ursula was and the circumstances that led to her taking the envelope as requested.

"Jean Hammond seemed to think that Ursula would know what to do with these things, Ursula didn't and so she went to see Rina Martin who also knew Jean Hammond and who has been something close to family for Ursula. And Rina, of course, went with her to the studio to introduce her to Cal when she went to pick up her portfolio. Ursula was of the opinion that Jean had been worried about something, but she was also of the opinion that Jean was suddenly getting old and that perhaps she wasn't as acute, mentally, as she had been. Anyway, she wanted to do the right thing so she went to see Rina."

"Of course, she did," Kendall said. "Who doesn't go to Miss Martin in times of crisis?"

Mac ignored him. "Rina contacted me hoping to get some advice. She had by then discovered that the studio had been stripped bare. And I have to say it crossed our minds that this was what the thieves were looking for."

Mac sat back and watched while the others examined the objects on the table.

"You've no idea who the individuals in the photograph might be," Kendall asked studying the picture.

Mac shook his head. "But one of them looks familiar, I just can't place him." He pointed to a man standing centre back of the group. He was tall, dark-haired and a little detached from the others who were smiling or laughing and generally having a good time. The photograph looked as though it had been taken at a party and the photographer had told everybody to get together in a huddle so that he could squash them all into frame. Everybody but this man at the back seemed to have a glass in their hands and had raised it in a toast.

"*I* know who he is," Yolanda said. "Or at least I think I do. It looks like Miles Cunningham. My mum likes to read true crime, particularly historical stuff, not so much the modern stuff because she says it's too close."

"Too close?" Mac queried.

"To now. She likes her criminals safely dead and gone, or at least in prison."

"Is there anything your mother doesn't have an opinion on," Mac asked.

Yolanda seemed to think about it for a moment and then shook her head. "If she does then I don't know about it," she said.

Kendall had been studying the image while Stella searched on her computer.

"It could be," Kendall said.

"I think it is," Stella confirmed. "Look at this." The image on the computer screen had been perhaps taken a few years after the one in the photograph and featured Miles Cunningham standing outside the Old Bailey with his solicitor, but there was no mistake, it was certainly the same man.

"Art critic rather than artist," Stella commented.

"And murderer," Yolanda said.

CHAPTER 16

Rina arrived home to a quiet house. The Peters sisters had gone off to their lunch club, one of three they attended during the week, and if she remembered right it was Matthew and Steven's day to wander along to the marina and spend a pleasant hour or two with friends there. She closed the front door and breathed a sigh of relief that she would not have questions to answer, that she could make herself a cup of tea and retire to her little room and have a think. It was only when explaining her connection to Miles Cunningham to Joy and Tim that she had fully felt just how important that brief friendship had been and how much it pained her when Miles had been accused of murder. Although the evidence had piled up against him, she had still found it hard to believe. What had happened seemed so impossible, but when he had pleaded guilty . . . Over the years she had put him out of her mind. Over the *Many* years. She had not actually seen the man since 1979, five years before he had been accused of murder.

She had not known him well, he had merely been a face at after- performance parties, gallery openings, late-nights spent with friends and the ever moving, ever changing crowd of artists, actors, casual acquaintances and hangers on that flocked to the better known of Rina's set. He and his wife had been pleasant and easy to chat to but that could have been said of most of the crowd that seemed to have drifted through Rina's existence at the time.

She remembered this as an exciting point in her life. She was right at the beginning of her career and working at anything and everything. She had been a knife thrower's assistant, one half of a not very successful song and dance act in a very shabby end of the pier show. She had, for a season, even been a Redcoat. Then had joined repertory companies and played multiple insignificant parts, often on the same night, only occasionally forgetting who she was. And she had met Fred and married him. It was perhaps the happiest time she had ever experienced. Now, in later life, she was content but it was a different kind of happiness, one born of experience and friendship and being settled. The joy she had felt back then was all to do with the newness of the world, or at least of her world.

She remembered that she had liked Miles but then she had liked a lot of people; she had always been disposed to *liking* people. It had been easy to strike up easy and casual friendships that sometimes deepened into something more but often remained as just bright spots of colour rather than complete works of art in their own right. This, she thought, was inevitable when the community to which she belonged was largely transient and mobile, drifting from job to job and place to place.

Miles and his wife had been two such bright spots. They were lively and charming and a little older than Rina, with two children and a house of their own. Miles was a journalist, officially an arts critic but he could turn his hand to most things. He wrote reviews of everything from restaurants to West End shows and even, she remembered on one occasion, a catwalk show held at one of the big London hotels. He'd stood in at the last moment and, though he admitted to Rina after that he knew nothing whatsoever about fashion apart from what his wife told him, he'd not made a bad fist of it.

Rina wandered through to the kitchen and set the kettle to boil turning as she did to gaze at the framed posters and flyers on the wall. Most of these were from the early days, cherished because they often featured Fred's name as well as her own.

She made herself a mug of strong instant coffee, feeling she really couldn't be bothered with anything more complicated, and took herself off to her little sitting room at the front of the house and closed and locked the door.

Three weeks after Fred's death and she had barely left their flat, the little bedsit that they had occupied together and which now, though it was tiny, seemed vast and empty because he was no longer there. She had occasionally remembered to eat and spent a lot of time sleeping and the rest crying. She felt wrung out with the tears, dry and empty inside and yet the tears still seem to flow as though they were intent on draining every drop of moisture from her.

Friends had called, had been sympathetic, tried to persuade her out of a self-imposed exile and on one occasion she had even made it to the top of the stairs but as she stood there the distance down the stairs to the front door had seemed so enormous, so long and stretched out that she could not face such an epic journey; to the dismay of her friend she had turned around and gone back into her room and shut the door.

Rina closed her eyes. Even now she could recall that sense of panic as she stared down what seemed like an endless flight of stairs. The way Barbara had gripped her arm . . .

"It's all right," Barbara had said, though Rina could hear in her voice that she had run out of ideas. That she had no idea how she might help.

"There, sit down. You want a cuppa?"

Rina had shaken her head. Just go, she wanted to say. Please just go, but Barbara had been kind and even in the depths of her grief she knew she could not throw that kindness back in her friend's face.

"I'll be all right," she managed. "Please, just tell them all I couldn't make it. I'm sorry."

And a little later Barbara left.

And then they had moved on, the little company she and Fred had worked for. She could not remember their schedule, only that it would be six months before they returned and though they promised to write and she knew they would write and promise not forget her, another part of her life had gone and Rina had no idea how to follow it.

She knew that she would have to find work soon. Rent for this tiny bedsit in off-season Rottingdean was cheap but still needed to be paid for. But she couldn't make herself care. Rina sat on the side of the small double bed she had shared with Fred her mind empty, her body drained, tears flowing and wondered how she could go on.

And then there was a knock on the door.

"Rina, it's Miles, open the door."

It took her a moment to remember who Miles even was and then when she did she couldn't think why on earth he was knocking on her door.

He knocked again. "Come on Rina, I know you're in there. Your landlady's given me special dispensation to come up so open the door, there's a love."

Because she knew he would not go away, Miles was persistent like that, she got up opened the door and then went back to sit down on the bed.

When other friends had come they had looked around the room as though startled by how much she had let things go. Some had even tried to tidy up. Some had coaxed her to eat but Miles had done none of those things. He had closed the door, moved a stack of clothing off the chair and drawn it up near to where she sat on the bed and then taken her hand. She had the feeling he hadn't even looked anywhere else, that there was no judgement, that there was no sense that he was about to give her good advice. He had just reached out and taken her hand and they had sat in silence apart from her sobbing for, well, she didn't really know how long. And after a while, much to her surprise, she realised that the tears had stopped.

"Where do you keep your suitcase?" he asked.

"Why?"

"Because Betty and I have agreed that you're coming back to stay with us for as long as you need. There's plenty of room and you shouldn't be alone."

"I can't do that."

"Yes, you can."

He had spotted the suitcase in the corner of the room and he brought it over to the bed before she could stop him and began to pack her things. She was horrified, realising that she hadn't done her washing, that he was packing whatever he could lay hands on and she . . .

"I can do it," she said.

He nodded, sat back down in the chair and watched as she folded clothes and tried to separate out what needed washing.

"I need to go to the launderette." Her voice was shaking, her hands were shaking, her whole body was trembling.

"We have a perfectly good washing machine at home," he told her.

Rina swallowed hard. She put her belongings in the suitcase and holdall and he helped to carry them downstairs and then dropped them in the back seat of the car.

Once he was in the driving seat he turned to her and said, "I'm not going to tell you it's all going to be all right, you've lost the love of your life and it's never going to be all right, not really. But you will be able to go on, you will have a life after this."

She stared at him not knowing what to say. Then she reached into her handbag and removed the little watch that Fred had bought her for their first anniversary. She hadn't wound it since the funeral. Miles glanced her way and then looked at his own watch.

"It's twenty minutes past one."

She set the time, wound the watch and fastened it on to her wrist then stared blankly out of the windscreen not really knowing where they were going or even caring very much until, a little time later, they pulled into the drive of Miles's house. Betty was waiting at the front door and she could hear the children playing in the garden and her feet sounded loud on the tiles in the hall that smelled of lemons and furniture polish.

Sipping her coffee, Rina remembered that Miles had car-ried her luggage upstairs to a little room at the back of the house. For the next two weeks she had done very little but eat and sleep, waking to the sound of the children playing in the garden or running up and down the corridors, to the distant sound of the television downstairs, to the quiet knocks on the door that signalled someone either bringing her food or telling her that dinner was ready in the kitchen. The house, she recalled, had a big dining room but family meals were in the long kitchen at the back. No one minded that she didn't speak, the conversation at the table had swirled around her and occasionally she caught a meaningful sentence and as time went on she even added the odd word, the odd response.

And then she had woken up one morning and when she looked out of the window, the garden had been white with frost, and Miles had been raking leaves into a big pile with the children helping him. And although the grief had still been like a cold lump in her heart and a lead weight in her belly she knew somehow that she was going to be all right. That Miles had been right; the pain would never completely subside, it would be there like a drumbeat, marking time to everything else she did in her life. But she would have a life.

She remembered how she picked up the little watch and fastened it back on to her wrist and set the time and stroked the face. "Oh Fred, I do love you."

She drained her coffee and took the mug back to the kitchen, rinsed it and set it aside.

She had left Miles and Betty's house about a week later and they had kept in touch for a while, postcards and letters, presents that first Christmas but, as often happens, as Rina had picked up the pieces of her life and Miles and Betty had gone on with theirs the contact became more sporadic. And then that dreadful day five years later when Rina had spotted her old friend's name in a newspaper headline. Horrified, she read about the deaths of Betty and the children, the two she had known and the new baby born only a few weeks before, and a man who had been staying with the family. And that Miles stood accused of their murder.

CHAPTER 17

Rina had left the copy of the photograph with Tim and Joy, knowing that she could easily make copies when she reached home. Now Joy and Tim were consulting the computer and doing a reverse image search to try and find out the source of the photograph but they'd so far come up empty. The photo did not seem to have been published to the public domain.

"Do you think she's all right?" Joy asked. "She seemed kind of upset. I mean it's not a nice thing to remember but—"

"We'll just have to keep an eye on her," Tim said. "She's angry with this Jean Hammond for having involved Ursula in something that, well, that Rina thinks might be dangerous."

"As she's got a right to be," Joy said. "Ursula's just a kid. If this Jean Hammond had felt threatened then she should have gone to the police or told her son or even talked to Rina."

"I agree," Tim said. "But it's a bit of a dilemma, isn't it. If you're the one everyone else looks to when things need sorting out, who do you ask when it's your turn to need assistance. Who would Rina go to, for example?"

"Well, us, of course. Like she did this morning."

"And if she thought she might be putting us in harm's way?"

"Well, she certainly wouldn't throw a seventeen-year-old girl under the bus and she'd probably consult Mac if it was that serious."

"But this Jean Hammond didn't have us and she certainly didn't have Mac. Her son lives in Exeter and she maybe didn't want him involved. No, I know what you're saying," he ploughed on as Joy seemed ready to object again, "but who would suspect Ursula of being in Jean's confidence or even be someone she'd entrust with collecting an envelope of random stuff? So far as anyone would be concerned, Ursula was just a kid who did some cleaning for Jean Hammond. A nobody, and so totally off the radar of anyone who might have a grudge against Miss Hammond."

Joy still looked miffed but Tim was relieved when she conceded the point.

"Well, OK, but it still feels odd to me. I mean a woman like Jean Hammond would have had access to a solicitor and friends who could uncover stuff and help her out. Why pick on Ursula?"

Tim thought about it for a moment and then said, "if you needed someone utterly trustworthy and who wouldn't ask awkward questions then George or Ursula would probably be top of the list, don't you think? A bit like Fitch," he added, referring to the man who would soon be marrying Joy's mother Bridie Duggan. Fitch had at one time been Joy's father's right-hand man. If you were in a different kind of trouble, you'd call Fitch and he'd be there. "Maybe Jean Hammond recognised that in Ursula. Or maybe she was just an old woman who didn't want to make trouble too close to home. Who knows? Anyway, the important thing is we help out now and as we can't make any headway with a reverse image search, let's take a closer look at the Miles Cunningham bloke. It's possible someone else in the picture might crop up in news reports or something."

Joy nodded and turned back to the laptop. Tim pulled up his chair beside hers. Seeing Rina upset disturbed him deeply. She was usually imperturbable and to see his friend and mentor shaken like this was rather like feeling the earth shake.

"Miles Cunningham," Joy was saying. "Look, definitely the man in the photo and that must be his wife, Betty." She pointed to a photo in the old news report that had come up on the Wikipedia site she was on and then to the woman sitting in front of Miles Cunningham in the photograph.

"It's a bit hard to tell," Tim said, "the picture's not clear. Funny Rina didn't pick her out."

"She said it took her a while to realise the man in the back row was who he was. I suppose you don't expect your past to come leaping out at you from nowhere, especially as it was such a bad time in Rina's life." She paused, reading the entry. Two small children, a baby, the wife, the young man who lived with them, all dead.

"How could someone do that?" she asked. "Kill your own kids?"

"No wonder Rina's not that keen on remembering any of this," Tim said.

* * *

Mac had made more coffee while Kendall and Yolanda called up general information on the Miles Cunningham case that was in the public domain. Stella had gone to make some calls to see how difficult it was going to be to get the original case records. They were likely to be stuck in an archive somewhere and so obtaining them might take several days. She would set this in motion and also arrange for full copies of the reports on the deaths of Christopher Hayes and Graham Jackson to be made available to Mac and Kendall. She was also going to talk to her bosses about extra manpower but she wasn't terribly hopeful about this one. They all suspected that Stella Fullhurst, their current liaison, might also be their full complement of additional investigators for now at least.

As Stella had already had contact with the SIOs dealing with the Hayes and Jackson cases Mac had suggested that she begin by logging everything and drawing together the threads and that Yolanda should assist in this. It was inevitable given that they now had three dead bodies, including Jean Hammond, that major crimes would get involved in this too and it would, he figured, be good to have the basic investigative foundations in place ready for that so that he and his little team didn't get sidelined.

In the meantime, Kendall had contacted his own bosses to start the arrangements for the exhumation of Jean Hammond's body. It was just as well, Mac thought, that the vicar had managed to squeeze her into the corner of the graveyard and she had not been cremated.

"So," Yolanda said. "In January 1984 police are called to the house then owned by Miles Cunningham and his wife in Woodingdean on the outskirts of Brighton. Neighbours had reported a woman and children screaming. They get there and they find Miles Cunningham sitting on his front doorstep with a knife on the step beside him and both he and the knife are covered in blood. When they go inside, they find a wife and three children and a young man, who had been lodging with them, all dead and Cunningham is sitting on the steps saying that it's his fault. He is arrested and charged and, I think much to the annoyance of the local and national press who would like a nice juicy court case, he pleads guilty and is sentenced to life imprisonment. He never offers a motive and he never explains what happened."

"No one else is looked for or looked at," Kendall continued as Mac set coffee beside his hand. "Thanks. we're going to have a lot of stuff to get through. We've got two and possibly three suspicious deaths and we're also looking at historical crimes. I have a sneaking suspicion life is going to get complicated. Though, to be fair, just because he's in a photograph, that doesn't mean Miles Cunningham is any of our concern now."

Mac nodded. Suddenly there were a lot more problems on the table than there had been at the start of the day when all they had really been looking at was a couple of stolen pictures and the theft of some art materials. "Unfortunately for us, that photograph was in an envelope belonging to a woman who was frightened and who is now dead — and who asked someone to collect in the event of her death. Which sort of implies she might have expected to die."

"Well, she was old," Yolanda said.

"Which is beside the point," Mac told her. "Agreed, this may not be relevant, but I want to be on top of everything so we have no further surprises. If it turns out Jean Hammond was—"

"Losing it and imagining things?" Yolanda said.

"I wouldn't have put it quite like that," Mac told her.

Yolanda had the grace to look apologetic. "But she might have been."

"OK, so she might have been. But maybe bring a little more tact to bear if you have to ask Cal Hammond any more questions about Jean Hammond's state of mind?"

"Cunningham was imprisoned but, presumably because he never gave any explanation and no one got their full dose of drama, there was a whole load of speculation and several books written at the time about whether or not he'd done it. The family of the lodger, William Tatum, tried to sue Cunningham for compensation after the house was sold but it looks like that went nowhere. He had a sister, Constance, who was determined someone ought to pay for her brother's death and that prison wasn't enough in terms of reparation."

"Who did inherit then?" Mac asked.

"No idea," Dave Kendall told him. "All I have so far are headlines and speculation not the nitty-gritty detail."

"There's one interesting thing, though," Yolanda said as she picked up her own coffee. "Although his solicitor lodged a guilty plea, there are suggestions that his legal team actually thought they could get him off."

"On what grounds?"

"On the grounds that he never actually admitted to doing anything. And the forensics point to reasonable doubt at the very least. Cunningham's footprints were found going into the building, in blood, which was then tracked through the house and out again, but which suggests he came in after the blood was on the floor."

"Or came back in," Mac objected.

"Sure, but there were other fingerprints on the knife, just smudges but overlaid by his. And it could be argued that he struggled to get the knife off someone else, and then he took a better hold on it and smudged their fingerprints, but a good legal team could at least have sowed the seeds of doubt . . . suggested that someone else had hold of the knife and Miles Cunningham took it off him. As it was, it never went to court but his brief, Robert Haven, had it put on record that he wasn't happy about the guilty plea."

"But he more or less admitted to the fact that he'd done it," Dave Kendall objected.

"No," Mac said. "He said it was *his fault* which is not the same thing at all. We have to remember that this is 1984, the Police and Criminal Evidence Act as we know it is just a twinkle in someone's eye at this point, or at most in its earliest iteration. Investigations were, sometimes, not as thorough as we hope they are now and police corruption was, well let's say, widespread. That's not to say it was endemic, I don't believe that, but what I do believe is that Miles Cunningham made it easy for no one to look any further. So, either he was protecting someone, or he genuinely felt responsible, or he genuinely was responsible—"

"Or he knew for certain that whoever had murdered his wife and kids wasn't going to kill again," Yolanda finished. "Everyone else had their throats cut, the lodger, this William Tatum, he was stabbed in the guts and was still just alive when the police arrived. This was also the days before trained paramedics, and ambulance drivers were little *more* than ambulance drivers back then. Had it happened today he might even have survived."

Mac saw Kendall looking thoughtfully at the young officer. Yolanda really had grown up, and he thought she had the makings of an excellent investigator, something he never imagined he'd be thinking. "Was there ever any investigation into this William Tatum, any suggestion that he might have been responsible?"

She shrugged her shoulders. "There's still a lot to look at but I've not seen any suggestion as yet, but I imagine someone, somewhere, did think about it. There have been a couple of books written about the murders, one close to the time and at least one since then, according to the references at the bottom of this page. They might be worth chasing up."

"Cunningham died in prison back in 1997," Kendall said. "He'd apparently been in bad health for some time. Died of pneumonia after a bout of flu, so he's not going to be able to help us out here."

Mac considered this. "At the moment I don't think we've got any idea about what might prove important and what might not, so perhaps you'd better add a reading of those books to the action plan and perhaps trying to find out who Cunningham associated with in prison and if they're still in the land of the living."

She nodded and added some bullet-point notes to her notebook. She had a bit of a gleam in her eye, Mac thought, obviously feeling that this was all very exciting. He tried not to smile at the thought that if this took off then in a few days she would be inundated with bullet points to add to the action plan, or multiple action plans by then, and might not be nearly as keen.

The door opened and Stella came back in. "Right," she said, "the original Cunningham files are being located and will be sent over. The case notes and evidence from the Christopher Hayes and Graham Jackson deaths are also on their way, most of those are electronic so should turn up in your inbox in no time but I've asked that the evidence box also be sent across, together with any ancillary hard copies of anything. Dave, do you reckon we can set this room aside or find somewhere else. We're going to need space and computer equipment and all the usual stuff."

Dave Kendall stood up and said he would go and sort things out. Mac and Yolanda brought Stella up to speed on what they had discovered so far. Yolanda, Mac noted, appeared to have about a dozen pages open and was flicking between tabs.

"I was looking to see what had been published about it," she said, "if there was anything more recent than those books I mentioned and you know the strange thing? There are two more books out this year, one is a memoir and the other is a novelisation based on the murders. That's not out yet, apparently there were some legal challenges which delayed publication."

"Interesting," Stella said. "Definitely an angle worth following up. Who's writing the memoir and is that out yet? And who's the author of the novel?"

"Um, right, the memoir came out in March and is published by a small press in Exeter. Prussic, that's the name of the publishing house."

She grinned as though, Mac thought, she was very amused by that.

"They seem to specialise in memoirs from journalists, police officers, members of the Armed Forces. They only bring out about five titles a year, but this one is from a local journalist who covered the Miles Cunningham murders and, though the book isn't exclusively about that, from the look of it I'm guessing that was the biggest thing he ever covered." She paused. "Now that is interesting. It seems he was related to William Tatum, the murdered lodger but it also looks as though he thinks William Tatum might have done it."

"Definitely someone to speak to," Mac said. "And the novel?"

"From a bigger publisher. Aldridge and Marshall. But the odd thing is they're keeping the name of the author back, just saying that this is 'a revelatory novel from an ex-journalist'. So, maybe someone who covered the case? I can call the publisher, see if they'll tell me anything." She paused. "Want to bet it's Clive Tatum?"

"It's very possible," Mac agreed. "Add it to the action plan but wait until we know what we want to ask."

"It's odd, isn't it?" Stella commented. "That two books should suddenly pop up this year."

"It is indeed," Mac said. "We do seem to have wandered a long way from two stolen paintings, I just hope we're not heading on a wild goose chase."

The two women laughed but he could see in their faces that they didn't believe that any more than he did.

CHAPTER 18

The tiny police outpost at the end of the promenade in Frantham on Sea usually closed at 6 o'clock. It had a staff of three, DI Sebastian McGregor, Sgt Frank Baker and the youngest of the team, Constable Andy Nevins. This evening it was almost seven o'clock and Mac was there alone. He was listening to a recorded statement that Jean Hammond had made to a Metropolitan police constable, following the theft of the jewellery and portrait sketch from Graham Jackson.

Graham Jackson and Jean Hammond had apparently never met. She had known his father, Rory and sketched his mother before his parents' marriage. This was the drawing that had been taken when Graham Jackson was murdered.

It felt like a spiteful act as well as a murderous one Mac thought, and though spite might seem like a far lesser crime, in Mac's experience it was a great driver of violence and cruelty and deserved to be acknowledged.

The interview itself was routine, requiring confirmation that Jean recognised the earring and had gifted them to the bride on her wedding day. By this time it was clear that Graham Jackson had been unlawfully killed otherwise, Mac thought, no one would have bothered asking about a long ago wedding gift. That the interview was recorded was a little unusual for a witness statement, but Mac had also used taped interviews when there was a high volume to get through. Civilian personnel were employed to type up anything that became relevant as the investigation progressed. It was interesting, Mac thought, to hear Jean's voice. Lively, a tad impatient, and, as Rina had commented, sharp as a tack.

The constable asked her about her relationship with the family. Jean had said:

I didn't know this generation. I'd never met the poor unfortunate Graham Jackson. I did know his parents and, yes, the earrings were probably a wedding gift. I vaguely remember owning a pair like that and giving them away. I've never been one for fancy jewellery. The portrait was drawn a few years before. Understand, young man, I probably drew everyone I ever met, sooner or later. You must practise your skills, keep them alive and develop them and to that end it really doesn't matter if you sketch a person or an apple. If people wanted their picture then I quite often gave it to them.

The constable commented on the earrings being expensive. Did that indicate a closeness to the couple?

My dear, it indicated that I liked them enough to go to their wedding. Rory was a sweet man, from what I remember. Greta was a lovely young woman. I presumably thought she would like the earrings and if she didn't then they could always sell them and buy something they needed. I think I gave Rory a tie pin. Does anyone wear tie pins nowadays? There was a bit of a fad for them back then.

Did I know that they were valuable? I doubt I gave it any thought. I'd no use for them, never had my ears pierced. Most likely I'd not had time to buy them a present so I looked through my belongings for something suitable. I really wouldn't read any more into it than that.

She was off-hand about the gift, Mac thought, and yet the family had treasured the jewellery and the portrait. OK, so maybe not the tie pin . . . though it was quite likely that had been given to another family member who hadn't known its history. Or perhaps Rory Jackson had known Jean well enough not to be sentimental about the gift. It was Mac's experience that women tended to be more romantic about jewellery than men . . . or was that just his aunt and his mother? Rina was very powerfully fond of her watch, but that had been a gift from her beloved husband, so that was different, wasn't it?

So why had Graham Jackson been killed? Yes, there had been theft but theft did not generally lead to murder, not even when a theft turned violent. No, Mac thought, this was back to spite and rage again.

A soft knock on the back door brought him to his feet and he opened it to allow Ursula and George to come inside. He would need her to make a formal statement later but there were questions Mac wanted to ask her specifically. This routine process would normally be dealt with by a uniformed officer but as he had known Ursula for quite some time now, and felt that she'd been through enough, he'd decided he would be the one to talk to her. Besides he also knew what questions were pertinent to the enquiry and this seemed quicker than trying to brief someone else, especially as they were still short on manpower.

"Thanks for coming over," he said. "How are the two of you?"

"We were doing OK," George said. "And it's almost the end of term so we were hoping to have a bit of a break, maybe go camping for a few days," he added clearly hopeful that whatever Mac wanted it was not going to interfere with their plans.

"I've never been much for camping," Mac admitted. "Where are you thinking of going?"

"Not too far, possibly just into Somerset or North Devon. We can only manage a few days away from work and we've both been offered extra hours through the summer which will be good, so we can put away some cash for the winter. But we're taking a weekend, adding the Friday and the Monday, and it will be good just to have a change of scene."

Mac nodded. George had grown up so much since he had first encountered him as a boy of thirteen. And Ursula, well, Ursula had always been possessed of maturity in advance of her years though not always in a way that Mac thought was good for her. They had both missed out on a lot of childhood.

"So, what do you need from me?" Ursula asked. "I really don't know what else I can tell you."

"We just need all of this in an official format," he reassured her. "And there are some specific questions I want to ask you, so I've got a better picture of what Jean Hammond was like in the months before she died."

Ursula was regarding him thoughtfully. "You're thinking this wasn't a natural death, aren't you?" she asked.

Mac hesitated and then nodded. They would find out soon enough and probably best they found out from him. "Evidence has come to light which has made us wonder," he said. "We've applied for an exhumation order."

He watched her closely to see how she would take that news and saw that she grew very pale.

"You really think someone killed her? Who would do that?" She turned to George and said, "I told you something didn't look right."

"What didn't look right?" Mac asked.

"Like I told George, Jean would never sit on the floor, not even on a cushion. There were seats all around the garden so she could sit down if she got out of breath or felt dizzy. She'd got folding chairs to take out there if she wanted to sit somewhere else. Once she got down on the floor she couldn't get back up again. She couldn't really get down on her own. If she dropped something she had those grabby things, you know like a litter picker only retractable. She had one in the kitchen, one in the studio and one in the stick stand in the hall. Or she'd wait until someone came to visit and then she'd get them to pick up whatever it was. It's stupid to think she could have sat down under that tree on her own, even if she'd managed it she'd have been stuck there."

"Did you explain this to anyone at the time?" Mac asked.

"I didn't really get the chance did I? This constable came over and told me I had to leave. He wanted to know who I was and what my business was and then said I'd got to go because Miss Hammond was dead of a heart attack. So I left and I drove home."

"And then you got Rina to go with you to collect your things. You waited until after the funeral."

Ursula nodded, anticipating the unasked question. "Why didn't I go before then? OK, there were two reasons. One was that I wasn't quite sure how I was to go about it. I don't know Cal Hammond, I'd never met him, I didn't have a number for him or anything like that so I didn't know how I was supposed to get into the studio. Then Rina mentioned going to Jean Hammond's funeral and I realised that she knew her. Then I remembered that Jean had mentioned Rina in passing, something about them being on the same committees. I must have mentioned her first but it was ages ago and I hadn't really thought about it. Then I thought well if Rina knows Cal then I can at least go and collect my portfolio."

"And the envelope?"

Ursula sighed. "Look, Jean got all upset about something before Christmas and then again a few weeks before she died. She went to a funeral at the end of November and that upset her a good deal. She mentioned having an argument with someone but I don't know who, but suddenly Jean was on about, what if she died suddenly? What if something happened? And she made it sound as though she was scared of somebody or something or worried about something unusual happening. Not just a heart attack. I tried to get her to talk to someone. Tried to get her to tell me what she was worried about, but she just came over all cryptic. Jean was like that. She was a lovely woman, but . . . especially this last few months, she could be a bit strange. Like she wasn't really in touch with reality sometimes."

"You think there were signs of dementia?" Mac asked, then added quickly. "Sorry, no, that's an unfair question."

"When I first met her she was pin-sharp, would have run rings round anyone and on just about any subject. Later, well it was becoming obvious that she was physically weaker and her mind seemed . . . well, not as sharp." She paused thoughtfully. "Or at least not about everything. She'd have days when she was really back to her old self and she'd just have bad days."

Mac nodded.

"The possibility of having a heart attack was something she lived with. She'd always got her pills in her pocket and a spare pot by the kitchen sink and another in the bathroom, just in case. I never thought that was what she was talking about when she said she needed me to pick up the envelope if anything happened. There was always that sense that she was talking about something else. I was thinking . . . well, I suppose I was thinking that she was overreacting but I didn't know what had set her off. She was kind of dramatic anyway. Jean Hammond made Rina look kind of low-key in comparison, she was that sort of woman. I liked her a lot but—"

"But you felt awkward about going to her place and taking something that didn't belong to you."

Ursula nodded. "That was my second reason for waiting. I decided I was just going to get my portfolios. I decided right up to the last minute that was all I was going to do but then I felt guilty and then Rina saw that I was hesitating about something and she distracted Mr Hammond and it was like, like my options had suddenly been taken away, does that make sense? So, I opened the second drawer down and I took the envelope and I slipped it inside my portfolio and soon after that I left."

She frowned.

"It's a funny thing though. Her mobile phone was in the drawer. She'd usually got that in her pocket with her pills. Cal tried to persuade her to have one of those radio alert things to wear round her neck. You know the things I mean? But Jean said that would just make her feel old and she promised she'd always keep her phone with her. But there it was, in the drawer."

Mac nodded. That was indeed odd. "Did you know she was growing cannabis?"

Ursula laughed. "Was she? Well from what I saw of the garden she grew just about everything else. And she made hand creams and teas and oils and things. She gave me some hand cream, I don't what's in it but it smells nice. Mac, I don't know what else I can tell you. George and I opened the envelope, saw what was inside, didn't know what to do about it and as soon as we could we went to see Rina. We would have gone sooner but what with college and work . . ."

Mac nodded. "You said Miss Hammond got worried before Christmas and then again in spring this year. Do you know what set that off?"

Ursula glanced at George and Mac got the feeling that they had discussed this at length already. "As I said, the first time was after she'd been to a friend's funeral. I don't know his full name, she called him Christopher and said that they'd known each other for a long time. I think he was younger than her because she said something about outliving him and that she never expected that would happen. I think he was an artist. She said something about them having friends in common and I might be wrong but he was a student of hers at one time. When she came back she seemed upset. I saw her a day or so later and she was really not her usual self. She kept talking about dying and how her time would come sooner than she thought and that somehow this Christopher dying was proof of that."

"And you mentioned that she'd had an argument with someone?" Mac asked.

"A right blow up, she called it. But I don't know more than that. To be honest I thought she was, understandably, just getting a bit maudlin. It must be hard seeing your friends die and going to their funerals especially if they're younger than you. And then she fell ill and she was really poorly with a chest infection for a while. She went away for about ten days over Christmas to stay with her son, Cal, and his partner. When she came back in the New Year she seemed much more cheerful."

"And this was when she talked about the envelope? When she was unwell."

Ursula nodded. "She showed it to me one day in the drawer and she said if anything happened to her, anything sudden and she should die I should be sure to take this away and that I'd know what to do with it."

"And you agreed."

"You know, Mac, she was a nice lady. She'd been very good to me and when she asked me to do that, she was really poorly. She could hardly get up the steps to the studio her breathing was so bad and I had to help her to get back down again. And then I helped her into bed and she was so worried I just agreed to whatever she wanted. And then I called her doctor, the number was on a list in the hall, and a few days later she texted me to say that she was going away to spend Christmas with her son and that she would still pay me for the days I didn't go over there but that I didn't need to clean the week before Christmas. She'd been unwell since she came back from the funeral and that was early December. Of course, I agreed to what she wanted because I thought that would make her feel a bit happier, I never really thought anything would come of it."

"And then she seemed to forget about it?"

"When I saw her in the New Year she was almost back to her old self. She did seem a bit quieter and a bit older and more frail but she had this painting to finish and she was very excited about it. She kept saying it was probably the last big thing she'd ever do, that it wasn't right to take on anything major after this because she might not live to see it finished. I kept telling her she was going to live forever."

Ursula's voice faltered slightly. She really had liked Miss Hammond, Mac thought. "And then she got worried again and she started talking about the envelope and about you taking it away?"

"Well, the first time was in February. She said she'd found out something bad about her friend's death. That it hadn't been natural causes. I mean, that would be enough to upset anyone but she didn't seem inclined to tell me more about it. Then about March time, late March, I arrived one day and she was upset about something. She was snappy and angry which was unusual. She could be sarcastic, and very acerbic but there was usually some humour to it, you know. I asked her what was wrong and she said something about people raking up the past and how they should leave well alone because they never knew what they were going to uncover. I asked her what she meant but she just kind of threw up her hands and said never mind."

"And you got no further than that?"

Ursula shrugged. "Not really. Though there was one thing, and I don't know if it's got anything to do with what upset her, but she had a bin in the kitchen for things that went on the compost, alongside the usual recycling and ordinary rubbish bins. I used to carry it down the garden and empty it into the compost heap. As a rule there wasn't much in it, veg or fruit peelings and tea leaves and that sort of thing, but that particular day there was a torn up book. I wondered why she'd not put it in the recycling. Actually, I wondered why she had torn up a book in the first place because Jean loved her books. I asked her about it, just in case she had, I don't know, got mixed up. She said that vile rubbish might as well feed something."

"Do you know what the book was?"

Ursula shook her head. "She'd torn the cover off because they don't break down in the compost too well. There can often be plastic in the covers, or printers' ink that doesn't do the ground any good, at least that's what she said. The rest of it she'd ripped to bits so I couldn't even see the title page. To be honest I was curious but it was also covered in tea leaves and pretty soggy by then and she was so vehement about it I didn't feel able to go poking about."

Late March, Mac thought. Was it pure coincidence that this was when the memoir had been published? Had someone sent Jean Hammond a copy? Had Jean Hammond known Miles Cunningham? He asked Ursula if his name had ever been mentioned.

She frowned. "Yes. She did a painting for him."

"A painting *for* him, are you sure?"

"I think so, it's an unusual name isn't it? You don't get many Miles. It was only small, by Jean's standards anyway. No more than A4 paper size, on canvas mounted on board. It was this man and two little kids standing in front of an old house and there was lightning in the sky. It reminded me of a Tarot card. The Tower Struck by Lightning one. I didn't know her well enough back then to ask her about it." Mac thought Ursula sounded regretful about that.

"When was this?" he asked.

"Not long after I started cleaning for her. So a bit over a year ago? May or June time. I was still getting the bus out there back then and that was a right pain. Jean used to let me hang around while I waited for the bus back to town and I sometimes watched her work. She said something about an anniversary and that she felt she should have done this a long time ago. I assumed he must be having a birthday or something and liked spooky pictures."

Mac was silent for a moment before asking, "There were flowers on the table in the hall, do you know who they were from?"

"Mr Goodman, Philip. He'd come over to dinner a few nights before, he always brings flowers and wine. He's a nice man."

"You've met him?"

Ursula nodded. "A few times. Jean would try and cook but to be honest it was getting a bit beyond her. Mostly she ate microwave meals and just added a few veg so, as she put it, it looked like she was making an effort. I suggested she just ordered in when he came round to dinner. During the pandemic a lot of the local restaurants started doing takeaway and those that didn't do delivery you could still go and pick things up. Most carried on with that even after things got back to normal. There were times recently when she paid me a couple of hours extra to stay on and go and pick up the meal for them. Both times it was when she was having Philip over." Ursula smiled. "She ordered extra so I could take some home with me, she was kind like that. They always seemed to be having such a good laugh together — both when he came over and when he phoned her. He'd call her two or three times a week or she'd call him. She said he was one of her oldest friends."

"And did she ever mention Graham Jackson? Or the theft of some jewellery?"

"What? From the house?" Ursula sounded alarmed.

"No, from Graham Jackson who was the son of an old friend. Sadly he was murdered."

"Murdered?"

"Unfortunately so."

"So that's two people she knew who were killed. This Graham Jackson and her friend Christopher. Mac that's—"

"Not a coincidence." Mac nodded. "I know. But I can't tell you much more than that. Did she mention someone called William Tatum?"

Ursula looked puzzled and then said, "I'm not sure. The name's familiar from somewhere. But I can't think where, sorry."

"Ursula, thank for you for telling me this. I'm going to need you to write all of this down."

Ursula opened her backpack and withdrew several sheets of paper. "Already done," she said. "It didn't have to be on any official paper, did it?"

Mac laughed. "Organised as ever," he said. "And I've got a list of the questions that I just asked you, do you mind adding your answers while you are here and could you also make a list for me of anybody you remember Jean Hammond mentioning, friends, delivery drivers, any of the committees she was on, anything like that."

"No problem," she grinned at George and then said, "We figured you'd have more for me to do, so George and I thought maybe you could go out and get some of that nice coffee while I was doing it?"

Mac laughed. "I can do that," he said.

He and George wandered along the promenade towards their favourite coffee shop. The evening was warm, dark blue skies out at sea suggesting it might rain later but at that moment pleasant enough for people to be out for an evening stroll. Mac had come to love this little bay, the small town of Frantham on Sea nestled in the gap between two headlands and the pebble and sand beach. Not as impressive or busy as Lyme Bay, just along the coast, or as conducive to fossil hunting but this was more intimate, somehow.

George glanced up to the flats above the row of shops, towards the one Mac had occupied when he had first come to Frantham. Mac knew that he was remembering. George's mother and sister had taken shelter there when George's violent father had been in pursuit of them and had then kidnapped George. Sadly, George's mother had committed suicide in the flat.

It was now back to being a holiday let and Mac could not sometimes help but wonder if it was haunted.

"So how are you both doing?" he asked. "You're both looking well but tired. I imagine your exams must be nearly over."

"Mine are, Ursula's got one more," George replied. "Then I start my apprenticeship in September, two days in college, three days in the boatyard at Lyme. There's a year of that and then I can go to work full-time. I can't believe how much has changed over the past few years since I first came here."

"That's true for all of us," Mac said. He had arrived in Frantham at more or less the same time as George and his family and had been in just as parlous a state. George and his family had been worn out by the need to keep running and hiding and Mac in turn by a child abduction case that had gone horribly and dramatically wrong. It had almost destroyed him. "Are you and Ursula—"

George smiled. "Kind of on and off. I mean it's never really off, it's just that sometimes . . . oh I don't know. We talked about it and it's like we'll never *not* be together it's just that sometimes we're more together than other times, if you know what I mean. We both still get scared when it gets a bit intense but we both know what we're doing, so it's OK, we can work it out."

"I'm glad that you can work it out," Mac said. "And how is Ursula, after this Jean Hammond thing."

"This Jean Hammond thing? Now *you* are being cryptic. You really think she was murdered?"

"It's something we need to find out."

"Well, Ursula was upset. And she was very upset that she couldn't go to the funeral. She really liked her and Jean offered her something different in her life. I think Ursula felt she was special because of that. She's always been interested in art and in making things but she's never really had the chance and Jean gave her that chance. That was really important. She has a lot of pressure from everyone else, her aunt's always on at her that she must get a good job, but no one in the family's ever stepped up to help her so she's always taken care of herself. So, I don't see how she can dictate really. But Ursula takes it seriously. I'd love her to turn round and say get lost, I'm gonna run away to a circus. But she won't. I want to make sure she keeps on drawing. She needs it, she needs something for her."

Mac nodded, admiring both Ursula and George's resilience. He opened the door to Tonino's little coffee shop. "Vanilla or gingerbread?" he asked. "I seem to remember she liked both."

"Vanilla, probably. So, who is this Miles Cunningham?"

Mac knew that they would just Google the question anyway so he may as well reply. "In 1980 he was accused of murdering his family and a young man called William Tatum who had been lodging with them. He pleaded guilty though there is an element of doubt. He died in 1997 so I don't know why Jean Hammond would have been painting anything for him. Or what the anniversary would be, unless it was the date of the murders. That was June, I believe."

George looked shocked. "But what's that got to do with Jean Hammond now. She obviously knew him if she was painting something for him or in his memory or whatever but—"

"I know. But right now George, I have no idea."

* * *

When Ursula and George had left, Mac walked up to Peverill Lodge to see Rina. The Rina Martin household were gathered in the big living room watching the television but when Mac arrived the kettle was put on, cake was produced and the questions began, the collective intelligence of the Martin household feeling that it had a vested interest in whatever Mac had come to ask. As it happened, Mac only had one question and that was if Rina had known Miles Cunningham.

"I had a feeling you might ask me that," she said. "After you left the other night, I realised that I did in fact recognise one of the people in the photograph. I'd put him out of my mind, I'd not seen him since just after Fred died and I suppose he got buried in the past, he was part of that painful time but the truth is Miles and Betty were very kind to me."

"We all knew him though, didn't we," Eliza said unexpectedly.

"Not particularly well," Matthew said, shaking his mane of grey hair "but he was certainly part of our wider circle of acquaintances."

The comment was greeted by general nodding.

"It's not so surprising, Sebastian," Matthew continued. "Miles Cunningham started his career as a journalist down on the south coast. One of the little, local newspapers, if I remember correctly. He was reporting on the kind of shows we were all in back then. Brighton Pier, one or other of the little theatres, that sort of thing. And unlike some of the so-called critics, he was generally very pleasant."

"Then he got better known," Steven said, "and gradually worked his way up to reporting on West End shows and reviewing television programmes."

Mac nodded, he knew that the Montmorency twins were older than Rina, so presumably were fairly well established when Rina was still starting out. Their collective trajectory would probably have paralleled Cunningham's.

"Then that dreadful thing happened," Bethany almost whispered. "We couldn't believe it, could we Eliza?"

"No, indeed we could not. We'd seen him only a few days before and he seemed perfectly normal then. It just goes to show, you never can tell what's going on in someone's head, can you?"

"You saw him? Where was this?"

"In Brighton, Mac dear. We'd been auditioning. We left the theatre and there he was, just walking along the street. So we all went and had a stiff drink. It had been that kind of audition," she added with a little shudder.

Mac hid a smile. "I don't suppose you can recall what you talked about."

The sisters looked at one another. "Of course we can," Eliza said. "That dreadful thing happened only days later, so you can imagine how we went over every detail, just in case there had been any hint, you know, of what he might be about to do."

Mac nodded and waited. Performers still, their instinct would be to wring every ounce of drama from the telling.

"Well," Bethany said, "we couldn't think of a thing. Not one little clue. It was mostly shoptalk, you know, who was appearing in what and how our work was going. He seemed his old, jovial self, wanting to know what we'd been up to and giving us his news." Her hands fluttered to her face and her mouth twisted as though in pain. "He told us about the new baby," she said. "Oh, those poor, poor little mites, what had they ever done to anyone."

Eliza took one hand and Matthew the other. Both turned accusatory gazes on Mac.

"There was gossip, of course," Steven said, taking over. "That the baby wasn't his, but I never could believe that.

Betty was a lovely woman. I can't believe she would have cheated on Miles."

"There was gossip, I remember, about Miles and other women, including that awful Constance Tatum, sister to the boy that died," Bethany added. "Of course, none of us believed that either."

"Indeed not!" Steven declared.

Again Mac waited. It was unusual for Steven to sound quite so vehement about anything. Matthew and the Peters sisters were nodding agreement, Mac noted. Rina was just out of his eye line; he'd have given a lot to have been able to monitor her reaction too.

"Why 'awful'?" Mac asked.

Steven looked uncomfortable. "Well, I don't like to speak ill of anyone and I know the young woman had a rough time growing up but she certainly didn't know how to behave. Flirting is one thing but she went well beyond that. If you listened to Constance, every man who saw her found her irresistible. The rows she had with Betty! Well I, personally, only overheard one of them but it was common knowledge."

"And yet they agreed to take her brother in," Mac said.

"They were kind people," Eliza said. "He had a horrible childhood and I believe they thought they could help and that maybe if Connie got back on her feet that would be good for her and for her brother. Though we did all wonder if it was wise. I know Miles and Betty worked wonders with their lodgers, but this was surely one step too far."

This time, Mac thought, *waiting might not be enough*. "Their lodgers?" he asked.

Again that exchange of glances.

"Well," Matthew said, "Betty inherited that great rambling place in Woodingdean. Wonderful views across the downs and out to sea. It was very run down, and it was far too big for them. But when they inherited the house no one wanted buildings like that. This was before the property bubble of the 1980s," he added knowledgeably. "Lord alone knows what it might have been worth now."

"Might have been?" Mac asked.

"It burnt down, Sebastian. Arson, of course. House, fence, garden shed and summer house. It was only because the alarm was raised so quickly that it didn't spread to the neighbouring house. Razed, it was. Funny thing was though, the privet hedge at the front was untouched and so were those stupid hydrangea things Betty had in pots at the end of the path. Not plants I've ever liked, I'm afraid. Just two days after the . . . murders, this was."

Like the others he seemed reluctant, almost superstitious about calling the crime what it was.

"Was anyone charged with the arson? Are you certain that was what happened?" Mac pressed.

"Mac, my dear, someone threw a Molotov Cocktail through the sitting room window at the side of the house," Bethany said. "By the time the fire brigade arrived the whole place was ablaze. And before you ask, yes, we're certain that was how it was. Someone witnessed it, you could see the front of the house from the road and a motorist driving by saw the arsonist. He called the fire brigade and the police from a nearby phone box but I don't believe anyone was ever caught." She leaned forward, confidentially. "You know, the motorist thought it might have been a woman. Imagine! He saw them hop over the fence into the next-door garden and then run out into a side road."

"A great many people were glad the house had gone," Eliza added. "A house like that, with so many deaths, so much blood soaked into the fibres, I imagine it would feel cursed. Haunted at the very least. Who would want to live there?"

Mac's thoughts were drawn to his old flat on the promenade. Holiday lets were one thing, he thought, but a permanent resident would surely have to be made aware of the history. Might even sense the history. Or surely the neighbours would enlighten them.

"And this William Tatum," Mac said. "Do you know how he ended up living there?"

"Well, I imagine Betty or Miles felt sorry for him," Bethany said. "It wouldn't have been the first time. They worked with some charity or other. I forget the name, I know it was a saint or something, Oswald, maybe? Or maybe not. He's the patron saint of soldiers, isn't he? Anyway, the charity was all about rehabilitation. They had a lot of space and not a lot of money. The charity paid them to act like a sort of half-way house, I suppose you'd call it. The lodgers would stay for a while and then move on and someone else would come and take their place."

"Usually it was women," Eliza added. "Betty was there on her own with the children a lot of the time, so usually it was a girl who would stay. Often a girl who, you know, had got into trouble."

So, an unmarried mother, Mac thought.

"I know it's really not that long ago," Eliza said sadly, "but there were still parents willing to throw their girls out because they'd got pregnant and couldn't marry the father. Betty would look after them when they came out of hospital, help them get back on their feet. The babies would often as not be adopted."

"We're talking about the late seventies, very early eighties?" Mac asked.

"Indeed. As I say, not so very long ago really. Times have changed, of course, and we should all be thankful for that."

Mac nodded. "So William Tatum was an unusual lodger."

"He was, but he was also a local boy. The girls would come from all over the place. I don't know how they came to offer him a place to stay but perhaps it was almost inevitable someone would start nasty rumours about him and Betty. There's always someone with a spiteful tongue. Though how anyone could say those things given the circumstances . . . He was hardly someone Betty would have been involved with. Not in that way anyway."

"I stayed there for a while," Rina said quietly. Mac turned to look at her and noted a certain reticence in her manner that was very un-Rina like.

"Oh, so you did!" Bethany's hands fluttered. "I'd quite forgotten that. You were so unwell after Fred departed."

"And Miles and Betty were kindness itself," Rina said. "I don't know what I'd have done if they hadn't stepped in. They gave me a place to stay and fed me, looked after me until I was ready to get on with my life again. That's why, when I read the reports in the papers, oh this was a long time after, I couldn't believe that Miles would . . . could have done anything so terrible."

"But he confessed, didn't he," Steven said sadly.

"As I understand it, he said it was his fault." Though Mac was still not sure that amounted to the same thing. "Did any of you know Jean Hammond back then?"

A general shaking of heads.

"No, we were theatrical people," Eliza said. "She was a painter. I don't think we moved in the same circles at all."

"It seems she knew Miles Cunningham," Mac said.

"Well, Miles was a critic. I imagine if his editor told him to go and review a painting exhibition then off he'd go and do it," Bethany told him.

"None of you recall him mentioning her?"

No one did.

"What about Christopher Hayes?"

Again, no recollection.

"And Philip Goodman?"

"Oh, of course we knew Philip," Bethany's eyes sparkled. "Such a funny man. You know he started out in the theatre, painting the flats. He was starting to get successful as an artist around the time we were all in Glasgow. You remember he sent us a collective invitation to his one man show and none of us could go because we were all up in Scotland?"

A general murmur of agreement followed. Mac could see memories being rekindled and knew he'd lose control of the conversation if the reminiscences began. Ordinarily, he'd have been happy about that but it was getting late and he was tired. He wanted to go home.

"It seems that he and Jean Hammond became good friends."

"Did they? How lovely," Eliza beamed at him. "He was one of those people who, you know the type, you don't see one another for years and then suddenly from across the room you'd hear this big, booming voice saying 'Eliza Peters, how the devil are you,' and there'd he'd be. Larger than life. You know when the new law came in allowing civil ceremonies? He and Tony had theirs booked in the first week. We were so happy for them. We all went, of course. There were so many people there. He'd hired this big reception room in a very smart hotel."

"Jean Hammond was there," Rina remembered. "I didn't really know her then, though I knew who she was. She'd done a painting for them as a wedding gift. You remember the grand unveiling?"

"Oh was that one of Jean Hammond's?" Bethany asked. "I do remember the fuss about a painting being unveiled, yes. I don't recall much about it though."

"That's because you'd been drinking champagne," her sister told her. "For that matter, so had I. I don't recall the painting either, but I do remember having rather a fabulous time."

"It seems Miss Hammond liked to create art for people she loved," Mac commented.

"I think she did," Rina agreed. "She once told me that early in her career it was all about getting established, making a living, satisfying the client when she was lucky enough to get one. Later in life, when she was well established and had sufficient money to last her lifetime, she had a great deal more latitude. It must have been a wonderful position to find herself in. She struggled in those early years just like we all did. Different discipline but the same sort of obstacles to overcome, I'd have thought."

Mac nodded and stood up. "I should go," he said. "It's late and Miriam will be wondering where I've got to."

He left, carrying messages of love and affection from all in Rina's household.

Rina walked him to the door.

"Are you looking into the Cunningham murders?" she asked. "What's going on, Mac?"

"It looks as though Jean Hammond's death might not have been as simple as we first thought," he said. "There have been two others that had, shall we say, similarities."

"The flower in her hand," Rina guessed.

"I never told you about that," Mac smiled. "It was an ordinary hydrangea flower, by the way, just like the ones at the Cunningham house but also annoyingly commonplace."

"And Miles Cunningham?"

"Was, as you know, in the photograph she was so insistent Ursula should take. So far there's not much else, but . . . Rina, it seems she painted something for him too. Last year, long after he and all his family were dead. Apparently, she referred to an anniversary or a reminder of some sort. This would be about a year ago or just over, in June, probably, around the time Ursula started working for her. I wonder if she meant the anniversary of the murders."

CHAPTER 19

Clive Tatum, second cousin of William Tatum, the lodger stabbed to death in the house of Miles Cunningham, lived about ten miles from Frantham.

Mac, being tied up elsewhere had dispatched DC Yolanda Cooper, accompanied by PC Andy Nevins to see if he would talk to them informally. Mac had been unable to reach Clive Tatum by phone, so it was perfectly likely they would get there and he would not be in. Just as likely that he would not want to talk to the police, on spec, in which case they would have to try something more official. Mac and Kendall figured that Yolanda and Andy would make a good team for this task. Yolanda, Dave Kendall said, could talk her way into just about anywhere — though once she was in she could be a little too abrupt for some people — and Andy, more diffident in manner, just as acute when it came to observation, would balance her more acerbic qualities.

Of the two, Andy, though he'd not been in the force for quite as long, had the edge when it came to involvement in murder enquiries, his first having occurred just a few weeks after Mac's arrival.

The two officers sat across the street looking at the very ordinary terraced house with a bright red front door and exuberantly planted hanging baskets swaying in what was quite a stiff breeze.

"Well, someone's in," Yolanda said as a figure moved past an upstairs window. She glanced at her watch. Ten fifteen. "Do writers get up early or do they sleep late like actors," she wondered.

Andy's look was quizzical. "How would I know," he said. "I know Mrs Martin gets up early but the rest of them like to sleep in a bit. I've not met many writers and I don't think journalists count."

He watched as Yolanda put her head on one side and considered this. "Journalists are different," she agreed. "And this Clive Tatum must be retired, I suppose, so do retired people get up late?"

"My nan gets up early," Andy told her, opening his door. "I'll bet yours does too."

Yolanda rolled her eyes. *She was good at that*, Andy thought. "My nan on my mum's side, I'll swear she's nocturnal. Watches the telly most of the night and then dozes off in the afternoon. But then, she spent most of her life on the nightshift, so . . ."

The street was quiet, well off the main road. Andy guessed the majority of traffic would be just the residents. He noticed a couple of curtains twitching as Yolanda knocked on the door. Guessed that police officers were probably a bit of a rarity round here where the houses, though modest, looked well cared for and there was a distinct absence of rubbish in the gutters. Andy was a bit of a connoisseur when it came to classifying streets.

The door opened and a short, rather round man peered out at them, clearly as taken aback as his neighbours by the sight of two young people, one in uniform and the other waving identification in his face.

"Mr Tatum?" Yolanda asked cheerfully.

"Yes," he replied warily.

"I wonder if we could have a quick word. It won't take long, but it's about your memoir."

He frowned and Andy noted the suddenly closed, unwelcoming expression. "I think any queries of a legal nature should be addressed to my publisher," he said. "I have to say, I'm pretty sick of being harassed like this?"

Andy and Yolanda exchanged a glance. So far as Andy knew no one had even contacted him yet. "Like this?" Andy asked. "Mr Tatum, has someone else been in touch? We've just come round to ask a couple of questions because there's a slight possibility your recollections might be able to help with a police investigation?" Even as he said this, Andy got the feeling that he and Yolanda were not in fact the problem. "Has someone else been harassing you?" he asked.

Andy watched as Clive Tatum reassessed the situation. Finally, he stood back from the door and gestured for them to come inside. "Beginning to wish I had never written the damn things," he said.

Things, plural, Andy thought. Yolanda was ahead of him.

"More than one memoir?" she asked.

Clive Tatum looked slightly uncomfortable and then shook his head. "Now if I'd had stuck to memoirs, I'd probably have been fine."

"Oh my God, you wrote the novel as well," Yolanda sounded triumphant. "I told you it was him."

Andy tried hard not to laugh.

"I suppose this is where I offer you tea or coffee," Clive Tatum said. He seemed to be giving in to the inevitable.

"That would be very nice, thanks," Andy told him. They followed the man through to the kitchen and Andy could see that Yolanda was ready to launch into her own questions. He wondered if he should hold her back and then thought, no, let her get on with it. See what comes out and then he'd see what needed to be asked to fill in any gaps.

"So, what made you want to write a novel as well?" Yolanda asked once they were seated in the middle room of the little terraced house, from where they could watch Clive Tatum busy himself in the narrow, galley kitchen.

He laughed. "I've always had this . . . Strategy. Make the most of whatever research you do, see how you can reframe it or reshape it for another article, or to sell to a different market. Often all it takes is a slightly different spin and you can make twice the money for half the work. I'd gone back through all my old notes and documents and interviews for the memoir so I thought, why not. I know I have to write it differently. I couldn't make it too obvious, and it was supposed to come out under a pen name. My thinking was, just about everybody involved back then are dead or too old to care."

"You were wrong about that," Yolanda said. "So I'm guessing there's some kind of legal query going on?"

He nodded. "Something like that."

Clive brought a tea tray through and Andy, as his instruction, set a small folding table down in front of the gas fire. He had been in a lot of rooms like this, standard terraced house layout, with space for the small two-seater sofa which he and Yolanda occupied and a fireside chair which was clearly the house owner's favourite seat.

"So this harassment," Andy asked, "that's about the novel?"

"Well in the main, yes, but the problem is the trouble could spill over and impact on the memoir, which happens to have sold quite well as these things go. I mean we're not talking about a bestseller here, but satisfying nonetheless. Enough for the publisher to want to put second edition into print but of course that's on hold now as well."

He handed them both mugs and Yolanda leaned forward, her expression intent. "So, what's been happening then?"

She was, Andy realised with a slight jolt, genuinely interested. Tatum must have realised that too because he leaned back in his chair and regarded her with a far more sanguine expression. "I guess I got stupid and overconfident," he said. "I had this idea that I could disguise what had gone on, but in such a way that anybody who was interested, or who had any knowledge of true crime, would get that this is what I was writing about. You see it always struck me as such a good human interest story, not to mention the question of why or if he did it."

"Miles Cunningham," Andy said. "He pleaded guilty. So that is a confession, surely."

"He came close to confessing. And yes, he pleaded guilty and so there was no court case. He was sentenced, life imprisonment of course, and he died in jail. He refused all attempts by anybody to get him to talk about it. The investigating officers, the press, friends. From what I can gather he barely spoke at all and he certainly would not discuss the deaths of his wife and children or of my second cousin. It was as though he closed the door on the entire episode, accepted his punishment and that was that."

"So, what's a novel about?" Yolanda asked. "I'm sorry but I don't see it as much of a story. Miles Cunningham lost it, killed his wife and kids and your cousin happened to be there, so he died too." She bit her lip, as though suddenly realising that she had seemed a little blunt but Tatum was definitely finding her amusing, Andy thought.

"Would it be possible to get hold of a copy of the novel?" Andy interjected. "And would you mind telling us who you think has been harassing you?"

Clive Tatum looked at him thoughtfully for a moment and then nodded. "You mentioned this was part of an investigation? Tell me what investigation, and what it is you want from me and I will do my best to give you any information you think might be useful. As far as the novel is concerned, well I guess it might be possible for you to have an earlier draft. I can't let you have a copy of the novel due for publication because I don't have a copy myself as yet. And I'm not going to offend my publisher or risk stirring up other problems by letting you have a copy of the proofs. If you need something like that you'll have to get someone higher up the pay grade to talk to their lawyers. But I can email you an uncorrected draft which will be close enough, I would have thought. Though I do need convincing as to why this might be required."

Andy nodded. "Fair enough. But as the novel hasn't been published yet, and presumably no one knows exactly what's in it apart from you and your publishers, who's been objecting and why?"

Clive Tatum sipped his tea as though buying time to think through his next words. "I said that just about everybody concerned with the incident is either dead or too old to care. Well, it seemed I was wrong. William Tatum had a sister, Constance, she died a couple of years ago. She had a daughter, Sarah. The thing was, Constance absolutely adored William. His death devastated her." He shook his head.

"Somebody, I'm not entirely sure who even now, suggested to her that she might get compensation from the Cunningham estate. One of the newspapers took up her cause and this was pushed for, but the fact was there wasn't really anything left in the Cunningham estate. Although Miles Cunningham had been earning a reasonable living and they were taking in lodgers paid for by a local charity, they were not particularly well off. They were still trying to run that great barn of a place, pay for the kids to go to private schools, waste of time and money if you ask me, but there you go. Cunningham's father was also in a care home and they were doing their damnedest to keep him there.

"All that was left after the family's deaths and Cunningham's imprisonment was the land that the house had stood on. It was suggested that be sold off and put into trust. I think the intention was that it would be there to pay for Cunningham's father's care but as it turned out that was unnecessary. The poor man died only a few months later. They tried to keep it from him, what had happened, but that was impossible of course. The shock finished him off."

"What about other relatives?"

"Betty was an orphan, had been raised by an aunt but she doesn't seem to have come into the picture very much after Betty was grown up. I remember she came to court to see the sentencing, and I did try to speak to her — as did just about every tabloid in the country. But she was married to a Frenchman and had been living in France for a while and as soon as the case was over that's where she went back to. Miles Cunningham's mother had died when he was in his teens, but she had been in and out of various mental hospitals long before that. Attempted suicide three or four times and finally succeeded. Of course, all this was fodder for the press and a popular opinion at the time was that he had inherited her mental illness and this had eventually led to murder."

"But you don't think that do you?" Yolanda said. Then added, "I'm sorry but we hadn't even heard about your memoir until yesterday so nobody's had a chance to get a copy and read it."

"An issue I'm sure I can correct," he told her. "And no, I'm not convinced that Miles Cunningham was guilty of killing his wife and children and I am not convinced that William Tatum was innocent. There are forensic findings that are suggestive of another explanation and I also knew Miles Cunningham and I find it hard to believe that he could have attacked his family."

"But you do believe he might have attacked someone who had murdered them," Andy said carefully.

"That I do, and in my memoir I explore that possibility. The memoir is not, to be honest, high-profile enough that it attracted much attention from the likes of Sarah, Constance's daughter. But the novel is another matter and the advance publicity made it fairly obvious that this was based on a real-life event, albeit very loosely based. And if you know the Miles Cunningham case it wouldn't take much working out. Constance must have heard about it, but by then she was too ill to take any kind of action. That has been left to Sarah. Basically, she's talking defamation. We have the lawyers working on it of course and I've no doubt the novel will come out, just a little late and with a few tweaks here and there. And I've also no doubt the advance publicity and the controversy will ensure that it sells much better than my memoir was ever going to. But in the meantime, it's all very unpleasant."

"You talked about harassment," Andy said.

"I did. Sarah looks as if she's about to work her way through money realised from the sale of the family home on lawyers who are to my mind simply leading her along making what they can while she still has the cash to pay them. I've had cease-and-desist letters and phone calls from her and from her solicitor, threats of court action and indeed there will be some court action. She even came to the house. She stood in the street and shouted abuse, I'm not entirely sure whether my neighbours were amused or insulted. This is a quiet street. But even though I am confident that events will turn in my favour in the end, it is very uncomfortable at the moment. And as I say even the reprinting of the memoir is being put on hold and I've no doubt I'm going to have yet another round of edits come back on the novel by the time my publisher's legal eagles have finished picking it over. That I can live with, daily hate mail is a little more difficult."

"Have you reported it?" Andy said.

"The local police know, and of course everything has been handed over to my publisher's legal department. I've kept copies," he added looking meaningfully at Yolanda and obviously anticipating her next question. "But I'm not certain my publisher would want me to share them with you. They won't want anything else slowing down the legal process so if you want them then I suggest your superiors apply for a warrant. And now, would you mind telling me what your mission for the day is all about."

Andy and Yolanda exchanged a swift glance.

"Did you know a lady called Jean Hammond, she was an artist," Andy asked.

"I may know her work, but I don't know her." He frowned. "Was that the woman who was found dead in her garden a few weeks back? I remember there was a big thing in the news because she was a famous artist."

"That'll be the one," Yolanda said. "Well, it turns out she also knew Miles Cunningham." From her bag Yolanda produced a copy of the photograph that Jean had left for Ursula to retrieve. She pointed to the figure of Cunningham standing at the back of the group. And then to Jean.

Clive Tatum studied it carefully. "This was a while ago. So . . . I'm not quite sure I see the significance."

"Do you recognise anybody else in the photograph?" Andy asked.

"One or two of the faces look familiar but I'd be hard-pressed to put a name to them. I'm guessing this was taken in the seventies?"

"Late seventies we think."

"Did you know someone called Christopher Hayes?" Yolanda asked. "He was also an artist."

"Christopher Hayes, yes, I knew him in passing. He wasn't somebody I knew well. I have a vague feeling Miles introduced me but it's going back a long way. What's all this about?"

"At the moment we're not quite sure," Andy said quite truthfully. "It's just these names have come up, in the course of an investigation so I can't tell you too much at the moment because there isn't really much to tell."

Clive Tatum looked sceptical. "Well, I will look over my notes and see if there's anything relevant." He stood up. "Now let me find you a copy of my memoir. You'd better give me an email so that I can send you a draft of the novel."

"Could you also give us contact details for Sarah . . . Tatum, is it?"

"Fredericks," he said. "That was her mother's married name. But I don't quite see what she has to do with anything?"

"Probably nothing," Yolanda said. "But you know what it's like; we have to tick all the boxes."

They were conscious of Clive Tatum — and various neighbours — watching as they walked back across the street to their car.

"What did you make of that?" Andy asked.

"That he is lying through his teeth about something," she said. "And is looking for an angle — how can he use our little visit, how can he turn this to his advantage because he's a canny old git."

"I thought you kind of liked him?" Andy said. "You gave that impression."

"I thought he was interesting," Yolanda said. "And yes, I'm inclined to like him in the way you'd like a reprobate uncle or something. It was weird the way he talked about putting a spin on his notes or his research or his articles or whatever so he could use them for something else, but my guess is he does that with absolutely everything, conversations, relationships, the works. Did you notice how bare the place was? I mean, no photographs, no pictures on the wall, no bric-a-brac."

Now she came to mention it, Andy had noticed that. "Maybe he just likes minimal," he said.

"My guess is that he's got used to not wanting anybody to find out anything about him that he doesn't want to volunteer and he only volunteers information that might get him a quid pro quo."

Andy laughed at her. "That's a bit of a stretch, drawing an inference like that just from the fact that he hasn't got any family photos on his mantelpiece."

Yolanda opened the driver's side door. "I'm right," she said. "You just see if I'm not."

CHAPTER 20

An incident room had been set up at the Palisades Hotel, courtesy of Lily and James Blake. The hotel being a convenient location and the newly renovated stable block affording the space they needed.

The Palisades was an Art Deco hotel, expensive and luxurious in its day but sadly run down in the years before Lily and James had taken over. The renovations had been slow but thorough and the main building now being finished they had moved on to the stable blocks. These were impressive, built around three sides of a courtyard with a massive clock tower set at the centre of the longest side. The stable block was older than the hotel, left over from the grand Victorian pile that had previously stood on the site and whose cellars still ran beneath the current building. The Blakes were hoping that eventually extra, self-catering, accommodation could be set up for families or visitors with pets, that needed a bit more flexibility than a hotel could offer.

The basic building work had been completed and some of the areas already subdivided, though there was still work to be done before it became proper holiday lets. Water and other utilities had been installed and it had been Mac that had suggested approaching the Blakes with a view to establishing the incident room there. He knew them well; they employed Tim as resident magician and had been obliquely involved in previous investigations, so he was pretty sure he'd get a sympathetic response — as indeed he had. The hotel was in a glorious location, halfway between Frantham bay and Lyme Regis, standing atop the cliffs with a long lawned garden running down to the South West Coast Path with Frantham an easy walk in one direction and Lyme and Golden Cap a slightly more strenuous walk in the other. The landscape surrounding the hotel, undulating and green, was popular with walkers and the main rooms faced the sea; massive windows providing a view of the seasonal changes; grey and bleak in winter, almost turquoise in the summer months.

The stable block backed on to a wooded area with a winding path through the trees that linked up to yet more footpaths. It was possible, should you have the energy and inclination, to walk from the Palisades into Bridport though Mac suspected most visitors took their cars.

Tables and chairs had also been provided by the hotel and a couple of massive hot water urns. Andy and Yolanda arrived to discover something that looked like barely organised chaos. Boxes of records from the Miles Cunningham investigation had arrived alongside evidence boxes from the deaths of Christopher Hayes and Graham Jackson. It looked also as though the team had expanded, with extra tables and chairs being moved into a far too small incident room.

Yolanda paused in the doorway and looked around. "You see that desk over in the corner of the room" she said, indicating an as yet unoccupied space. "I think we should lay claim to that."

Andy could immediately see her point. There was just enough room for them to have a chair on either side and a couple of laptops and the deep windowsill would make extra space for storage. It would also give whoever was sitting closest to the window a good view over the rest of the room and therefore a sense of what else was going on.

"Right," he said. "Give me your jacket and your bag, you go and nab a couple of laptops and we'll move in."

She rewarded him with a broad grin and Andy made his way across the room and began to pitch camp.

Mac came in a moment or two later and spotted him. "How did it go with Clive Tatum?" he asked. "And how did it go with Yolanda?"

"With Yolanda, absolutely fine. With Clive Tatum, well we both agree there are things he's holding back but we got a copy of his memoir," Andy indicated the book on the desk. "And he's promised to email a draft of the novel. It may not be exactly as it was intended to go to press, but it'll hopefully be close enough. It also seems that William Tatum's niece, and her mother, that's William Tatum's sister, Constance Tatum, before that, were on the warpath and didn't want either book published. The sister didn't know about the memoir until it was out, and Tatum thinks that would have slipped beneath her radar anyway, it being with a small publisher. But she got wind of the novel and she's the one that's been creating the problems which is why it's subject to all of these legal enquiries right now. Constance Tatum, or Constance Fredericks as she became, died about eighteen months ago from cancer."

"So presumably before the novel was even due to be published."

"Yes, but the publisher had an article about it in *Publishers Weekly*. It was part of a debate about using true crime in fiction and it got picked up, he thinks, in one of the Sunday supplements. Anyway, she got wind of it and she was furious because he implied that William Tatum might not be as innocent as she believed him to be. Obviously, names and circumstances had been changed, but he himself admits that it would be clear to anybody that knew about the original murders to draw parallels.

"Anyway, she died, but her daughter is busy spending everything her mother left in trying to get the book stopped. Clive Tatum reckons the lawyers are just stringing her along, his publisher's lawyers think this is just a matter of time before the objections are cleared and Sarah Fredericks won't have a leg to stand on. But he reckons hardly a day goes by without something coming through the post or email threatening him. He's passed all this on to the publisher's legal team but he let us have copies." Andy indicated the stack of paper lined up against the edge of the desk. "And he reckons the controversy will just convert into book sales in the long run."

Yolanda arrived at that moment carrying two laptops. She looked, Andy thought, momentarily put out that he had claimed the seat with his back to the window and an outlook across the room.

"I thought we might swing the table round," he said, "that would mean we can use the windowsill and also bring one of the little filing cabinets over to put in that corner." Yolanda brightened at the prospect and Andy wondered why that pleased him so much. He realised with a slight shock that he actually liked her a lot and was suddenly very aware of Mac scrutinising them and the slight smile playing at the corner of his boss's mouth. It had been a while since Andy had been in a relationship and Yolanda hadn't mentioned anyone significant, Andy thought, so maybe . . . He pulled his thoughts back to the job in hand.

"She certainly seems to have inherited her mother's anger about William Tatum."

"Well she needs interviewing, certainly," Mac agreed, "particularly if she's been sending hate mail to Clive Tatum. Have a word with the local constabulary and find out what action's been taken."

"We'll add it to the action plan," Yolanda said.

Mac smiled at her. "I'll leave you to get yourselves . . . established," he said. "If you take my advice, you'll make sure you're thoroughly ensconced in the next half-hour or so, we've got three more team members arriving and they're all going to be wanting space. If it looks as though you're going to be difficult to move, they are less likely to want yours. Get the Clive Tatum interview written up, I'll be wanting you both to brief the team later. Oh, and Andy? DI Kendall and I both agree you'd be better off in civvies for the moment. Acting DC, OK. You've got the experience for it."

Andy stared after him as Mac made his way back across the room.

"Well, get you," Yolanda said, grinning.

For the next few minutes they organised their space and then logged into the computers. Andy was gratified to see that Clive Tatum had already sent across the draft of his book. DI Stella Fullhurst came over and dropped a stack of photograph albums on the desk.

"Another little job for you," she said. "If you can go through and see if any of the photographs in the book match those in the group photo that features Miles Cunningham. I've had a quick glance through and it looks as though she labelled her photos in pencil on the back, so fingers crossed we'll be to get some identities. Yolanda, did you go into the Hammond house when you were there?"

"Only to make sure the doors were locked. Mostly I just stayed in the garden and the studio."

"Pity, you might have spotted something. I expect she had other photographs on display so we might have to try and get hold of those."

When she left Andy eyed the stack of thick, expensively bound books. "OK," he said, "we need to divide this up. How about I get the record of the interview done, you start on those. You might be better at matching faces than I am. You can read through the report and add anything you think I've missed and then I'll give you a hand with the face matching."

She nodded, handing over her notes so that he could collate the information they had gathered. "What do you think of him now we've had a bit of time to consider?" she asked.

"Clive Tatum? I don't know. He's not a man I'd trust but that's not a feeling I can justify. I'm quite looking forward to reading his memoir and it should be interesting to cross-reference whatever he's written with the evidence gathered at the time." He sighed. "We don't even know if this is relevant. I mean, what do we have? This little thread that Miles Cunningham and Jean Hammond and a few other people knew each other a long time ago. If it wasn't for this photograph, we wouldn't even be looking at something that happened forty-odd years ago."

"True, but this Jean Hammond seemed very keen that somebody got hold of the photograph and the other stuff if she died suddenly. It's funny though isn't it, Ursula was initially just her cleaner, and they ended up friends. I mean, Miss Hammond clearly valued Ursula enough to the extent that she trusted her with something she clearly thought was important."

Andy nodded. "I think it's easier to understand if you've met Ursula," he said.

* * *

One person who was not so happy about this task being entrusted to seventeen-year-old Ursula, a person he had never met, was Cal Hammond.

Apparently, the police had contacted him about the envelope and about Ursula's statement that Jean had been worried, even scared, and frankly he was furious. That afternoon, he found himself at Rina's door, determined to know more.

Rina led him into the big living room. Sparks of anger were almost visible, flying off the younger man, and she hoped that the presence of Matthew and Steven might dilute him a little. She was frankly in no mood to deal with someone being offended just because he hadn't been consulted. She had the grace to remember that she had been just as cross — or rather just as hurt — when Jean had not come to her immediately with her anxieties but Rina being Rina was putting that behind her now and felt that Cal should do the same.

"What right had she to take those things? Come to that, what right had you to bring her over there knowing what she was going to do. She took something from Jean's home, she took something belonging to Jean, she didn't consult me or ask me. It's theft, Rina, nothing more nothing less and you facilitated it."

"Sit down and get a grip on yourself," Rina told him bluntly. "Jean asked Ursula to take the envelope away if anything happened to her and seemed to think she would know what to do with it. Ursula wasn't sure whether she should carry out her wishes or not, it seemed like such a strange thing to ask and she was also worried about upsetting you. She doesn't know you any more than you know her and she couldn't come to you and tell you what was going on because she had no idea how to get hold of you, even if that had felt like the right thing to do. Right up until the moment when she took her portfolios from the desk, she was in two minds about whether or not to carry out Jean's wishes, but then maybe her conscience got the better of her. She had promised, she was simply keeping a promise and if you've been to the police or the police have been to see you then you know that what was in the envelope was nothing valuable so far as we know. In fact, I think they're still trying to make sense of it."

"Which is not the point," he persisted. "You brought her to Jean's home to what is now *my* property, you allowed her to take something that was not hers. You even distracted me, Rina, I'm realising that now. You could have talked to me about it."

"Had I known what Ursula had been made to promise then I probably would have talked to you. But why should she talk to you? As I said, she doesn't know you from Adam. The fact that Jean asked *her* to do something and not you, however strange that might seem to Ursula, made her feel that perhaps it was something you wouldn't approve of, or wouldn't understand, or that Jean had some reason for not asking you, for not telling you what was going on. And did you, did you know she was worried or frightened?"

Cal's face was red, incandescent.

Matthew, who had done what he usually did whenever they had visitors, had disappeared into the kitchen and now brought out coffee. "You'll have to give it a moment," he said indicating the cafetiere, "before you plunge it."

"I don't want any coffee," Cal said, through gritted teeth. "I want an explanation."

"And you've had one," Rina told him coldly. "Jean Hammond asked a favour from a young woman who had become her friend. That young woman carried out that favour. That is all. It was not theft, it was not deceit, it was keeping a promise."

"Whatever was in that envelope was my property. How do I know she didn't take something else out of it? How do I know there was not something valuable in there? I'll be taking this further Rina, I'll see her charged."

"Now listen here," Rina told him. "Stop spouting such nonsense and get a grip on yourself, man. Did you even know that Jean was afraid? No. So now you're feeling guilty but let me tell you this, guilt is no excuse for threatening a young woman who has done nothing wrong. Any more of this Cal and you can get out of my house now and *I'll* be reporting you for threatening behaviour."

Cal looked stunned for a moment. He rubbed his hands across his face and Rina could see that he was trembling.

Matthew plunged the cafetiere. "I'm going to add some sugar and a little cream," he said. He set the cup and saucer on the little table beside the chair that Cal was seated in. "Now anger following grief is understandable but don't add bad manners to your sins."

"Quite," Steven said. "It's very hard when we miss something we should have taken note of, or someone we love fails to confide."

Cal stared at the Montmorency twins as though they were just beyond his comprehension.

"Now drink your coffee," Rina said. "Let's talk about this logically and calmly."

It was clear that Cal was still deeply distressed so Rina took a seat close by and waited for him to gather his thoughts. Eventually she said, "I understand Jean came to stay with you at Christmas."

"Yes, so why didn't she say something then. What was worrying her? She'd been to a funeral of an old friend, she seemed completely all right until then. Then she was ill and we thought, Etta and I, that she was out of sorts because of the funeral and because she felt unwell. Jean never liked being unwell, she was a dreadful patient."

"Ursula seems to think that something must have happened at the funeral but she doesn't know what. Only that Jean seemed very upset and distressed and yes, frightened. Ursula says that she seemed better by New Year, after she'd been on her visit to you, and that all was normal again until February, when she seemed to think there was something odd about Mr Hayes's death. Then in early March Ursula thinks that someone sent Jean a book that upset her. Jean tore it into pieces and put it in the compost, but after that she was talking about this envelope again, how Ursula must collect it should anything happen to Jean. She seemed to think that Ursula would know what to do with it. As it happened, Ursula had no idea which is why she came to me and why I contacted Mac, Detective Inspector McGregor."

"They're going to exhume her body. Why would they do that? She had a heart attack. She'd seen her doctor the day before and we all knew she didn't have long. But they're saying there are similarities with a murder. They're saying Christopher was murdered, Christopher Hayes. That's whose funeral she'd gone to. She just told me that an old friend had died, nothing about him being murdered. Why didn't she tell me about that after the funeral? She used to tell me everything."

"Did you know him? Christopher?" Rina asked.

"I knew who he was, of course, but I didn't know him well. He and Jean kept in touch but I'd not seen him in years. He was just an artist, not even a particularly famous one. Who'd want to kill him? And now they think someone maybe killed Jean. I can't believe this, Rina."

"It's quite possible she had no idea that Christopher Hayes's death was suspicious until later. I looked him up on the internet and his body wasn't exhumed until February. Perhaps by then she didn't feel right about telling you. Jean was a complex and unpredictable woman, you know that better than I do. That timing certainly fits with when she started to be upset again. She might well have found out about the suspicious circumstances then."

"Your policeman friend hasn't told you anything else?"

"Mac isn't a gossip," Rina told him. "He has to be careful what he says as I'm sure you'll realise."

"I suppose so, yes. I'm sorry, Rina, it's just so hard being kept in the dark. Even harder knowing there are things that Jean didn't tell me about."

"I'm sure she never meant to hurt you," Rina said. "I'm sure she probably just thought you deserved to be getting on with your own life."

She wasn't sure anything she said was actually helping. Rina leaned forward and handed him his coffee knowing that sometimes it was easier to talk when you had something in your hands. "Did the police show you what was in the envelope?"

He nodded. "A photograph of a lot of people I didn't know and a key. They don't seem to know what the key fits and neither did I. What does it all mean, Rina? Was she just losing it? Was she just becoming paranoid or senile or something? I should have had her to live with us; maybe being on her own in that place was just too much."

"Jean loved The Willows and she would never have moved in with you, you know that. She was so proud of you and she knew you had a right to your own life and to be honest I think she just wanted to live hers. She wasn't lonely, Cal, she was busier than she'd ever been, involved in just about everything that was going on in the local community. Jean was a doer you know that. You have done nothing wrong."

"But she needed help and she didn't ask me."

"Perhaps she was worried you would overreact or perhaps she was worried that she couldn't give you a logical explanation, that she just had a bad feeling. Sometimes it's hard explaining ourselves to those we're closest to. Sometimes it's easier with a stranger or someone who doesn't know us as well, who isn't going to be so hurt or anxious."

"But what was she worried about? Was she being threatened, did she know someone wanted to kill her?"

"I think if she had felt the threat was that specific, she might actually have confided in the police," Matthew said logically. "If there had been an actual threat, something evidentiary then she could have taken it to the authorities. But something more vague, something more ephemeral is difficult to explain and difficult to justify."

"Perhaps when they find whatever the key unlocks they will find more information," Steven said.

"The police will do their job, we have great faith in Sebastian," Matthew added.

"Sebastian?"

"Detective Inspector McGregor," Rina told him. "It's a name he prefers not to use. And Matthew is right, the police will do their job. I know it's hard to stand by and feel helpless, but just now you have no option. If you're looking for someone to blame then blame whoever frightened Jean, not a young girl who befriended her."

Cal took a deep breath. "I want to talk to Ursula," he said. "I want to hear from her what Jean said and what she did. And I'm still not sure there was nothing else in that envelope . . ." he went on, his wrath suddenly flaring again.

"If Ursula says that was all that was in the envelope, then you may be certain she's telling the truth," Steven told him sharply. "That girl is honest as the day is long and I will not hear a word said against her."

Rina looked at Steven who was positively vibrating with rage on Ursula's behalf.

"Steven is correct," Rina said. "That young woman is totally honest and could be trusted on any matter and maybe that's what Jean saw in her. She knew that Ursula would do her best to follow her instructions and she did."

"I want to speak to her."

"Not while you're in this kind of mood." Rina told him. "When I'm sure you have completely calmed down, I *might* ask her. Ursula owes you nothing Cal, not an explanation, not even her time."

"He never did drink his coffee," Steven commented after Cal had gone. "Do you think he'll make trouble for Ursula?"

"I should tell Mac about his visit," Rina said. "Just in case. I imagine he'll cool down when he gets over his fit of pique. It must hurt to think that his guardian, the woman who had been his only family for so many years, did not confide in him over something that seems to have turned out to be desperately important."

"Which raises the interesting question of why she didn't," Matthew said. "I know the explanations you gave him were perfectly reasonable but you can't help but wonder, can you? Was she trying to protect him? She has after all been protecting him since he was ten years old and these habits are hard to shake."

Matthew had a point, Rina thought.

None of them had noticed, as Cal left, the figure in the cream raincoat standing on the other side of the road.

CHAPTER 21

By the time the end of the day briefing came around, Yolanda had identified two more people in the photograph by cross-referencing the pictures in Jean Hammond's photo albums. Neither she nor Andy had initially recognised a very young Clive Tatum, glass raised, on the front row. *Age was a bastard*, Yolanda thought. He had not been bad looking in his day. The second identification was a woman who it turned out was an actress living in New York and who had not been back to the UK in years. A quick search revealed that she had died of natural causes some years before.

"But what's really interesting is that, when Andy and I went to see Clive Tatum this morning and we showed him the picture he didn't point out that he was in it. He claimed not to recognise anyone apart from Miles Cunningham and, seeing as he'd been writing about Miles Cunningham, he could hardly deny that one. He didn't mention recognising Jean Hammond in the picture either, which seems equally odd."

"Did he seem at all concerned about the photograph? Would you have said he reacted?" one of the team asked.

Yolanda shook her head. She and Andy had discussed this as soon as she had realised who she was looking at in the front row of the partygoers.

"No, he seemed really casual at the time. But Andy and I, we talked about this and we decided that, in retrospect, that in itself was a bit odd. He was really quite cranky when we first arrived, accusing us of coming to harass him. It turns out that he *is* being harassed, as Andy's already told you. Then he seemed to settle down and decide that we were not the ones being annoying. He *seemed* quite open, telling us about the problems around publication and about Constance and Sarah Fredericks but, thinking back, we've come to the conclusion that maybe he thought giving us a lot of information about one thing would stop us asking about another. It meant that the photograph became just something he dismissed in passing and we didn't follow up maybe as hard as we could have done. I mean if someone says they don't recognise anyone in a photograph you tend to take them at their word. But now we know he was in it . . ."

"Definitely worth going back and having another go," Mac said. "Yolanda, add that to your action plan for tomorrow and I'll be coming with you."

Yolanda nodded. She could see Andy was slightly put out by not being included in this enterprise and Mac said, "Andy I'm sorry but I've got a very tedious job for you. We still don't know what that key fits, the best bet is it's a locker of some sort. We've queried the local banks but Jean Hammond does not seem to have had an account with a security box anywhere, at least not under her own name. You've got the local knowledge, so take the key and go round to local banks, solicitors, anywhere she might have had a lockbox. If you need assistance we'll provide it but a local face, and one from Frantham rather than Exeter or Dorchester, might pay dividends here."

Andy nodded. Yolanda could see he wasn't looking forward to that particular job.

There seemed to be no more questions for her, so Yolanda sat back down and listened to the rest of the briefing. The only major thing of interest was that they now had a copy of the statement from the thief who had tried unsuccessfully to dispose of Jean Hammond's earring, along-side some other jewellery.

"He reckons he bought them in a local pub," an officer Yolanda did not know told them. "He's going to be re-interviewed but—"

No one, Yolanda figured, *was going to be holding their breath.*

Why would Clive Tatum have lied about the photograph, she wondered. It was just a group of people at a party.

She made arrangements with Mac about meeting him the following morning. She was definitely looking forward to challenging Clive Tatum.

* * *

Andy Nevins was wearing his comfiest boots. He knew that queries had already been made at the larger branches of local banks and the bigger solicitors' offices, which were known to have facilities for storing valuables, but Andy had a hunch that Jean would not trust these bigger, more corporate affairs. Cal Hammond hadn't known anything about a key to a security box and as far as a solicitor was concerned, if their name and number wasn't on the list in the hall then Cal did not know who that might be.

Andy could have phoned around, but he had long since learned that people respond far more efficiently and directly when you turn up at their offices. He'd also reasoned that Jean was much more likely to trust somebody that she'd been on a committee with and, knowing that a lot of local solicitors also served as charity and community trustees, he had of course started with a call to Rina. She had in turn provided him with a list of people who might fit the bill and Andy planned to start with these, cross-referenced with those closest to where Jean lived and also to those she actually liked. This second criteria, Andy found, had narrowed his options down by about half.

He decided to start with the smaller towns first and to prioritise the long-established firms that might have been

163

around when Jean Hammond first moved to Dorset. People were creatures of habit, Andy figured, they tended to use the same solicitor for conveyancing and wills and any other day to day stuff. They changed their legal advisors about as regularly as they changed their banks, and less often than they shifted their energy suppliers.

He decided that if he didn't strike lucky with the personal approach, he'd just have to spend the afternoon with a phone book and hope for the best.

At the first two offices he visited in Honiton, the town geographically closest to Jean's house, he drew a blank. He chatted for a time to secretaries, talked to partners, commiserated about Jean's death — several people he spoke to knew her from committees and charities. He did however come away with the suggestion that he might try and speak to Walter Heath, a man now semi-retired but who might have acted on Jean's behalf. Happy to at least have a lead, Andy drove to Frantham thinking that he probably should have started closest to home and saved himself a trip.

Walter Heath's office turned out to be a tiny little place just off the promenade.

Andy had been told that Walter had officially retired, had been for years, but he wasn't able to quite give up working. "He can't have more than a dozen or two dozen clients — all people he's known for years. Frankly it's a toss-up whether they or he dies first, the man's ancient and so are most of his clients. But I know he and Jean used to get on like a house on fire."

And so Andy found himself wandering down the little alleyway between the fish and chip shop and the dry cleaners and into a building even he, native of Frantham, could not recall previously being aware of. A small brass nameplate announced that this was indeed the business premises of Walter Heath and a note on the door informed callers that he would be back in five minutes. Andy settled down to wait.

It was in fact more than fifteen minutes before a very elderly gentleman with a rather fine walking stick sauntered down the alley to where Andy was standing. He looked a little surprised to see someone there and Andy was quick to introduce himself, not wanting the elderly man to feel threatened. A moment later he realised this was indeed a mis-judgement on his part. Walter Heath did not look concerned about anything and from the careless way he wielded what looked on closer inspection to be a very heavy walking stick, with a solid brass knob, Andy decided that Mr Heath was probably a lot more resilient than his evident age suggested.

"Come along in," Walter said. "You're lucky to catch me. I'm only here for a few hours a day, people know to ring me at home if they need me at other times. Supposed to be retired you know, but I get bored. So I come down here, have a chat to my neighbours, a walk along the promenade and on Thursdays I have fish and chips."

"Pity it's only Wednesday," Andy said. "I've had a busy morning, I'd probably have joined you."

"Well, I'm always quite happy to have fish and chips twice in a week," Heath said. "But let's start with business and see how we go. So, what brings you here?"

Walter Heath's office on the ground floor was small and quite sparse. A desk, filing cabinet, a couple of chairs and a narrow table on which was set a kettle and the makings for tea or coffee or hot chocolate. Walter explained that the upstairs was now used for storage, rented out to one of the local businesses. He only had need now for this tiny office, everything else he did from home. He made them both mugs of strong tea and they settled on either side of the narrow desk.

"This key," Andy said. "It was found among the posses-sions of Miss Jean Hammond, the artist. I believe you knew her?"

"I did indeed. Great loss, Jean was a spirited lady. Fine mind. So, you want to know if I have the box this key fits?"

"I'm hoping you do."

Walter Heath nodded. "I was told it would be a young woman who came to collect Jean's possessions."

Andy was momentarily taken aback. It would appear that Jean had assumed Ursula's knowledge of her affairs was greater than it actually was, if she thought that she would have known to come to Walter Heath. "That would be Ursula Beckett," he said. "Unfortunately, I think Jean missed that piece of information out when she gave her the instructions."

"Ursula, yes that's the one. Small and blonde and fiercely intelligent, so I'm told. I never actually met her, that was Jean's description. Unfortunately, yes, Jean always assumed people knew more than they actually did, she never had the patience to spell things out and as we get older we all tend to get a little more forgetful." He looked regretful for a moment as though this was not something he wished to contemplate unless forced.

"But you have the box that this key fits?"

"And I have my instructions to give those contents only to Ursula Beckett," Walter Heath said firmly.

Andy sighed. If this man had been a close friend of Jean Hammond's than he supposed he should expect some awkwardness. "I'm sure it's OK to hand it over to a police officer," he said.

"And I'm sure it's not. Jean Hammond was my client and I must carry out my client's wishes. Now if you could get hold of Ursula Beckett and get her to come over here then perhaps we could all eat fish and chips together?"

Andy knew himself to be at an impasse. The quickest way to get Ursula's number was another phone call to Rina. He also got George's mobile too, just as backup, and it was actually George he got through to first. Andy explained the situation and a few minutes later Ursula called him back and told him it would be at least an hour before she could get there. That, Andy thought, would have to do.

"Did it take you long to track me down?" Walter Heath asked.

"Me, personally? No, you're the fifth person I asked. Mr Sanders at Barlow and Sanders sent me your way. Other people have been chasing this down for a couple of days but when it became obvious she didn't have the security box at a bank or one of the bigger solicitors, Mac, I mean DI McGregor, thought it might be a good idea for me to use local knowledge. I figured Jean Hammond would want to leave anything important with someone she knew and trusted and it didn't seem to me that she was the kind of woman, from what little I know of her, that would be particularly interested in shiny new solicitor's offices that all looked like branches of fast-food outlets."

Walter Heath laughed. "No, indeed," he said. "Jean very much preferred a person-to-person approach. She liked to know who she was dealing with. She thought very highly of Ursula. I'm looking forward to meeting the young lady."

"Presumably you know that Ursula was meant to collect an envelope with various items including the key?"

"Jean did mention that yes."

"Did she say why she wasn't leaving this task to Calvin Hammond? I mean, he is her adopted son."

Walter Heath looked thoughtful and then said, "Actually she's his guardian. He took her name by deed poll but she never formally adopted him. A legal document had been drawn up by his parents because they had no close relatives that they wished to entrust their son to, and Jean was a good friend even though she was quite a lot older than they were. So she was his legal guardian, but going through the formal adoption process at the age that Jean was back then might have been difficult and so she decided, on my advice as it happens, that she would leave things as they stood. She had no wish for anything to occur that might make the boy less secure than he was or that might suggest that other people would have a claim on him."

"A claim on him." It seemed like an odd way to put it, Andy thought.

"The parents were not rich, but they were comfortably off and there was a house, I suppose some odd bits of jewellery perhaps. People have fought over less and no one wanted young Cal to be caught in the crossfire. The will tied everything up very tightly. Jean was to be the guardian, everything that was saleable should be sold and put in trust for Cal and an allowance was put in place for Jean to help her with the financial demands of raising a young boy. Jean Hammond was well off in her own right and only called upon that allowance on a few occasions, when Cal needed something in particular. I remember she drew down some money when he wanted his first car, and again when he went to university, she was keen to make sure that he had money available to him should he need it and after all the money was his, it was merely in trust."

"When did that trust . . ." Andy paused not quite sure what the terminology was. "When did he get the money in his own right?"

"When he was twenty-five, which I suppose seems like an old- fashioned sort of age these days. I believe it enabled him to buy his flat in Exeter or at least put a substantial deposit down. Jean didn't benefit from Cal's parents' estate, she didn't need to, but I imagine there would have been others who would have been eager to claim more of an allowance than she did."

"And were there challenges to her guardianship?"

"It was some time ago but from memory there were two. I believe one was an aunt and one a more distant relative. They did make trouble for a while, and Jean was very eager to keep all of this upset from Cal. The child was ten years old and he'd just lost his parents. To have this unseemly squabbling over him would have been distressing and I know she did manage to keep most of this away from him. I suppose it was less than a year before they gave up, the will had been drawn up tightly and securely and they didn't have a leg to stand on. Cal was living with Jean; Jean was more than capable of looking after him despite being older and I believe they were very happy together.

"But I also believe it set a train of thought on Jean's part, that Cal should not ever be upset or frightened or distressed, as he would have been had he known that these other relatives had been picking over the bones, as it were. They were perhaps things she chose not to tell him even when he became an adult with a life of his own. Of course, she had the perfect excuse by then, that he was entitled to live his own life and that she was entitled to live hers. She could be a very awkward and stubborn woman at times, despite all of her positive qualities. When Cal came into her life everything else seemed to take a back seat. Cal and work; that was it. It wasn't until he left home that she started to pick up her old friendships again. She'd kept in touch, but it was nothing like the old days."

He paused, his gaze suddenly far away as though contemplating those distant times.

"And did she confide in you? Ursula was convinced she was frightened and definitely upset by something, especially after Christopher Hayes's funeral and then again in March when we think somebody must have sent her Clive Tatum's memoir. Did you know about the memoir? Did you know Clive Tatum?"

Heath nodded. "Yes, to both. Though it's been many a year since I've seen him. Clive Tatum was a much younger member of our general circle so I never knew him well and, I must admit, I'm a little suspicious of journalists. Jean told me he'd written a memoir and that the Cunningham murders featured prominently. She didn't go into any details. I assumed she was distressed, late last year, initially because Christopher Hayes had died. Then we found out he was murdered. To find out your long-time friend has been murdered is going to upset anybody. And then the Clive Tatum memoir, well some coals should not be raked over; some fires should be allowed to go out."

"I'm not sure I understand," Andy said. "I've not yet read the memoir, but I believe he raised the possibility that William Tatum might not have been an innocent party in the murders. Do you have any thoughts on that?"

"And what thoughts should I have? I wasn't there, I am not an investigator. Miles Cunningham did not deny murder. If Miles Cunningham chose not to raise doubts in anyone's mind about his guilt, then does that not suggest that he was guilty?"

"That's a very political answer," Andy said. "Sounds like you're sitting on the fence, if you don't mind me saying so."

Walter Heath smiled, there was actually something wolfish and sly in his smile, Andy thought, that belied the affable easy-going manner. Retired he might be, but Andy didn't think this man had given up thinking about or having opinions on anything. He would have an opinion on this, but whether he was willing to share it or not . . .

"OK, so what if Miles Cunningham came home, found his wife and kids dead, caught William Tatum in the act? He takes a knife, he stabs Tatum. He's in a rage, not in control of himself. What if it's not the murder, the killing of Tatum, that upset him so much as the fact that he was so enraged he didn't even think about it. I know his mum was in a psychiatric hospital and that she killed herself when he was only about twelve, and that's a tragic thing to happen both to the mum and the kid. There's . . . anecdotal evidence . . . that this got to him, in a big way, that he was afraid he'd end up like her." He paused, studying Walter Heath's expression.

The old man nodded. "Go on."

"Supposing, just supposing, that scared him so much that when they accused him of murdering his family as well, he wasn't even sure he hadn't done it. He maybe had killed William Tatum in an act of revenge. He felt he was guilty, therefore he just accepted his guilt. He wanted to be locked away just in case he might do something else. Does that make sense?"

"It might have done, to anybody that didn't know Miles Cunningham."

"And did you know him?"

"I knew him. Jean knew him, Christopher Hayes knew him. We all ran with the same crowd, and he was a nice man. He was also an ambitious man and in business he could be somewhat ruthless. He could also be ridiculously kind, as could Betty. What I'm saying is, when the news came out about his allegedly having murdered his wife and children and this other man who lived with them, this William Tatum, we all found it very hard to believe."

"Did you know William Tatum?" This was turning into a proper interview, Andy thought, and he really ought to take notes. He was afraid that if he did it would stop the flow of conversation. He would have to see if anything useful came out first and if it did then it would be formal statement time. He had no doubt that Walter Heath knew exactly what he would be thinking.

"As I've said, I knew Clive Tatum in the sense that he was an acquaintance, not what I'd have termed a friend. I hadn't properly met William Tatum, just seen him in passing. So no, I didn't really know him. What did take me by surprise was the fact that the Cunninghams would have given him a room in their home. Previously they'd given shelter to a succession of young women. And I do mean given shelter. There was never a hint of impropriety. They helped them get back on their feet and pick up their lives again. Of course, after the deaths, Constance Tatum put it about that Miles was exploiting them. That he had seduced and exploited her."

"But you never believed that?"

"Of course not! Constance was a troublemaker. I heard that her brother was the same, at least according to Clive Tatum. As I told you, I didn't really know William. Clive Tatum would have it that William was not a good person. But being not a nice person does not automatically make you a potential murderer."

"What did William do?"

"According to Clive, he was a liar and a cheat, a thief, petty and otherwise. He liked to stir up trouble, start arguments and stand back and watch them develop. He'd also had a dreadful childhood, abused and neglected until both he and his sister were taken into care, as a result of which they were very close. He and Clive were of a similar age, William being about three years younger, and for a while I heard he

171

did seem to be leading Clive astray. However, I also heard from sources I'm more inclined to trust that it was the other way around. That William wasn't really very bright and was very easily led into trouble. But I can tell you very little from first-hand experience, I'm afraid."

"Sources you trust?"

"Jean Hammond and Christopher Hayes. Jean went as far as saying that William was too unintelligent to be leading anyone astray. That he was more child than man. Clive's part of the family had more or less ignored what William and Constance were going through and I don't think Constance forgave them, though Clive had no part of that of course as he was just a child himself. Jean always said that they could have stepped in and helped but they chose not to."

"Jean knew the family?"

Walter Heath thought about it and then said, "I'm not sure she knew them when the children were small, not when William and Constance were little things, but she certainly knew them all when they were in their late teens and early twenties. Clive and William and Constance. I suppose she must have found out about their history. Jean had a way of drawing out information from people."

Andy took out his mobile phone and found the copy of the photograph that had been in the envelope. He handed the phone to Walter. "Do you recognise any of the people in that photograph?"

Walter Heath felt in his pocket for his reading glasses and Andy wondered if he should have told him how to zoom in on the screen, but he needn't have worried, the older man was perfectly competent.

"Now then, let's see. Well Miles Cunningham of course, standing at the back and refusing to smile as he usually did. Then there's Clive on the front row, and that actress, she went to Hollywood and I forget her name, changed it to Sophie something. Did rather well for herself. Standing just in front of Miles, that's Betty his wife and next to her is Jean. Goodness, you forget how young we all were. Jean was a little older of course, the grand dame, acted as a sort of house mother or mentor to the younger ones.

"We were a mixed sort of group, old artists, older actors, neophytes, complete newcomers. It was a friendly crowd. Then there's Christopher Hayes, you see there standing to the right of Miles. He was quite a bit younger than Jean but they'd been friends since his college days. He was a student at Ruskin when she was doing her first stint as a drawing tutor. Couldn't tell you about these two," he pointed to two young women at the front of the group, glasses raised as though in a toast. "Then there's Rory Jackson, now he wasn't a regular part of our group, or he wasn't in the sense that he was an artist or an actor or anything like that, he was training to be an engineer. Nice man, started his own business I believe."

"Jackson," Andy said recalling the name of the second murder victim, Graham Jackson.

"Significant? Take my advice, never play poker young man. You know where this was taken don't you?"

Andy shook his head.

"Well, it was at the Cunningham house. I recognise the tiles in the hall and the staircase behind. They had quite regular parties. We all used to bring a bottle or two and quite often a sleeping bag, it has to be said. The Cunninghams were a cheerful pair, and it seemed we often ended up there, a big group of us."

He paused and Andy could see the sadness in his gaze. "Thank you," he said. "This is all proving very, very helpful."

Walter Heath seemed to gather himself. "Well, you'd better get some of this written down hadn't you, young man. Young Ursula should be here soon and I don't know about you, I'm hungry as a hunter and I imagine she will be too, so when she arrives, I'm going to dispatch you to get us all some chips. I'm sure Inspector McGregor will have some petty cash he can reimburse you with."

CHAPTER 22

While Andy Nevins was getting acquainted with Walter Heath, Mac and Yolanda were on their way to Exeter to question Clive Tatum and find out why he had failed to identify himself in a photograph. Before leaving, Yolanda had called the local station who had been dealing with Clive Tatum's complaints about hate mail and abusive phone calls. She had learned that they had been unable to make contact with Sarah Fredericks and that the letters had been posted from a variety of locations all along the south coast.

Old fashioned poison pen letters were something of a novelty to Yolanda, Mac realised. The prospect of reading them later seemed to quite excite her.

They had driven from the Palisades back on to the Honiton Road and down the dual carriageway through Honiton and then on to Exeter. Mac could never drive this route without recalling the day Joy's father had been run off the road and killed. There were so many locations hereabouts that now had violent associations that seemed so at odds with the soft landscape, but Mac found he could not love the place less just because of that. This was home now. Home and family.

They arrived in the quiet street and parked up in the same place that Yolanda and Andy had the day before. As they approached Mac logged that the house had an empty feel to it, a sense of no one home and when they knocked on the door there was no answer. He stepped back and looked up at the curtained bedroom windows. The curtains were still drawn. Was Clive Tatum not up yet?

Mac knocked again.

Yolanda peered through the window into the living room. Unlike many of the houses on the street, Clive Tatum had foregone net curtains.

"Anything?" Mac asked.

"I'm not sure. I can't see through properly but it looks as though something's been knocked on to the floor."

Mac glanced at her, she was standing on tiptoe but was still not tall enough to get the angle she needed. He took her place by the window and saw that she was right. A book and a smashed glass lay on the floor by the front door, which like many terraced houses opened straight into the small front living room.

Between this house and the next a shared passageway led to the back gardens and Mac led the way, Yolanda hot on his heels. He pushed the gate open and hammered on the back door. A neighbour looked over the wall and asked what all the noise was about. Mac introduced himself and asked if they'd seen Mr Tatum that morning.

The woman shook her head. "And the funny thing is, he didn't put his bins out this morning. It's rubbish collection day and he always puts his bins out first thing. You're not allowed to leave them on the front overnight, there are bylaws. The council can fine you."

Mac nodded. *Right*, he thought, that settled things. "I don't suppose you know if anyone's got a key to the house?"

The woman looked alarmed. "You think there's something wrong with him?" she asked. "Well, I don't have a key, but I'll bet there's something in the shed you can use to get the door open." She indicated a small shed at the bottom of her garden.

Mac left Yolanda still knocking hard on Tatum's door, just in case he was asleep and there be no real emergency.

175

Mac came back a few minutes later having found a nail bar, rusted and clearly not used in a long time but it would do. In a few minutes he had acquired a lot of the neighbour's life history; her name was Nan, she was a widow and these were her husband's tools that she really ought to have taken better care of, but what use did she have for a lot of old hammers and saws and no one else seemed to want them . . .

Mac came into the yard and bolted the gate behind him, just in case Nan should decide to try and follow him in. He pushed against the back door and inserted the nail bar into the small gap. It took a couple of attempts but then there was a rending sound of tearing wood and he broke the lock free of the jamb and the door flew open.

"Stay here," he told Yolanda. "If there is anything wrong then the less people trampling around the better."

She looked reluctant but she nodded.

The door to the staircase in the middle room was open and Mac went up, instinctively trying not to touch anything. The stairs were steep and the house was silent. He stood on the landing at the top of the stairs and glanced down the hallway. Doors stood open to the second bedroom and the bathroom. The master bedroom was at the front of the house and that door was closed. Fishing a glove out of his pocket Mac opened the door and stood on the threshold.

Clive Tatum lay on his bed, fully clothed, propped against his pillows, his hands flopped on the blankets, one clasped around something. Mac did not have to go further into the room to satisfy himself that Tatum was dead.

* * *

Back in Frantham, Ursula arrived with George and Andy was duly dispatched to the fish and chip shop at the end of the alleyway. He had fought this briefly, thinking he really ought to be there to witness the first conversation between the solicitor and Ursula but Walter Heath had shooed him away and assured him that nothing would happen until he got back. When Andy returned, George had found another couple of chairs from somewhere and they were all seated around the desk, the key laid in the middle as though it was some prize exhibit.

Food was handed out and Andy Nevins was reminded of Rina Martin's house, when nothing important seemed to happen without the accompaniment of sustenance. What was it, he wondered, about older people that meant they always needed to eat or at least drink tea before discussing anything. Then he thought that actually wasn't a bad idea and reminded himself that if he had anything he really needed to get off his chest he would go back to the family home and sit in his mother's kitchen and drink tea and dunk biscuits while they sorted it all out between them.

The key, Walter Heath told them belonged to a strongbox. He had the second key for the original lock and this was one that had been added because Jean was not convinced the original was safe enough. He didn't know what was in it, just a lot of papers and diaries, so far as he could tell, and Jean had entrusted this box to him in the November of last year when they had both come back from Christopher Hayes's funeral.

"She got somebody or other, maybe the young man who did her garden, to fix a hasp and staple to the old box and this key is for the padlock. She kept that, I kept the old one and she made me promise to look after the box until she sent this young lady for it. I wasn't to entrust it to anybody else and if Ursula did not come to collect the box, then all was well and Jean said that she would just let things take their course. But, of course, being Jean she didn't tell me *what* was going to take its course. I asked her if eventually I should give it to Cal and she said definitely not. In fact, her exact words were: 'Walter, if it comes to that, chuck the bloody thing in the sea.'"

"I'm not sure I understand," Ursula said. "Why would she not want Mr Hammond to have it?"

"Your guess, my dear, is as good as mine."

Andy dipped a chip in tomato sauce and then asked, "Mr Heath, who were Calvin Hammond's parents?"

"I never really knew them. They were friends that Jean acquired when she moved to London. Their names were Colin and Deirdre Tripp, and from the way Jean spoke about them it seemed they were distant relatives of her mother's. I know she saw a lot of them, was very fond of them. I believe they had a flat in the same old building Jean lived in so presumably that was how they became so close. They were younger than her but age never bothered Jean. She liked young people. She must've got to know them about fifteen years before young Cal went to live with her because I know she was at their wedding and then Cal came along, and she was his godmother and then became his guardian. You have to understand we didn't totally lose touch but we weren't seeing as much of one another at that point. After the Cunningham murders we all drifted apart. It was as though the heart had gone out of our little tribe and we all crept away into our corners and tried to make lives for ourselves. I think . . . on some level we were all ashamed."

"Ashamed?" Andy was puzzled.

"I get that," George said. "I think we both do."

Ursula nodded.

"It's like contamination," George went on. "My dad was a criminal, he was violent, he was evil, and me and my mum and sister, in the end we spent a big chunk of our lives running away from him and even though we hadn't done anything wrong, it was like he had infected us. Like we were kind of unclean because of what he'd done. Nobody sees you for you, they just see you as connected with this man."

Andy stared at him. He knew George's history, knew less about Ursula's, but it never occurred to him that George should feel this way or have any reason to.

Walter Heath was nodding. "That's a good way of explaining it," he said. "Jean and I really picked our friendship up again when she moved here, back to the south coast. In fact, I helped to find the house. It was in a bit of a state but it was clear it would be perfect for them when it was done up and so it was. I think she and Cal had a very happy time living there."

"How long before what happened with the Cunninghams was this photograph taken?" Andy asked.

"Six months perhaps? I don't know if I was at that particular party or not, but Sophie whatsername went away to America a couple of months before the Cunningham murders."

Andy glanced around the table and it seemed that everybody had just about finished their meal. He was conscious that this was not so much about food now, as about Walter Heath's wish to put this off. Now why was that, Andy wondered. He screwed up his chip wrapper and thrust it into the fish shop carrier bag and looked directly at Walter Heath. "Don't you think we've dithered enough," he said.

"I suppose we have. What I said about after the Cunningham incident, about the murders, about feeling ashamed. I don't want that feeling to come back. Jean is dead and gone, whatever she entrusted to me, what good it can do. Can it change the past?"

"You do know that Jean's body is going to be exhumed don't you," Andy said, suddenly realising that this news was probably not common knowledge. "You do know we're now treating it as a suspicious death."

It was clear from the look of shock on Walter's face that he had not and Andy felt immediately guilty for being as blunt as he had. He noticed Ursula reaching out a hand and gripping that of the old solicitor.

"I think Jean was tired of hiding whatever it was she was hiding," she said. "She asked me because I *wasn't* an old friend, because I was just someone she happened to like and she thought she could trust. And she could trust me, and I'm not going to let her down now. How do we know what to do unless we know what we are dealing with?"

Walter Heath nodded slowly. "Quite right my dear."

* * *

Before Walter could produce the strongbox from wherever he had hidden it, Andy received a phone call from Yolanda telling him about Clive Tatum's death. Andy took the call in the alleyway.

"The boss wants you to finish up whatever it is you're doing and then get over here," she said. "As soon as the CSI tell us we can, he wants us to look around and see if we notice anything moved or missing."

"And it's definitely not natural causes?" he asked.

"Well he's not been stabbed or had his head bashed in or anything, but he's laid out on the bed, fully dressed, propped up on pillows and he has a bit of plant in his hand."

"Oh," Andy said. "I guess that settles it then."

He went back into the office. A substantial wooden box now sat in the centre of the table. Andy wondered where the solicitor had been keeping it. An already stale smell of chips hung in the air. He thought absently that he would be carrying that particular perfume around with him all afternoon.

Ursula picked up the key, she seemed hesitant but then suddenly reached forward and unfastened the padlock. The solicitor inserted his own much older key into the original lock and turned it with a loud click.

"So, let's see what we've got in here," Walter Heath said.

Andy moved so that he could see the contents as Ursula opened the lid. Part of him wanted to go racing off to join Mac and Yolanda at the murder scene. Part of him was desperate to see what was in the box. He was slightly disappointed to see that it was as Walter Heath had suggested, just full of paperwork. Diaries perhaps, what looked like old school exercise books, photographs. What was so important about this lot? He groaned inwardly knowing that he would probably end up being the one to log it into evidence. That was supposing any of it was actually relevant.

"Um, that was Mac on the phone, I mean DI McGregor," he corrected himself noting Walter Heath's amusement. "I have to go and join him. Perhaps I should take that box with me."

"I don't think so," Walter Heath said. "My instructions were to give this to Ursula, so until she has examined the contents and decided what she wants to do, it should remain here."

One look at his face told Andy that Walter Heath would not be shifted and, as he didn't have a warrant to take the box, there wasn't a lot he could do about it.

"Fine," he said. "But we will want to see it. It could have bearing on the murders, you know that."

"And it might not," Walter Heath told him solemnly. "Now off you go, I have your number and so do Ursula and George. We will be in touch as soon as we've looked over the contents and, if she'll permit me, I'll be able to advise Miss Beckett what to do next."

"As long as you're not going to charge me," Ursula said heavily. "Because Mr Heath, I don't think I could afford you."

* * *

The CSI was still at the house and Andy was somewhat disappointed to find that Miriam Hastings was not among them. He liked Miriam. But then, he reminded himself, this was not exactly their patch. He assumed that another SIO would be along to take over from Mac in due course.

Mac and Yolanda were in the garden, talking to a woman next door who stood with her arms folded defensively, a thick cardigan pulled around her body even though it was a warm day. She looked shocked Andy thought, but then murder usually did that to people. Threw them completely off balance, shook them to the core.

Mac came over to speak to him and Andy filled him in about the box.

"I should have insisted he give it to me," Andy Nevins said uncertainly.

"You had no right to insist," Mac reminded him. "Fortunately, we know Ursula and my guess is—"

"That she and George will head over to Rina's, and Rina will extract anything important from the contents, even if

Ursula can't. I'm not sure what to make of the solicitor," Andy confided. "He was apparently an old friend of Miss Hammonds and he seems kind of protective of her and now of Ursula."

"We'll deal with Mr Heath later," Mac said. "Just now I want you and Yolanda to examine the scene, see if anything's changed since you saw it yesterday."

Apart from Clive Tatum now being dead, Andy thought.

The CSI had marked a common pathway and Andy and Yolanda made their way inside. "You been upstairs?" Andy asked.

She nodded. "Mac wanted me to look so I could compare the scene to that at Jean Hammond's place. I expect he'll want you to take a look before they take the body away."

Andy nodded, not sure he was enthused by the idea. But it was experience he couldn't afford to waste, he supposed. "And was the scene similar?"

"I suppose so," Yolanda said, but Andy could hear the doubt in her voice. She paused, looking around the small front room. Andy looked too, noting the book lying on the floor and the broken glass that had first attracted Yolanda's attention when she had looked through the window. The book had fallen from a shelf just inside the door. The glass was a heavy jar that Tatum had used as a bookend. Its twin stood at the other end of the shelf.

"Poetry," Andy said, catching the surprise in his own voice. Why should he feel surprised that the journalist liked poetry? "Victorian? Edwardian?" The volumes were obviously a set, pocket sized, cloth bound with gold blocking on the covers. The book that had fallen was John Keats. He noted Byron, Shelley, other names he did not recognise.

"Mostly romantic poets," Yolanda said. "The books are from the Everyman Library. I googled it; they were like cheap editions that most people could afford. A bit like Ladybird books. My mum had a load of those from when she was a kid. Passed them on to me."

Andy had never heard of Ladybird books. To his eye, these volumes on the shelf did not look like cheap editions.

They looked pretty valuable. "I can't see that anything else has been moved," he said. "We noticed when we came before that he didn't have much personal stuff on display. No photos or knick-knacks."

Yolanda nodded. She led the way back into the middle room where they had interviewed Clive Tatum. "Not much going on in here either.

"Come upstairs with me," Yolanda said suddenly. "Like I said, I expect the boss will want you to see the body before we leave and I want to ask your opinion on something."

"OK," Andy said a little surprised at her change of tone. He followed her up the narrow stairs and into the master bedroom. The CSI and photographer were still at work. They paused as Yolanda appeared in the doorway.

"I don't need to come in," she said. "PC Nevins just needs to view the scene."

The CSI smiled, her mouth hidden but Andy could see the eyes crinkling behind the mask.

"So, what am I looking at?"

Yolanda fidgeted as though suddenly wishing she'd not suggested they come upstairs. He tried to help her out. "Does it look like the other scene? I mean, superficially, I suppose it must but . . ." he hesitated, not quite sure how to phrase the question. "Does it, kind of, feel different?"

A fleeting glance told him that she was checking first that he wasn't being patronising, but she seemed to make up her mind that it was a genuine question. "You ever get odd feelings about things?"

"Sometimes. Not as much as some people do. What do you feel about this? Compared to Jean Hammond, I mean?"

They had been speaking softly, not sure they wanted to be overheard by the technicians of the forensic team. How a scene *felt* was, Andy thought, not in any of the textbooks or investigation manuals.

Yolanda turned and he followed her down the stairs. Once back in the middle room she paused and said awkwardly, "Jean Hammond looked calm, like she'd just gone to sleep. I had to stay with her for nearly three hours, on my own, but it was OK, you know. I felt sad for her but that was all. I wouldn't want to stay with Clive Tatum, alive or dead for three hours and maybe that's all it is."

"Or maybe it's that his face was all screwed up like he was scared or in pain," Andy said.

Yolanda looked startled. "It wasn't that bad," she said.

"No, OK, not that bad. But his mouth was twisted like . . . you now when someone has a bad taste in their mouth?"

Yolanda turned and went back up the stairs, Andy following.

"Sonia," she asked, "I know he had a bit of plant in his hand, but has anyone looked in his mouth?"

"His mouth? Well, no, that's a job for the pathologist." She glanced out of the window, "Speaking of which, the mortuary ambulance has just pulled up."

"She can't just open his mouth," Andy said. "That might contaminate evidence."

Sonia shrugged. "Sorry, he's right, but look, I'll make a note in the log. They'll look anyway. We've already noticed there's traces of something on his lips."

"Thanks," Yolanda said. She looked vindicated, Andy noted and relieved as though she'd thought she'd just been letting her imagination get away with her.

"OK, Andy," Mac said, "there's not much more you can do here. Phone Ursula and see where she is, see if she's gone over to Rina's yet. If not suggest she does and that you will meet her there. I want an inventory of everything that's in that box and I need to get a quick sense if anything obviously pertains to the case . . . Any part of it. And if you can persuade Ursula to hand everything over, so much the better."

"Would you apply for a warrant if not," Yolanda asked.

"Andy can just go and see what she's got first," Mac said. "And just hope that it clarifies some of the questions we've got. No sense anticipating complications."

CHAPTER 23

Her mother had taught her the art of hatred, Sarah thought, taught that one thoroughly. She thought about the dead, testing out her feelings to see if she felt any remorse, poking at the memories like a child might poke at a loose tooth. The truth was she could barely recall what she had felt when they had died. She rehearsed their names like a roll call, adding the bare facts to the list. Clinical and sparse. Christopher Hayes. The old man had not been long for this world anyway and he'd not known what was going on. Thought she was just another in the rotation of carers that called at his home and let themselves in. The front door key was in a small, secure box, opened with a key code but it hadn't taken much effort to discover what it was. She had watched for a couple of days when the carers arrived to get him up or put him to bed or bring his meals, standing at the bus stop outside the house, seen but unnoticed until she had watched for long enough to have worked out the full four-digit code.

She wasn't even sure what the man was supposed to have done, only that her mother hated him.

The younger man, Graham Jackson, well he had just been unlucky, she supposed. His family had left by the front door and she had walked in through the back. She had realised immediately that this was not Rory Jackson; too young, too slight of build but he had seen her by then, so she had killed him anyway and taken some jewellery just because she felt she ought to take something. Then she had seen the picture Jean Hammond had drawn, the pretty young woman with far too much happiness in her eyes. Jean had never drawn Constance; a fact that had always rankled with Sarah's mother.

Jean Hammond, who had painted that filthy picture, told Sarah she should be grateful. That she could sell it. As though the money would make up for all the years of misery. If Jean had only helped back then, William might still be alive, Sarah might have had a father and her mother . . . her mother might have been a different woman.

Possibly.

But Sarah, even as she took a metaphorical step back and looked at her situation, knew that was unlikely to be true.

But who would want to buy a picture like that, even from the hand of the famous Jean Hammond? It was as though she had stripped Sarah naked and exposed her past and her pain to the scrutiny of the world. That alone was deserving of hatred — and on her own account this time, not just because her mother willed it.

Because Sarah had realised that she was stronger than Constance had ever been; she knew that for certain now. Connie had persecuted her daughter, taught her to hate, spent a lifetime complaining and cursing and railing against the hand fate had dealt her. Sarah had actually done something about it.

She recalled with deep pleasure having watched the light go out in Jean Hammond's eyes.

And then there was Clive Tatum. So surprised to see her and so unable to do anything about it. But it wasn't over yet. Sarah hadn't *nearly* finished yet.

* * *

Back in Frantham, Rina stood against the rail of the promenade, her back to the sea for once, watching the summer crowds ebb and flow. They were mostly young families enjoying the sunshine with a few couples here and there and older people wending their slow way.

A young couple came to stand not far from where Rina was waiting; two women, maybe just into their twenties, walking hand-in-hand and then standing close beside one another leaning on the rail and looking out to sea. The one closest to Rina had a rainbow of piercings climbing all the way up her ear. She must have sensed Rina looking at her because she turned with a slightly apprehensive look. Rina smiled and touched her own ear.

"That's pretty," she said.

The girl returned her smile. "Thanks," she said.

Steven and Matthew Montmorency came bustling out of the little supermarket and across to where Rina was waiting for them. "You wouldn't believe how busy it is this morning," Matthew said.

"Well, never mind," Steven soothed, "only one more place to go and then we can all go home and have a nice sit down."

"It will be almost teatime anyway by then," Rina observed.

The two girls moved off, their fingers brushing and then interlocking. Moments later they were absorbed by the crowd.

"The young have no idea how beautiful they are," Steven said softly.

"Or how lucky," Rina observed, thinking how different it had been when she and the Montmorencys had been that age.

"Fragile victories, Rina," Matthew said. "We can never afford to assume they are safe. Right," he added, seeming to gather himself. "The radio was on in the shop. Rina, there's been another murder. A man in his seventies."

"Did they say who it was?"

"The police have made no statement," Matthew said, "but the news did one of those 'locally named as' statements. They say his name was Clive Tatum."

"Oh," Rina said. "That's the author of the memoir Jean was so upset about."

"Which is not a good sign," Steven commented. "Sebastian's life is going to get even more complicated, I fear."

Rina nodded.

"I need to go to the post office and then we're done," Matthew said. He took off ahead of them, marching down the promenade, his mane of grey hair streaming behind him in the wind.

Rina and Steven followed more slowly. Steven's knees were hurting him today, badly enough that he had borrowed one of Rina's collection of sticks. Rina often carried a walking stick, not because she needed one but because she rather liked them and she also found that it encouraged the less surefooted of her housemates to put their reservations aside if they saw Rina striding out as though her stick was a fashion accessory.

She took Steven's arm, became acutely aware of the unevenness in his gait and the stiffness in his back. He was ageing much faster than his ersatz twin; his on stage partner and his companion since the two had been in their teens and just starting out in show business. What, she thought — the thought itself filled with pain — would happen if one of them were to die and the other be left alone. Could either of them survive that?

It was never asked or talked about, not even within the privacy of Peverill Lodge, if these two were a couple. They had been born and grown up in a time when that would have been a criminal act and the habit of caution had never quite left them. And the only thing that mattered, Rina considered, was the fact that two people had loved one another for more than half a century.

"He's got more energy than I have," Steven said ruefully as Matthew finally paused just before the police station, the post office being on the road that ran parallel to the promenade.

"He's got more energy than the whole lot of us put together," Rina laughed, thinking, not for the first time, that Matthew always reminded her of some kind of large hound. A Saluki or a Borzoi, something slightly unusual at any rate.

"Has Mac said anything more about the Jean Hammond death," Steven asked prompted by the proximity of the police station.

"Not really. I've only had time for a quick word but Miriam seems to think they'll be escalating the investigation and, as you know, Jean Hammond's body is going to be exhumed."

"That's going to be hard on Cal," Steven said. "So, they definitely think it could be murder, then?" He shook his head sadly. "Bad enough to lose someone you love but then to find out that someone deprived them of whatever time they might have had left. Do you know what the police will be looking for when they exhume the body?"

"Well, I guess they don't know for certain, though I agree, they probably wouldn't be doing the exhumation unless something really significant had turned up. Miriam did say the opening of an investigation was down to something found at the scene that matched something in another case, but of course she couldn't elaborate."

"No, I suppose not. Any thoughts about this new death?" He turned his head to look speculatively in her direction, the washed-out blue eyes intensely interested.

"Well," Rina said. "Jean had a bit of plant clasped in her palm. What would you bet that this new victim also died with a flower in their hand?"

* * *

They made an odd little procession walking from the solicitor's office to Peverill Lodge. Ursula, George, carrying the box, and Walter Heath dabbing his elaborate walking stick to the ground on every second step. Andy Nevins, who had arrived at Heath's office just as they were about to leave, walked beside him.

"Why wasn't your name on the list in the hall?" George heard Ursula ask Walter Heath as they walked along. "If I'd known about you, I'd have known who to ask for advice." She'd paused. "Though I'd probably still have talked to Rina first."

Heath seemed amused by that. He had a gigantic laugh, George thought, it fairly shook the walls. "She just had my number on speed dial in her phone," he said. "We'd seen a lot more of one another since Cal left home and she felt she could take on more responsibilities. Once he'd gone off to university, when he turned eighteen, she picked up a lot of her old friendships and interests and I'm happy to say that I was one of them."

Ursula had nodded. "She did mention you several times but I didn't know you were her solicitor." She frowned. "That's a funny thing, actually, she'd left her mobile in the drawer with the envelope. Usually, she stuffed it in her pocket in case she needed to call someone in a hurry."

"Jean never bought anything without a pocket," Walter said fondly. "Odd about her phone though," he added.

"I . . . I almost took that too," Ursula said. "It felt out of place, you know? Then I didn't; that felt like overstepping—"

It might have been better if she had, George thought. Then the police would at least know if she'd had any odd calls — though he supposed they'd be able to get her phone records, anyway.

"I'm not even sure if Cal would think to contact me," Walter said thoughtfully. "If he needed to speak to someone about the will or whatever, then I'm sure he'd have the number for her regular solicitor and I expect Jean would have apprised them of everything necessary. I do have a copy of her will for safekeeping and she asked me to be her executor but she lodged her will with the Cotton Brothers, they saw to the conveyancing on the house and dealt with all of that stuff. We renewed our original acquaintance when she came back and I happened to mention the house to her, but I didn't start to deal with any of Jean's legal affairs until much later. I'm happy to say our relationship grew into friendship after that."

"So, I suppose you know Philip Goodman," Ursula said. "I like him. He made her laugh."

"I do indeed know Philip," Walter told her. "He and his partner and I manage to have dinner together at least once a month and often we all met up, Jean as well, and spent an evening together. As you get older the friends you had in your youth somehow become even more important. Jean had a good few years on the rest of us, of course, but you'd never know it. She complained about her knees and her dizzy spells and we all knew she wasn't in the best of health, but she was in all other ways just the same as always."

"The others are all artists," Ursula said. "Were you?"

"You could say I'm a failed artist," Walter said. "I still dabble but it became obvious, to me anyway, after my first term at college, that I didn't have what it took. So, much to my father's relief, I dropped out as they say and the following year took up the study of law. I'm a much better legal eagle than I ever would be an artist."

They had arrived now at Peverill Lodge and George rang the bell.

It seemed that Rina and the others had only just arrived back and it was Bethany who opened the door. "Oh my goodness, what a lot of visitors," she exclaimed happily.

They were soon ensconced in a big living room, the box taking pride of place on the dining table. Walter Heath was introduced to the Peverill Lodge community and everyone gathered around Ursula. She looked slightly self-conscious, George thought, now that she was the focus of everyone's attention and preparing to open the box.

"I have advised Ursula that the police will definitely want to see the contents of this box and that it would be better if she handed it over personally, because we do suspect that some of these items are pertinent to their enquiry," Walter Heath said.

No shit Sherlock, George thought.

"PC Nevins here tells me that Inspector McGregor will probably be over to see you later anyway, as he assumed that Ursula would be bringing the box here. Apparently, you, dear lady, are considered to be the oracle above all oracles."

He was enjoying himself, George thought. This was probably more fun than he'd had in ages. He was inclined to like Walter Heath. The solicitor had assured Ursula that Jean Hammond had provided sufficient funds for anything that Ursula might need to do and when George queried this it turned out that Jean Hammond had long kept Walter on a retainer. She had him look over her contracts, her stocks and shares and general investments and keep an eye on the other houses that it seemed she owned and that were currently rented out. George had realised the woman was well off, but not *that* rich. He wondered if Mac realised just how much Cal Hammond was going to inherit. Having never met Cal Hammond and therefore having no emotional investment in the game, George felt quite free to consider that the man had motive for murder. It made about as much sense as anything else.

"And in that light," Walter Heath continued, "we thought we might come and see what the oracle has to say. And Ursula assures me that you have a means of copying these," he went on, "and as there is quite a lot of material, I suggest we might make a start?"

Rina viewed her guest with what was obvious amusement but she nodded. "We need to be organised about this. George there's an all-in-one scanner and printer in my room, you can work out how to use it I'm sure. What I suggest we do is that we review each of these documents quickly, just to get an overview and then make a copy. By the time Mac comes over this evening we should have made a complete inventory. Andy, no doubt you need an inventory for your records, so I'll get you pen and paper and you can make two copies, one for us and one for Mac."

George glanced at Andy who was looking as though he might object but he then thought better of it and shrugged. "Right you are Mrs Martin."

He had, George reflected, known Rina for longer than either George or Ursula but he still couldn't get out of the habit of calling her Mrs Martin. George suspected that Andy was still a little bit intimidated by her.

"Now," she said turning to the solicitor, "where do you suggest we start?"

"With a quick glance through the exercise books," he said. "And I would like to add that I'm not very comfortable with this. While I totally understand Ursula's reasoning, I suspect that the police will be very keen to get hold of these records, so to cover ourselves I suggest that Andy here telephones his boss and emphasises that we may well have evidence he could make use of and that perhaps we get the copies made quickly and have a proper read later."

Rina looked surprised, she glanced at Ursula and then across at George who nodded. "I think he's got a point," George said. "The rest of the stuff looks a bit less interesting, but the exercise books are dynamite. So, Rina it's probably a good idea to get those copied first just in case Mac turns up too quickly. It would also be quicker to photograph the pages on a mobile rather than make copies on your machine," he added.

"Good idea. We have several smart phones at our disposal, so let's get started. Andy, as Mr Heath suggested, you had better phone Mac and let him know what's going on. We've got a box of those disposable gloves in the kitchen, under the sink, perhaps we should use those when handling the documents. Now I have my phone, and Ursula and George both have one."

"As do I," Walter Heath said. "So, let's crack on shall we."

He really is enjoying himself, George thought. Eliza brought out the gloves and they began.

CHAPTER 24

In her hotel room, Sarah watched the press conference. An inspector talking about Clive Tatum's death and that a major enquiry was now underway. The event was being held in a large room that did not look like a police station and at first she was puzzled by that, but as she watched she realised that this was a dining room or ballroom or something inside a substantial hotel. As the news report cut to a reporter standing outside, summarising the events of the previous day, she was able to see the exterior of the building. It looked vaguely familiar; she was sure she'd passed it at some point recently.

She half listened to the summary; the reporter was talking about Clive Tatum as a retired journalist with a solid local reputation. That the police were linking his death to others, including that of the artists Jean Hammond but had not released details as to why. That her body was to be exhumed the following day . . .

Bored now, Sarah turned the television off and lay back on the bed. Beside her lay a stack of notebooks, some of them going back years, the latest entry made just a few days before her mother died. Her mother's words, admonitions, demands, punishments all recorded in the greatest detail so Sarah could not have the excuse of forgetting.

No one is unworthy of your hatred, her mother had said. *No one is worthy of your love.*

Not even you, mother, Sarah thought. *Not even you.*

CHAPTER 25

Mac arrived at Rina's just after eight o'clock after a very long day. Andy had called and showed him a video of the contents of Ursula's box and Ursula was going to leave it at Rina's to be collected as she had to go to work that evening.

"So, you've got another murder then," Rina said as Mac settled himself in the fireside chair.

"We do indeed and as you've probably heard on the news it's the journalist Clive Tatum. And the scenario is very similar to others, not just Jean Hammond's."

Rina raised an eyebrow. "Others? I saw your press conference but you were, shall we say, a little oblique."

"There are two more that we know about, I hope no more than two. And this is confidential information, I don't have to tell you that. The connection was only made a couple of days ago thanks to young Yolanda. If she hadn't been intrigued by the bit of plant that Jean was holding in her hand and if she hadn't mentioned this at a briefing with someone from the art and antiques division, the connection would not have been made. As it is, we seem to have two previous deaths with a Jean Hammond connection. One late last year and one this spring."

Rina nodded. "Hence the exhumation."

"Which is tomorrow at dawn. I wish I knew the bugger who first came up with that tradition, deserves a punch on the nose. What's wrong with midday or early afternoon or even teatime."

"Once these things are established they tend to stick around," Rina agreed. "Is Cal going to be present?"

"I don't think so, no. He has the option or he could send a legal representative if he wished to, but I did talk to him and we both agreed there was nothing to be gained by him coming. He's shocked enough as it is and all he really wants to know is if the post-mortem turns up anything we didn't know previously. It's the toxicology results that are going to be crucial here."

"We'll make this quick, then," Rina said, I'll bring you up to speed on what we've found and then you can get off home to get some sleep. Andy and Yolanda can give you a proper briefing in the morning.

Mac awarded her a wry smile. "So, what was in the box?"

Rina handed him an inventory. Andy had taken his with him and she had made a copy of the one he had left behind for her. "As you can see there are a lot of old photographs, some journals from various times in Jean's life. It seems she got very enthusiastic about keeping them for a while and then she'd lose interest, like the rest of us do. But it's the note-books, like school exercise books that are probably going to be the most relevant. What puzzles me is why she kept them all this time."

"Were they hers?"

"Well no, that's the thing. They seem to have belonged to William Tatum."

"Really? Very odd. According to Clive Tatum, his cousin, William Tatum, was a thief and a liar," Mac said. "I take it you've had a look through them. Would you say there was any suggestion that he might have been the killer of Miles Cunningham's family? I know Clive Tatum was fairly convinced this might have been the case. Andy read his memoir and gave me a summary. That theory also seems to be central to this novel that's no doubt going to sell in the millions now the author is dead."

Rina had a curious expression on her face.

"What?" he asked.

"Well, that might be Clive Tatum's version," Rina said. "But from what I could glean from the writing and drawings in the exercise books, William Tatum might have been a grown man but he had the mind of a child."

"I'm not sure I understand what you mean, surely school exercise books would have been written in when he was at school."

Rina shook her head. "All of these seem to date from when he was living at the Cunningham house. I can't be sure but it looks as though Betty was setting him little lessons to try and improve his spelling and his writing and was encouraging him to draw. There are things like *'Today is Tuesday and Betty helped me read a book.'* Betty, presumably, or someone with decent handwriting anyway, has written the date at the top of each page. The Cunningham's were trying to take care of William Tatum. He was about eighteen or nineteen when he went to live in their house, physically at least. But I wouldn't say his mental age is much more than seven or eight years if that. I'm no expert of course, but if that is the case . . ."

Mac realised he was staring at her. If that was the case then it changed so much, it altered the whole complexion of the murders. "I heard he wasn't very bright but if he had the mind of a child then that's a very different matter. Surely this would have come out at the time?"

"Would it? I know this isn't distant history but from what I remember of the seventies and eighties there was not nearly so much support for families of kids with learning difficulties, and if that family was dysfunctional, which I understand it was from Walter Heath, then maybe they didn't have access to the help they needed. Isn't it possible he just fell through the cracks? Children do now, even with a system that's supposed to have improved and you know how little support teens that have been in care get from the authorities.

I know everyone does their best, but it's not like being part of a close and loving family is it?"

"But Clive Tatum would have known the truth." Mac said. "Why lie? And it doesn't mean that William Tatum wasn't the murderer."

"Yes, he would have and no it doesn't but it does perhaps make a little more sense of Miles Cunningham's statement that it was all his fault. If he brought William Tatum into his home then his sense of responsibility must have been overwhelming. Especially if he then in fact killed William Tatum because he believed William had slaughtered his family."

Mac thought about it. "However, any way you look at it it's a tragic set of circumstances. Is there any sense in the books that William Tatum was violent?"

"It's hard to tell. He talks about having tantrums and Betty telling him off. There is one sentence when he says that he frightened Betty and the children but he doesn't say how, just that Betty said he must say sorry to everyone. However, it's far from conclusive. One interesting thing though, he talks about Jean coming to visit and that he likes her and that he has asked if he can go and live with her and he thinks she might say yes."

"So, what happened," Mac wondered.

"Hard to know, but there are a few people who were around back then and who might remember. Walter Heath hasn't got a clue, he knew that Jean visited the Cunningham house but then so did they all. He's pretty certain that Jean was on some kind of residency up in Manchester when the murders happened. But he suggested that Philip Goodman might know more about Jean's involvement with the Cunninghams and he was kind enough to arrange for me to go and visit Philip tomorrow."

"Rina, it's not your place to be investigating."

"Of course, it's not. I'm simply *visiting*. Philip Goodman and I shared a mutual friend in Jean Hammond so it's natural perhaps that we should get together." She smiled at Mac as if recognising that he was becoming increasingly irritated.

"He is also quite happy if you tag along," she said. "That way everybody's curiosity will be satisfied and you can do your investigating."

"Rina—" Mac gave up. At least, he supposed, she'd told him what she was up to this time. And it would be a useful contact to make. "I have the exhumation tomorrow morning," he said.

"I know, at dawn, so you should have handed everything off by about eleven which is when I suggested to Philip Goodman we would be arriving."

"I should go on my own," Mac told her sternly.

"Of course, you *could*," she said. "I'll see you in the morning, then."

CHAPTER 26

Very early the following morning Mac stood in the corner of the churchyard, with Andy Nevins and one of the Cotton Brothers' solicitors, representing Cal Hammond's interests, beside him. The coroner was dealing with the gravediggers and the funeral directors and there was not a great deal for anyone else to do apart from bearing witness to what Mac always thought of as an indignity.

He recalled the motto of the coroners' service, *Civitatem Servamus Mortes Loquimur.* We represent the living but speak for the dead. The coroners' office might speak for the dead, Mac thought, but it was up to the likes of him to act upon their words. A few hardy journalists had gathered in a quietly gossiping knot at the corner of the road. Mac recognised his friend, Andrew Barnes, among them and nodded a greeting. No doubt Andrew would be coming to him for the inside story before long. Mac was fine with that; he was one of the good guys.

He had spoken to Cal the night before to make sure he'd not changed his mind about attending. Cal had sounded subdued and tired but was adamant that he could not bear to watch Jean being ripped from her grave — his words — and Mac had promised to call him as soon as he had any news.

He'd also had a quiet word about Ursula and sensed that Cal felt somewhat embarrassed by what he'd said about her to Rina. *So he should*, Mac thought.

He thought about William Tatum. In the end he'd had very little sleep, sitting up late and reading the relevant chapters of Clive Tatum's memoir and then the printouts of William Tatum's exercise books. Rina, knowing he'd probably prefer not to handle the originals until they had been examined, had been thoughtful — was that the word? — enough to have printed copies for him.

He felt unjustifiably miffed by that. She had taken liberties with what might be evidence. Though, he asked himself, had she really done anything of the sort? Jean Hammond had left Ursula in charge of these particular documents. If Ursula hadn't had a Rina Martin she might, not knowing what to do with all of this random mess, have just shoved the box under her bed and forgotten about it. Or she might have handed it over to Cal and he'd have done something similar. As soon as they had realised the contents of the deed box might be important, they had informed him. It was down to Mac that he'd not managed to collect the box until that evening and Rina had assured him that they'd handled documents only after donning gloves.

Beside him Andy Nevins moved restlessly. This was a new experience for the young officer, Mac knew, but Andy had seen worse in his short career and Mac knew that he was well able to cope. The digging had started while it was still dark, lights brought into the tent surrounding the grave. No one had said very much; Mac had the sense that even the diggers were trying to do their work as silently as possible. The closest houses were maybe fifty yards away from the churchyard wall and he had been aware of lights coming on in bedroom windows, of faces glancing out before curtains were tightly drawn. There were a few silent spectators, some in their dressing gowns and others almost formally clothed as though attending a memorial service. He had attended exhumations where there had been protestors or grieving families, unable to cope with this latest indignity. This group at least was quiet and calm.

"Mr Hammond didn't want to be here, then?" Andy asked.

"What could he do if he came," Mac asked, though he felt, as he sensed Andy must do, surprised that Cal and his partner hadn't decided to come and witness this most sombre of events. Even out of curiosity — or was that odd too?

There had been a pause about half an hour before. The diggers having accomplished their task but now waiting for first light before lifting the body from what was supposed to be its final resting place. Mac found that he was watching the sky, willing the sun to rise and fancying that he saw a lightening of the horizon.

"Mrs Martin's here," Andy said quietly.

Of course, she was, Mac thought. He turned to look over the churchyard wall. Rina stood on the corner of the road and she was not alone. Beside her were George and Ursula and an older man leaning heavily on a walking stick that Mac did not recognise but who Andy told him was Walter Heath. They made no move to come any further, just stood quietly, respectfully and as Mac watched they were joined by other silent spectators. Some carried flowers, one or two were crying openly. A young man came over to Ursula and spoke to her, shook Rina's hand, seemed to be introducing the young woman with him. Who were they? Mac wondered. People who knew Jean or those who were simply curious?

The coroner came over and announced that the body was to be brought up and Mac moved closer to the tented ground to witness the event. Dawn had arrived, with violet skies touching the cliffs and a paler blue above the sea and, Mac felt, the promise of a perfect, early summer day.

He watched as the coffin was lifted up, formally checked, was taken out of the tent and carried to the waiting funeral ambulance.

"To Jean, may all her travels be joyful," a voice said and Mac twisted around to look at the gathering on the opposite side of the road. "To Jean," other voices took up the toast and Mac was astonished to see glasses raised, bottles passed along the row and through the crowd. Ursula stepped off the kerb and, not looking at Mac, came over to the churchyard wall. She carried flowers and she laid them down on the low stone wall. Others followed and as Mac watched more and more flowers appeared, the mourners laying them down and then walking away. By the time the coffin had been loaded almost everyone had gone, just a small knot of people remained, watching the funeral ambulance as it drove away. Then they too drifted off, Mac imagined, to carry on with their day having done what they came for and been satisfied.

"Wow," Andy Nevins said.

Wow indeed, Mac thought.

CHAPTER 27

Mac collected Rina at ten thirty, not quite sure how long it would take them to get to Philip Goodman's house along the coast road. He guessed it would be no more than twenty minutes but he preferred some leeway.

"This morning," he said. "What was that all about?"

"A lot of people felt they should pay their respects. The exhumation seemed like such an intrusion and if she has been murdered that's, well, that's going to impact on a great many who knew her."

"But how did they all know to come. I know it's impossible to keep a lid on these things but it looked almost like a flash mob, everyone turning up like that and then fading away again."

"I think Walter put the word around and there were people I knew of course and Ursula and George wanted to be there. Her gardener turned up as well, he was very fond of Jean."

"Gardener? Yes, she would have had a gardener. Worth speaking to," he added.

"He and his partner have just been away on holiday, they only came back a couple of days ago. He was rather shocked to find that Jean's death might not have been natural causes after all. I should warn you that you might find some irregular plants growing in her garden, unless Cal's had the sense to get rid of them of course, but perhaps that has more to do with Jean than her gardener if you see what I mean."

"Irregular plants? OK, I think I understand. When did he last see her, do you know?"

"Three days before she died, she seemed in good health and good spirits and she showed him her latest painting. It was essentially complete, he said, she was just fiddling with it and was preparing to put a temporary coat of varnish on it. I don't know about these things but he seemed to be saying it needed a permanent coat putting on in about six months' time. Apparently, oil paint takes a long time to dry. They'd previously had a long conversation regarding what plants should be in the picture. He had lent her some books on the language of flowers and traditional meanings. He liked her a lot."

"Most people seem to have done. Though I understand she could be quite irascible at times," he added.

"No doubt the same is said of me," Rina said comfortably. "Did you have the chance to look through William Tatum's writing?"

"I did yes. Frankly Rina it does not make for easy reading. The young man might have had learning difficulties but he was perfectly capable of feeling rage and pain and, it seems, lashing out. It looks like Betty had to have words with him several times over the way he was treating her children. He said she wanted to send him away and he seemed to have an idea that he was going to go and live with Jean Hammond."

"That was the impression I got," she agreed. "Let's hope Philip Goodman can shed some light."

Philip Goodman and his partner lived in a stone cottage high up on the cliffs. Thick hedges surrounded the garden, protected by dry stone walls but Mac guessed the winds would still cut across fiercely in the winter. There was a gravel pull-in close to the house and a car already parked there. Mac drew up beside it and he and Rina made their way to the front door between low, lavender borders. The house was smaller than he had expected. Somehow, he had thought Philip Goodman would have a place on a scale with Jean Hammond's but this was just a small cottage probably no more than two up two down. The front door opened straight into the living room and Philip Goodman stood back to allow them to go inside. He was in his eighties, a little bent, blessed with wrinkles and neat cropped white hair. He also had a lovely smile and a welcoming manner.

He offered coffee and took an old-fashioned tea trolley through to the kitchen so he could push the tray along rather than have to carry it. He impatiently brushed off any offer to help. Rina noted a slight tremor in his left hand.

He was curious about the exhumation of course but seemed satisfied that Mac could tell him little. Rina had brought her copies of William Tatum's books with her. He flipped through the pages pausing occasionally to read a passage or examine a picture.

"I remember William and Constance," he said. "Constance was a couple of years older and she was very protective of young William. You know that they were in care for quite some time?"

"I believe their family was dysfunctional and abusive," Mac said.

Philip nodded. "The father was a drunkard and violent with it. He was also a compulsive gambler and when he lost it he took it out on his wife and children. Do you know what happened to the wife?"

"No," Mac said. "We've only just started looking at William Tatum."

"And that bollocks Clive Tatum put out that he might have been the killer?"

"He seems to have been prone to violent outbursts," Mac said cautiously.

"And is that any surprise? Look, children learn by example and if the only example he'd had for years was a man who came home and beat seven shades out of . . . You know they saw their mother die, William and Constance. They tried to stop the father but there was nothing they could do. The neighbours called the police and it took four officers to pull the man off but by then it was too late. The children were taken into care of course but it was far too late by then, if something had been done earlier there might've been a very different outcome. As it was, they were disturbed and frightened and aggressive."

"How old were they?" Rina asked.

"Constance was twelve and William was about ten. He was badly injured trying to protect his mother, spent some time in hospital afterwards, brain damage they said. He was certainly never the same again, according to his sister. In those days they would have said he was slow I suppose, that's if they were being kind. I believe the terminology has changed now. I just hope the help that children get has changed too. It was an appalling situation. Constance felt so responsible; she was the eldest of course and felt she should have looked out for her little brother. The truth was she had done all she could and she continued to do so for quite some time after."

"Did you know the family when the children were young?" Rina asked.

Philip Goodman shook his head. "I got to know them when the Cunningham's took William in. It was supposed to be for a couple of weeks, but it ended up being about eight months in all. Constance had been offered a job, a good job but it meant leaving William and how could she do that. She knew the Cunninghams and she knew that they occasionally took in lodgers and though William wasn't the kind that they usually accommodated, they agreed. As I say it was supposed to be just for a couple of weeks while she sorted something else out but that something else didn't materialise. William seemed to be doing fine, he liked Betty and he had something of a crush on Jean. She was quite a frequent visitor, as were we all."

"A crush can be a powerful emotion," Mac observed. "Did Jean realise?"

"We all did, he followed her round like a little puppy and she was very patient with him but then Jean was very patient with most people. The only people she couldn't tolerate were the deliberately ignorant or people who were so full of themselves they couldn't see how badly they were doing things. Jean must have been fifty I suppose, the Cunninghams were in their mid-thirties and there were a lot of younger people who used to come to the house. A lot of us saw Jean as a kind of mentor, she was always very generous with her advice and time. She was also still a very beautiful woman." He smiled. "I suspect William wasn't the only one to have a crush on Jean Hammond, though I think William's was a lot more innocent than some."

Mac produced the photograph that had been taken at the Cunningham house and laid it on the table.

"God, that's a blast from the past. Unusual to see Jean in the picture, she was more often than not the photographer." He laughed. "You see what I mean about her still being beautiful?"

Mac nodded.

"I didn't recognise her at first," Rina said. "I only got to know her about eight years ago so the only picture I had in my mind was of her as an old lady."

"Age isn't kind. I wasn't bad looking either back then, was I?" He smiled. "And there's Clive, and there's Sophie as she became, fine actress. Where on earth did you get this?"

Mac briefly explained about Ursula and Jean's request and what they had found when they unlocked the box.

"How very strange. I wonder how it was she had William's exercise books."

"There is anecdotal evidence that William believed he was going to live with Jean," Mac said. "Do you believe there was any foundation to that?"

Philip Goodman looked puzzled. "As I said, William certainly had something of a crush, he was certainly very fond of her, very attached, and I know from time to time he would ask her if he could go and live with her. You know how children do, when they are feeling unhappy, when they have a favourite aunt, that sort of thing. I never really thought any more of it than that. I didn't get any impression that Jean did either."

"Jean was not around when the Cunningham murders happened," Mac said.

"No, she'd got a teaching gig up in Manchester. She was earning decent money from her paintings by then but even so she liked to have a backup plan and in those days she actually enjoyed the teaching, mixing with the young students. She said they reminded her of why she wanted to be an artist in the first place — that they asked questions she had forgotten to ask. Frankly I never really fancied the idea myself, too much like hard work."

"Were you . . . are you an artist," Rina asked suddenly conscious that she knew very little about this man.

"I'm a sculptor my dear, or at least I was. Old age isn't kind to the joints. I had reasonable success and now the government pays me for existing and Tony and I rub along reasonably well. We managed to buy this place when we still had some money. Tony, would you believe, was an accountant and actually has a *proper* pension." He grinned at them and Rina found herself returning his smile.

"Why would Clive Tatum put forward the theory that William was the killer?" Mac asked.

Philip Goodman thought for a moment, tapping his fingers on the arm of his chair. "He was as shocked as we all were when Miles was accused and when he refused to defend himself. It was all so totally out of character. It seemed impossible. Everybody is capable of lashing out, but Miles adored his wife and children and I mean *adored*. He hadn't had the easiest of upbringings which gave him a lot of sympathy for other people, but when he settled with Betty and the kids in that great rambling house it was like he had finally found where he belonged." He paused. "I still don't believe he killed them."

"Then why didn't he defend himself?"

"Guilt. I think it's as simple and as complicated as that. I don't know what he felt guilty about, possibly not being able to look after them, to protect them, but whatever it was . . ."

"Guilt at bringing a killer into their home?" Mac asked provocatively. "That seems to be what Clive Tatum implied in both his memoir and his upcoming novel."

"Novel? I didn't know he'd written a novel. A pity he won't benefit from the increased sales I suppose." His was tone sour, Rina thought. "He sent me a copy of the memoir, he sent one to Jean, he sent one to anybody who had known him back then. But what struck me as strange is, he never came to us beforehand, asked us what we remembered or what we thought. It's as though he had made up his mind what had happened and that was that. And he was maybe anxious about showing anybody until the book was a done deal, out in the world. Perhaps he was worried we might contradict him. Jean and I talked about this quite a bit and I have to say she was utterly incandescent. She thought he was blaming a young man who could not defend himself; who could never have defended himself, without evidence or consideration."

"He was careful to present these ideas as just that, ideas, possibilities. He never said definitively that William was the murderer," said Mac, playing devil's advocate.

"But he left little room for doubt regarding what he thought, didn't he?" Philip Goodman returned. "It seemed to us, Jean, Christopher Hayes and I, that he was purely intent on making money from scandal, that he was digging up the past when it should have stayed buried."

"Some coals should not be raked over, some fires not rekindled," Rina said. "That's very much what Walter Heath said to us."

"Walter and I were of the same mind on this."

Mac picked up on something Philip had just said. "You said that Christopher Hayes agreed with you that Clive Tatum was just out to make money, but Mr Hayes was dead before the book came out. Did he know about it?"

"We all knew. Clive was very excited. He didn't tell us when he first got the publishing deal, but about a month before Christopher died, before Christopher was murdered, we were all invited out to dinner. That was unusual for Clive, he was not exactly known for throwing his cash around even when he had it. But he decided that he wanted us all to go out to some Indian place, very nice food, I forget the name . . . Anyway, there was me and Tony and Jean and I think he'd invited Walter but Walter couldn't come along. Walter did not exactly like Clive so he may have just made an excuse. Christopher really wasn't well enough to attend but we all went to see him afterwards — apart from Clive, of course — and took cake and some Indian sweets that were rather lovely. His carer had already put him to bed, but we had a little picnic in his room."

"Who let you in?" Mac asked. "I understood he lived alone."

"Oh yes, quite right. He had one of those key safe things next to the front door. Told me what the number was so we could let ourselves in. Poor lamb, he was so very ill by then." He paused and Mac could see that there were tears in his eyes.

"Anyway, it turned out that this meal that Clive had organised was an opportunity for him to announce the publication date and show us the cover and give us some idea of what he'd written. Well suffice to say something of a row blew up. Jean was appalled and told him so and we took her side. He kept going on about evidence and how the evidence did not support Miles being the murderer and we all knew that already. We all knew at the time that if he'd actually launched an appeal, or even spoken up, even pleaded not guilty and had a trial, the chances were there would have been reasonable doubt."

"But he would still have felt the guilt," Rina said quietly. "Whatever the cause."

Philip Goodman shrugged. He got up and went back through to the kitchen to make more coffee and Mac knew he was just buying himself some time, that he was finding this very painful. Rina left her chair and went to look out of the window. The sea was flat calm today and the sky that kind of deceptive blue that she knew, from experience of this coast, would blow up into a storm before the day was out. A photograph caught her eye and she picked it up, turned it so Mac could see. If he wasn't mistaken this was Jean Hammond as a young woman, the photograph was black and white but Mac could imagine the soft curls had been blonde, the scatter of freckles across her nose. The eyes were large and rather beautiful and the gaze direct, questioning.

"She was approaching forty when that was taken," Philip Goodman said as he returned to the room, pushing the tea trolley. "She always looked much younger. Some people do I suppose. You look at that picture and she looks at least ten years younger and she didn't really change, not for a very long time. She seemed to age after the Cunningham murders, like she carried guilt as well."

Rina replaced the photograph. "Guilt, why?"

"Even then Clive was making accusations about his cousin. Clive as you may realise was much younger than the rest of us. He professed himself determined to be a journalist, was busy trying to make a name for himself and this was a gift for him. Not only was it a series of brutal murders occurring at a house he had visited many times and committed by someone he knew well, but he had a direct involvement. He knew the background. I supposed in modern parlance he knew what spin to put on it. You could say that this launched his career. It must have seemed obvious to him that he should end his career by exploiting the same story, forty odd years on."

"And Jean wondered, if she'd taken William out of the situation, would everyone still be alive," Rina said.

"We all wondered, not just about that but if there was something important that we hadn't noticed. If there was something we could have changed."

"And what do you think now," Mac asked quietly. "Do you think it was Miles Cunningham who killed his family; do you think it could have been William Tatum?"

"I think what I have always thought, that it was someone else who came into the house, someone the police didn't bother looking for, someone who attacked Betty and the children. William tried to defend them. That's exactly what I believe he would have done. Betty was kind to him, as was Miles."

Rina seemed to be wondering if she should put her next question or leave it be. In the end she said, "There is some evidence from the exercise books that William left behind that Betty worried about the way he behaved. That on occasion she had to reprimand him for treating her children badly. She didn't punish him, but she did try and make him aware of what his behaviour ought to be. As we mentioned earlier there were certainly outbursts of anger, rage perhaps. He must have been difficult to manage. Someone with the strength and perhaps the urges of a grown man and the mind and emotional capacities of a young boy."

A look of distaste crossed Philip Goodman's face and for a moment Mac thought she'd gone too far, but then he relaxed. "No, of course you are right, there were problems. But as I've already said, how could there not be problems given the background. I admired Betty and Miles for offering him sanctuary. I honestly don't think they expected to still have him living there beyond the initial couple of weeks and they were not pleased with the way Constance behaved. She became very difficult to contact, very non-committal about her brother. It was as though she was satisfied that her brother was in safe hands and now she . . . Well, I guess she wanted a life of her own. She had a new job, she'd found herself a place to stay in the local YWCA, and in reality she had no means of looking after her brother. She had promised to stay in regular contact but I think she was very bad at that. I remember Miles getting very annoyed because he kept calling the Y and she wasn't returning any of his calls. A few days before everything happened, I know he went along the coast to Bournemouth where she was working and he camped out in the reception area until she came home. By all accounts they had a major row."

"And what was the outcome of that? I don't imagine Constance wanted to come back and collect her little brother if she was beginning to get her own life on track, however much she cared about him. Besides she couldn't house him at the YWCA. It's a big ask when you are just, what twenty, twenty-one? To make yourself responsible for another person who you know will be totally dependent on you?"

"Did Miles and Betty think that Constance had deliberately dumped her responsibilities on them?" Mac asked.

"By then I think they did. I believe they had tried to get social services involved and set things in motion to get him into some kind of home or hostel. But these things would take time now I expect and I'm sure they would have taken a lot of time back then. Then, of course, after . . . after William and the others were dead Constance tried to get recompense from the estate. She wanted money, she wanted to apportion blame. I suppose she wanted to feel that she was in no way responsible for what happened to her brother. Suddenly, there was no one she cared for more."

"Perhaps she felt guilty too," Rina said. "Perhaps this was her way of handling it."

"Or she was a gold-digger, determined to take advantage of the situation," Philip said coldly.

Harsh, Mac thought. But true?

"Did you know her well enough to form that opinion?" Rina asked.

Philip's face flushed with sudden anger. This time she had gone too far, Mac thought. "And how aware of this do you think William was?" he cut in, by way of distraction though aware that they were still treading on very sensitive ground and that Philip Goodman was uncomfortable with the answer he would have to give.

"I think they felt very resentful and although they were doing their best with William, I know the strain was beginning to show. Betty and Miles were having arguments and that was very unusual for them and I do know that Betty was arranging to go away for a little while. Not a formal separation or anything, just a break away to stay with family and she planned to take the children with her. I seem to remember the police making a big thing of this at the time, reporting that she was threatening to leave him and he was angry and that was the motive. Then there were the rumours that Connie spread. Rumours about her and Miles. Nonsense, of course, but it left a bitter taste. It was all very difficult and it was at this time, this stage, that William said he wanted to go and live with Jean. I believe at one point he had even packed his bag."

"There's something about him doing that in one of the exercise books," Rina said. "It's a drawing of a boy sitting on some steps with a suitcase beside him. He's written something like 'waiting for Jean to collect me'." She paused. "He still saw himself as a boy," she said. "In his own mind he'd not grown up. Did Jean even know what was going on?"

"I doubt it, not till afterwards. She was already up north. It wasn't like today, with everybody having mobile phones and WhatsApping one another and texting every five minutes. It was landlines and call boxes and letters. I remember when we heard about the murders, I tried to call her but I couldn't reach her and in the end she heard it on the national news. She was absolutely distraught, couldn't believe it. It was several days before she could come back down south and see us, she couldn't just walk away from her residency. She called us every day and we talked but none of us came to any easy conclusions. We just could not believe that Miles had killed his family and we could not believe the alternative either. I know William was difficult, I suppose you might even say he was unstable, but a killer? No. It had to be someone else, it just had to be."

They were all silent for a moment, thinking things through, and then Rina asked, "Was Clive at Christopher Hayes's funeral?"

"Yes, yes, he was. Didn't stay for the wake. I think he knew he wasn't really welcome. I only exchanged a few words and I'm not sure Jean even spoke to him. She was still furious. It was a good turnout, a lot of old friends and acquaintances. Word spread that Clive had written the memoir, I didn't know about the novel at all. What was the man playing at? He was tackled by several people about the . . . appropriateness of the book, of his bringing all of this pain up again. So far as I could tell he was unrepentant. Laughed it off."

"So, was that what Jean was so upset about after the funeral?"

Philip Goodman hesitated. "In part. And she was far from well as you probably know, so—"

"In part?"

"I don't know," Philip Goodman said. "She wouldn't say. Only that she had heard from someone we'd not seen for a long time and that it had upset her."

"You have any idea who?" Mac asked.

"Not for certain." He hesitated as though not sure whether or not to commit. He doesn't want to be any more involved, Mac thought. He feels he's said enough.

"Your friends are dead and their deaths are suspicious," Mac reminded him gently. "Jean Hammond and Christopher Hayes and, not to put too fine a point on it, you were part of that same group."

"You think there's a threat to me?" He tried to sound blasé but the tension in his voice was all too apparent.

"We should take no chances."

"Who would want any of us dead?"

"A man called Graham Jackson, was murdered in very similar circumstances. I believe you knew his father?" Mac pointed to Rory Jackson in the photograph.

"I knew him, yes. Though not well. Why would anyone kill his son? Look, I'd not seen him in years." Philip laughed, it sounded forced. "Funny thing, we'd all got Rory down as a confirmed bachelor, he never seemed to get involved with anyone. Then we heard he'd got married, had a child . . . but that was an age ago."

"So, who do you suspect had been in touch?" Mac asked.

"Oh, Lord. Look it was just an impression. She said to me one day, did I know that Constance had died? I didn't. As far as I was concerned Constance was in the past, I'd seen her perhaps twice since . . . she was never a friend and after the murders we all drifted apart. Jean had told me that she'd heard she'd died of cancer and that her daughter had been in touch. I never even knew she had a daughter. Then Jean told me that the daughter had been in touch again more recently and was demanding what she claimed Jean owed her. She seemed to be saying that her life would have been very different if Jean had helped out more."

"And you think this upset her?"

Philip Goodman rubbed his eyes with the heels of his hands as though suddenly wearied by all the questions. By the weight of memory. "I'm pretty certain of it," he said. "We all felt guilt. I know when Connie's daughter got in touch that Jean felt she should help out though Lord knows why. She had no obligation to the woman."

"Help out, how?" Mac asked.

"She painted something for her though I never saw the picture. She wasn't prepared to give her money; so far as Jean was concerned, that all belonged to Cal. But a painting could be sold and would likely be worth a great deal and the only thing Jean would be sacrificing would be time. It was a very Jean Hammond kind of solution."

"We've been told that Jean had an argument with someone, probably Clive Tatum, at Christopher Hayes's funeral," Mac said.

Philip Goodman shrugged. "I didn't witness it but she may well have done. Clive certainly cleared off in a huff, so it's possible she just picked up where she'd left off at the restaurant. Jean was like a terrier with a rag when she got going."

* * *

"What did you make of that," Mac asked as they got into his car to drive away.

"I think he's a man in denial," she said. "I also think that old sins, as they say, cast long shadows and perhaps old guilt does the same."

"You're thinking about Jean's commitment to Cal, that perhaps she was making up for the time she didn't do anything to help."

"But what could she do? This was not her fight to get involved with. You can't go around sticking plasters on everybody's hurts. All that happens if you try that is that you end up trying to mend a broken leg with a bit of sticky tape. Then eventually you just run out of plasters. Mac, there is so much we don't know even now."

"It's not really your job to know Rina," Mac reminded her.

"What's it got to do with a job description, it's common humanity."

"Sticking plaster . . . Broken leg . . ." Mac commented.

"Doesn't apply in this case. But the thing is what was Jean actually trying to tell us and why couldn't she have come straight out and said something? Let's think this through. She knew about Constance's death early last year. That was just before Ursula went to work for her. Ursula said Jean was painting something for Miles Cunningham. The name meant nothing to her but the picture was of a man and two children, standing outside a big house. Ursula said Jean thought it was about time she did this, but she didn't know Jean well enough at that point to ask many questions. In retrospect it seems an odd thing to do but it probably had something to do with this daughter of Constance Tatum and the anniversary of the murders."

"The picture Philip Goodman talked about. I must ask Walter Heath about it," Mac said. "He may know something about the arrangement she made."

Rina nodded. "Then Jean found out about the memoir. Last October, that must've been, if it was just a few weeks before Christopher Hayes died. Then her friend Christopher dies and she's naturally upset. And if Clive Tatum was at the funeral and boasting about his book then that probably upset her even more. And then she has this contact from the past in the shape of Constance Tatum's child. Then after Christmas, when she's already been very ill, they find out that Hayes had been murdered. Must've been a major shock. So, at that point she reminds Ursula about the envelope."

"OK, so we have a basic timeline, though we know also that she had put something in the envelope before Christmas, not necessarily what Ursula ended up with of course."

"What makes you think that?" Rina asked.

"Nothing in particular, it's just that she seemed so certain that Ursula would understand what to do with the contents so I do wonder if originally there was perhaps something that told her to go and see Walter Heath. Or something that pointed back towards Clive Tatum and William Tatum. The contents of the box are interesting, but much of it seems random, nothing to do with what happened with the Cunninghams or the Tatums."

"We all have boxes of memories and junk," Rina said. "I keep all sorts of random stuff and I know the Peters' sisters do and Matthew and Steven. Photographs and cards and notes and sometimes I look at them and think why on earth have I kept that and sometimes I really can't remember. Other times a photograph will remind me of something else and I understand why I kept that card or that menu or that receipt. She might have known that the exercise books were important, but perhaps everything else just lived in that box and she was reluctant to take it out."

"It's as good an explanation as any," Mac said.

"When will you get the results of the post-mortem?"

Hopefully the prelims tomorrow. The coroner's office aims to get the body back in the ground as soon as possible. It's always distressing for the relatives."

Rina nodded. "I wonder where Constance Tatum's child is now," she said.

"Sarah," Mac said. "Her name is Sarah Fredericks, that was her mother's married name. We're trying to track her down. According to her place of work she took all the holiday owing to her but told no one where she might be going and no one's heard from her since. But do you know what's interesting?

There's a dedication in the front of Clive's memoir. It says: 'To Sarah, hoping that one day she will understand.'"

"Ouch, "Rina said. "The arrogance of the man, Talk about rubbing her nose in it."

"Indeed," Mac agreed.

* * *

Sarah had been watching the lunchtime news and the coverage of Jean Hammond's exhumation. It didn't bother her that the woman's body was being exhumed and that this might reveal that her death had been far from natural. Sarah was far beyond worrying about details like that.

No, what enraged her, what was beyond everything was the sight of all those stupid people gathered to watch, to raise their glasses to the ridiculous, infernal woman. To lay flowers.

She caught sight of individuals she recognised among the crowd. Of the young girl who stepped forward first to set her flowers on the churchyard wall, who was crying! Crying for that old woman. For someone who never deserved anyone's tears.

Sarah remembered she had watched the girl leave Jean Hammond's place one day, the first time she had visited. The time Jean Hammond had promised her that she would give Sarah something in recompense for all she had lost.

"That's Ursula," Jean had said. "She's such a dear."

"Such a dear," Sarah sneered. "Such a bloody dear." And then Jean had expected her to be grateful for that fricking painting.

"Sell it," she'd said. "I've had papers drawn up so you're named as the official owner. I can give you the names of a couple of galleries that would be happy to handle that for you, though—"

Sarah remembered how she'd paused and then added, "You'd probably be better off putting it into a specialist auction. The commission wouldn't be as high."

"Commission?"

"Oh, there's always commission," she had said airily. "But it's a simple enough process and there'll be plenty left for you, even after they've taken their cut."

She'd been so off-hand, Sarah remembered. So bloody casual about it all. She was lucky Sarah hadn't flattened her there and then. But she hadn't been quite prepared; not then. That exaltation was still to come.

CHAPTER 28

Mac dropped Rina home and then called Yolanda to request that she contact Walter Heath and ask him what they knew about the painting Jean Hammond seemed to be doing in memory of the Cunningham family. He had a routine business to take care of, checking in with the Frantham office, content that the small town was being well taken care of by Sergeant Baker, though he was bemoaning the absence of PC Andy Nevins.

"Everyone and his dog popping in to ask why he isn't around and worried if he's ill," Frank Baker said. "They're used to seeing him on the promenade and having a chat."

By the time Mac returned to the incident room Yolanda had several answers for him.

"The birth certificate for Constance Tatum's child named her as Sarah Ann, but she wasn't Fredericks. It looks like Constance had Sarah before she married Jack Fredericks in 1983. Sarah was born the same year as the murders happened, in 1980, and on the birth certificate it has 'father unknown'.

"Interesting," Mac said. "So, she went away to work, leaving her brother with the Cunninghams, and presumably got pregnant while she was away. Though we know she was at least hinting that Miles Cunningham was the father. And do we know what happened to the marriage?"

"Ended in divorce about five years later. Jack Fredericks didn't adopt Sarah but she was using his name and carried on using his name. She finally changed from Tatum to Fredericks by deed poll when she was eighteen, but there's no evidence that Jack Fredericks was still around. I asked Walter Heath if he knew anything about the marriage and he said he knew it had happened, didn't know anything about the husband but he remembered rumours that Jack had gone missing after the divorce. It happened too long ago for it to pop up on the internet, but Andy remembered that one or two of the local newspapers further along the coast had been digitised so he suggested I called that friend of yours, the journalist? Andrew Barnes? And he managed to find some info for me. Sent it over and says you owe him coffee and an exclusive."

"I bet he did," Mac said.

Yolanda frowned. "It's OK to have done that, isn't it? Andy reckoned it would be all right. That he was a decent guy?"

"No Andy's right, he is a decent guy. He's helped us out before. What did the newspapers say?"

"That Jack Fredericks' family were looking for him. He seems to have disappeared and his ex-wife said she didn't know where he was. Apparently, she made quite a lot of accusations about him, violence and so on, which they refuted but it looks as though it got quite messy."

"Drama seems to have followed Constance Tatum around," Mac commented. "It seems odd, if Constance's accusations had any foundation, that her daughter should choose to change her name officially to her stepfather's."

"I suppose her mother carried on using Fredericks' name, so that was how the daughter was known. If there was no formal adoption then Sarah was still officially a Tatum. Maybe she didn't want to be Tatum on any of her official paperwork."

"A good point — but she could have changed it to anything she liked."

"But if everyone already knew her as Sarah Fredericks she might have had a lot of unwelcome explaining to do."

Mac nodded. "I suppose in terms of convenience it makes sense," he agreed. "Did Heath know about the painting?"

"Better than that, I have a picture . . . of the picture and I know what happened to it. Walter Heath handled the paperwork."

"Paperwork for what, for the sale?"

"Not sale, no. Jean Hammond gave the painting away, no strings attached, the recipient could sell it if they wanted to, lift up the nearest drain and post it down if they wanted. She gave it to Sarah Fredericks."

"That's quite a gift. How much was it worth? And why would she do that?"

"Well, what she initially told Walter Heath was that she was worried about Constance's daughter now being alone in the world, after her mother had died, and she felt it would be a nice thing to do. What he persuaded her to tell him afterwards, was that Sarah was playing up, threatening to drag up the past and accusing Jean of making promises she didn't keep."

"Promises? To William Tatum?"

"Walter thinks so. Apparently, Jean was really tight-lipped about the whole thing. When he tried to press her she just told him to leave it alone and just draw up the damned paperwork. He reckons she was very out of sorts anyway, even for Jean Hammond. If this was going to be a gift, or whatever, and it sounds to me like it was almost blackmail, but if it was always intended as a gift for Sarah Fredericks then, as Walter Heath also felt, Miss Hammond chose a really odd subject."

Yolanda turned her laptop so that Mac could see. "That's the picture?"

Ursula had described this image to him but he'd not really been able to visualise it. Mac could only really see representations on the internet of the Jean Hammond paintings that had hung in her dining room and representations of *The Wedding Coat*, the last commission she had done. The two pictures she had chosen to keep, and which hung in the dining room had been quite small — as was this picture. One of them had clearly been a portrait of Cal as a boy. He had climbed up into a tree and was looking down on her, or looking down on the viewer and he was surrounded by objects hung from the tree like Christmas baubles. There had been a kitten, a toy alligator, books, sweets, a whole variety of, Mac liked to think, Cal's favourite things. He remembered being very surprised that the picture had been left at Jean's house. If someone had painted something like that for him it would have been treasured, it would have gone everywhere with him even into the grotty flat where he first lived when he came to Frantham on Sea. In this case, Jean had perhaps decided she wanted to keep it with *her* but why did Cal leave it at the house after she died? It seemed like such an odd thing to do.

The second picture showed a high hill with something that was not quite a church standing at its summit and a procession of people wending their way upwards. Mac had no idea what that was about, but he liked it.

Then there was *The Wedding Coat*. Rina had described it as joyful and Mac concurred. She had also mentioned that much of Jean's work was quite melancholy but the painting she had done for Sarah Fredericks went far beyond that. He would have described it as emitting barely contained fury. It was quite simple and again quite small, and as Ursula had described depicted a man and two children standing outside a large house.

"Yolanda, do we have a picture of the Cunningham house anywhere?"

It seemed this had already been anticipated. "Andy found one. Here."

She handed him a printout and they both stared from that to the screen. "It is the same house, isn't it?"

"More or less," Mac agreed. "Complete with a damned great blue hydrangea." That, he noted, was the only really strong colour in the painting. The rest was almost monochrome. "I imagine she painted it from memory and so there will be certain details that will differ, but yes, it's the

Cunningham house. And I think that's Miles Cunningham. It certainly looks like him."

Yolanda nodded slowly. "So, who are the kids? The Cunninghams had three including the baby. This is a boy and a girl and they did have a boy and girl but . . ."

"They look older than the Cunningham kids had been, I think they were five and three and then there was the baby. These are what ten, eleven? Yolanda I'm wondering if these children represent Constance and William. At about the ages they were when their mother was killed."

"That would be creepy," Yolanda said.

"And provocative. Not exactly the best time of their lives was it. So, what's Jean Hammond trying to say and who's the message for?"

"It looks like the bloke is trying to keep a distance from the kids, or is that just my imagination," Yolanda said.

Mac studied the picture. She could be being fanciful, but he understood what she meant. There was a slight gap between the man and the children and there was a sense that his hands and arms and every part of him had been drawn inwards, arms wrapped around his body as though he was cold or upset or holding in his anger. The man was looking down, the children staring outwards, challenging, their gaze uncomfortable for the viewer.

"It might be worth a lot of money," Mac said, "but would you want to live with it?"

"It looks like she might have mixed the ghosts into the paint," Yolanda said.

"Do we know where the painting is now?"

"I spoke to DI Fullhurst and she says it hasn't come on to the market. Of course, it might have gone in a private sale to someone, she reckons there are collectors who just like to stick things in a safe until they get more valuable and with Jean Hammond dying, I suppose that price is just going to go up and up."

"And any progress on finding out where Sarah Fredericks actually is?"

"Certainly not at her Bournemouth address, hasn't been there for a couple of weeks. The landlady says she paid her rent up till the end of this month. Andy talked to her on the phone, he reckons she sounded kind of relieved that Miss Fredericks wasn't there anymore. She said if Sarah Fredericks didn't turn up in the next couple of weeks then she was going to let the place to someone else. Andy wanted to know if she was a good tenant, if she had any friends the landlady knew about, asked the usual questions but the landlady was very cagey. All he could get out of her was that she didn't have any visitors and that she paid her rent on time."

"Might be worth a follow-up call, or even a visit," Mac said. "Add it to the list of possible further action and, in the meantime, if we try and get a warrant, so the local police can have a look around her room, or maybe if the landlady is unhappy with her tenant she might even let them in."

Yolanda was smiling. "Andy already asked her, said there were welfare concerns."

"Nice one, Andy."

"The landlady said she was quite happy to let us in. She lives on the ground floor. So we thought we'd run it by you first, but he's made arrangements to meet a local officer and go over there first thing tomorrow, if you've no objections."

"And where is he now?"

"Assisting DI Fullhurst with something or other," Yolanda said. "Actually, she's given him a whole load of printouts of Jean's work and she's got him trying to match them to people in the photo albums. I think she realised that this picture looked like Miles Cunningham so . . ."

Mac nodded. "We urgently need to find Sarah Fredericks," he said. "Yolanda dig up absolutely everything you can on her, be ready to brief the team later. Talk to Cal Hammond, see if he can remember Jean mentioning her. Talk to Etta, his partner, if you can, it's just possible a woman might mention something to another woman that she wouldn't tell her son, especially as she seems to have been very protective of Cal. And see what you can find out about Cal Hammond's family and how they died, who they were. Walter Heath reckoned they were distant relatives."

"That's a lot, sir, if you want it for the evening sermon."

"And you're capable of doing it. If you want to split the workload go and steal Andy back. Tell DI Fullhurst I've asked for him."

CHAPTER 29

Rina had a theory about people, in fact Rina had lots of theories about people but one of them involved gardening. To her mind people that created gardens generally had a streak of unnatural optimism in their makeup. You might never see the tree you planted grow to full-size but you planted it anyway, in the belief that one day it would and other people would enjoy it. She also believed that gardeners were magnetically attracted to other gardeners. This pet theory had led her to believe that Jean and her gardener, Sandy, might have been friends. And now she had met him at the exhumation she was even more convinced of the fact. Sandy had spoken fondly of Jean as a lady who knew her plants.

He was working when she called so she assured him that she would only take a moment or two of his time and she just had what might seem to be an odd question. "Did she ever mention painting something relating to a man called Miles Cunningham? You might even have seen it, a painting with a house and a man and two children. She painted it last spring, around the time that young Ursula started to clean for her."

To her surprise Sandy laughed. "Oh, that," he said. "That was a strange one. She was in such a funny mood when she painted it, dashing it off she was like she wanted rid."

"Did she say who she was painting it for?"

"I don't remember. She said something about it being to pay off an old debt. I made a joke about it being a big debt then, knowing how much her work was selling for. Then she said something about it being worth it, just to get someone off her back. She didn't want to paint the picture, or maybe she did but she was cross about it all the same. You never knew what Jean was thinking, not really."

"Did she ever mention someone called Sarah, Sarah Fredericks or Constance Tatum?"

"Not that I remember. That policewoman phoned and asked me the same thing, the one who was there on the day Jean died. Yolanda."

"How do you know about Yolanda being there?" Rina asked.

"Oh, when she finished locking up, she took the keys round the neighbours. I do their garden too; they thought it was really off, leaving a young woman like that to look after a dead body. The colonel wanted to complain to somebody, I suggested he try the chief constable," Sandy sounded amused at the idea. "When she called to ask me about this Sarah Fredericks I asked her if she was the girl that had been at Jean's place when she died and she said she was. We . . . er . . . talked about plants for a bit."

"And so you went round and removed the more unusual ones, then," Rina asked.

Sandy's laughter echoed down the phone. "That part of the garden was strictly Jean's domain. My responsibilities ended on the other side of the shed and it says as much in my contract. Jean liked to have a clear contract for everything and everyone, and frankly I'm quite grateful for that in this case. Jean never had much time for what she saw as stupid rules," he said.

"How much could she still manage to do for herself?" Rina asked, remembering the little patch of garden behind the shed and wondering if she quite believed Sandy.

"The bit behind the shed was mostly raised beds. I put some in other parts of the garden too, so she could perch on the side and do a bit of weeding. She still liked to plant stuff so I'd found this long extendable planter thing, so she could make the holes, drop the plant in, poke it around a bit, stay involved. So long as she took her time, she was able to do quite a bit. She hated getting old but she deserved a few more years of it, she really did."

Rina let him get back to work and turned her attention back to her computer. She had been looking for the picture that Ursula had described to her but could not find it. Wherever it was, no one had posted its likeness on the internet, so far as she could tell. So what had happened to it, where had it gone?

Something ate at Rina, concerning Sarah Fredericks, but she wasn't quite sure what it was. Having drawn a blank with the picture she turned her attention to looking for the woman and for Constance Fredericks nee Tatum. A bit of searching brought up the funeral notice; it didn't really say very much. The service at the local crematorium, beloved mother of Sarah, sister to William . . . Now that was unusual, Rina thought to mention somebody who was long dead and considering she had spent practically all her adult life avoiding being a Tatum, why mention it now.

Rina searched further, finding nothing of significance. It seemed that Sarah Fredericks and her mother had never done anything of sufficient interest that even made the local news. She switched her search to Miles Cunningham, assuming that as the murders happened pre-internet she would just find later rehashing of old information and in part that was true. There was mention of the books that had been written at the time and also of Clive Tatum's memoir and now some reports of Clive Tatum's death, Rina noting that presently, in the local news at any rate, protests against yet another new supermarket seemed to be grabbing the headlines rather than the sudden death of an ex-journalist.

She found articles about the novel that was being written, based on the Cunningham murders. And the legal challenge that Sarah Fredericks had been bringing which seem initially to be based around the idea of defamation. As she read further, it seemed that Constance Tatum and then her daughter had eventually seemed more concerned with the fact that someone else was making money from a situation with which they had been intimately involved. In which they had lost a brother and an uncle. Constance Tatum or Constance Fredericks, as she had become, was still pursuing compensation for her brother's death up to the time she died. Some things could become a lifelong obsession and it seemed this was one of them.

Rina found that she was getting quite depressed by it all and she was about to give up and call a halt for the day when an email alert popped up from Joy.

"We thought you might find this interesting," Joy had written and there was a link to a magazine article.

The article referenced a book written in 1994. The volume mentioned was a book on murder houses; Rina was familiar with the genre, people writing about the sites of famous or infamous killings. She had always associated it with a kind of specialist tourism like the Jack the Ripper tours in London. There were always, she thought, people who were curious about where unfortunate events had taken place and she supposed, in all honesty, she might be one of them, though she generally preferred her historical murders to be really historical rather than living memory. This particular book seemed to be about houses in the south of England that had been the scene of violent crime and was part of a series, based on different areas of the country. The article mentioned the Cunningham house and the fact that this prime piece of real estate was still empty, unsold, left to nature even ten years after the murders had taken place. In the more recent article about hauntings and local dramas, the Cunningham house was only mentioned in passing.

"In 1994 the author, S A Freer, reported that a grey lady, ubiquitous but popular with ghost hunters, was seen on several occasions. At other times the figure of a man standing

*with two children could be glimpsed standing outside where
the front door was believed to be. The site was not sold on
until 2002 when it was finally redeveloped. A block of ten
flats now stands where the Cunningham house once stood,
together with parking for the residents. We could find no
further mention of ghosts."*

This story had to have influenced Jean's painting,
Rina thought. Which meant that she must still have been
keeping a close enough eye on what went on, related to the
Cunningham murders and their aftermath, for her to have
been aware of stories and perhaps even of the original book.
Was there a grey lady in the painting? No one had mentioned
one. But why paint the ghost of a murderer and two children.

And surely the Cunninghams had three children.

Rina gave up. As Sandy had said, you could rarely get
any kind of insight into what Jean was thinking. The whole
point of her art was that it was tricksy and deceptive, inviting
the viewer to create their own interpretation of what at first
might look like straightforward pictures.

More because it was annoying her than because she
thought it might be useful, Rina called Mac and told him
what Joy had found.

"Yolanda actually managed to get hold of a print of the
picture," Mac told her. "It seems that Jean entrusted one to
Walter Heath because he was dealing with the recipient of
the painting, our elusive Sarah Fredericks. Ursula was right
about the subject matter; a man that looks like Cunningham
and two children, standing outside what was definitely the
Cunningham residence, complete with blue hydrangea. We
think the children might represent Constance and William."

"The so-called ghosts, if the reports are right," Rina
mused. "Jean has to have heard the rumours. The subject
matter seems, well, odd, to say the least, for a painting
intended for William Tatum's niece."

"I know, we're still trying to work that one out. Was she
being deliberately provocative?"

"Knowing Jean, quite probably."

"I'll get Yolanda to email you a copy over just to satisfy your curiosity. And Rina, I'm looking at the picture now, Yolanda has just enlarged it for me and there is a grey lady. It's subtle, but there is a woman looking out of one of the upstairs windows. What do you make of that?"

"I don't think Jean Hammond was the kind of woman who believed in ghosts," Rina told him. "But she was the kind of woman who believed in making a point. And I'm presuming Sarah Fredericks would know what point she was trying to make, because I'm buggered if I do."

* * *

Sarah drove to where she had parked her van. She'd moved it around quite a bit, parking in different places, checking for CCTV cameras, always parking her car — what had been her mother's car — a street away and approaching on foot. Caution was inbuilt into Sarah's personality, caution and fear, though this last week or so the fear had diminished. Nothing really mattered now. Who could hurt her now her mother was gone?

Sitting in the drivers' seat she mentally inventoried the contents of Jean's studio, now crammed in the back of the van. She had really wanted to set the whole place on fire but had been concerned about the blaze being seen. The nearest neighbours were some little distance away down a narrow lane, but a blaze of the magnitude Sarah had envisaged might well have raised the alarm.

No, she had been right to take this stuff away, get it out into the open somewhere, deal with it where the blaze would catch quickly and that hated woman's life be consumed and cleansed.

Sarah drew a deep breath, anticipation and pleasure swelling inside her. Paper and canvas and paints, all would burn well and, she thought, she knew just the place for it to happen.

CHAPTER 30

Donald Nelson had been farming for all of his adult life and could not imagine doing anything else. A public footpath ran across his farm and over the years and with the cooperation of the local rambling groups and local authorities, Nelson had eased the path from the middle of one of his fields to across by the hedge. He had installed new gates and stiles and generally had no trouble with the locals who used the path regularly or the tourists who, in the summer months, usually found it by accident. The tourists were often put off by the cattle in the field and large signs warning them to keep their dogs on a lead, alongside the more humorous but pointed reminder that he would not be responsible if the dog got loose and the cow happened to sit on it.

In the last ten years he'd had two incidents where tourists had failed to take note of the signage and dogs had come off badly. One had been injured by a protective mother and one had been shot by Nelson himself when the dog attacked a calf, tearing at its legs and throat and injuring it so badly the vet had to put it down. Nelson had even more trouble with the fly tippers, a problem exacerbated during the pandemic but which hadn't seemed to get much better since all of the council tips reopened. Three times in the last year he'd had to call the local council and the police to get incidents investigated when inconsiderate bastards had pulled into the gap beside the five barred gate and strew their waste all over the verge, but this time was beyond everything.

Donald Nelson had been crossing his cow field heading back towards the road when he saw the van draw up and he knew exactly what was about to happen. Nelson and his two dogs broke into a run, certain that they probably couldn't reach the vehicle in time to stop the dumping taking place, but hopeful that he might actually get a registration number. He had seen these vile nuisances in action before and they were bloody quick. He could see a person chucking black bags out of the back of the van, and other stuff not wrapped up, but couldn't make out what it was. Briefly as he crossed into the second field and clambered over the stile, he lost sight of both van and individual, but they came back into view as he raced across the second field and towards the five barred gate, where the van was pulled up. The dogs were barking now and Nelson shouting which in hindsight was probably not the best thing to have done because the figure heard them, saw them, leapt into the van and accelerated away. It was only when he reached the gate that Nelson realised that whoever it was, not content with just dumping their rubbish, had actually set it ablaze.

"Damn and buggery," Nelson was incandescent now, flinging open the gate, dogs in tow. The bigger of the two seemed intent on chasing the van down the road before Nelson called it back. The number plate was mud coated and he could make out only three characters. He already had his mobile phone in his hand and he took a photograph of the swiftly receding vehicle, hoping that something in the picture would help the police. Then he spun around proceeded to stamp frantically at the flames licking at the stack of paper and rags. He kicked out at one of the bags on the verge and heard the chink of bottles. What the hell?

Instinct made him grab for the bag and pull it aside, out of reach of the flames. He stamped down again, blessing the thick leather of his boots but anxious that he wouldn't be able to bring the blaze under control before it spread.

"Out of it," he yelled at the dogs, who seemed intent on helping him. They backed off, milling excitedly, yapping and barking at the unexpected sights and smells. It was only after several minutes of frantic stamping and kicking, and worryingly hot boots that Nelson was finally satisfied he had quelled the fire.

Angrily he kicked out at the bag of bottles. It chinked again and a smell he half recognised rose up, cutting through the scent of burning paper and smoke. He drew back his foot to kick again and then paused, bent to look at what was in the bag. Thinners, turpentine, oils with names he did not recognise. Cursing loudly, Nelson pulled the bag further away from the still hot ground, his body reacting with relief that he had instinctively pulled this bag away from the flames.

Even a quick glance at the rest told Nelson there was something odd about this load of rubbish. There were pictures and picture frames and drawings and, where the bags were splitting he could make out paints and his thoughts immediately went to the artist that had been found dead, just a couple of miles from his farm. There had been local rumours that her place had been stripped out and then fresher rumours that she was going to be exhumed and she might not actually have died of a heart attack. A little more prodding and poking made him even more certain that this might indeed have something to do with Jean Hammond. She was something of a local celebrity and even Nelson, not really interested in art, knew a bit about her and the art books bursting out of one of the bags certainly looked expensive.

He knelt down, flicked open one of the covers and his suspicions were confirmed. Jean's name was inscribed on the flyleaf and on a second that he looked at.

Donald Nelson swore again. He called the dogs to heel and then he called the police and it occurred to him as he spoke to the call handler that at least this time he wouldn't have to pay to have the rubbish cleared up.

* * *

238

Mac, Andy Nevins and Yolanda stood looking at the piles of rubbish lying at the entrance to the farm gate and Mac could see that Yolanda was genuinely upset. She had, as they had come to understand more about Jean Hammond's life and about the woman herself, become oddly fond of her and to see this old woman's life strewn so carelessly across the grass verge was distressing.

Mac had more pressing concerns though. "Storm's blowing in soon," Donald Nelson said.

Mac nodded. He should really get SOCO out here but, looking at the rapidly darkening sky, he could see that half this stuff would be ruined and any evidence destroyed should he leave it in situ. Glancing at his own car and at Andy's he figured they could pack this mess of bags and pictures and books and Lord alone knew what else into both and still just about see out of the rear windows. He made an executive decision. The Palisades was the closest secure location, that way if they did have to come back for a second load they might just beat the rain.

He told the young officers what he had decided. "I'll go and get the Landy," Nelson said, "she's parked just along the road" and Mac got the sense that he was just relieved to be able to hand off responsibility for this literal mess as easily as this.

Donning gloves, they began their task and Mac had reason to be glad when Nelson reappeared ten minutes later. The weather was closing in and it was becoming obvious that Mac had been overly optimistic about what they could actually get in the two cars.

He handed the farmer a pair of gloves and the packing resumed with careful haste.

"Sir," Yolanda was staring at the ground, an oddly excited look on her face. "Sir, I think these are the missing paintings."

"What?" Mac went over to where she stood and realised that she was probably correct. The dimensions and subject matter certainly fitted with the paintings missing from Jean Hammond's house.

"Get them in the Land Rover," he said, selecting the vehicle that was less packed. "Careful now," he added.

"Valuable are they?" Nelson asked curiously. "Well, well." He stacked the paintings as securely as he could atop the rubbish bags and books.

The car doors closed just as the rain began to fall, thick, wet and heavy as only summer storms could be, Mac thought.

Yolanda settled in the passenger seat. "Why steal her stuff just to dump it and destroy it? Doesn't the thief know just how much those pictures are worth?"

"It's possible," Mac said, "that whoever stole Miss Hammond's belongings has no means of fencing them."

Yolanda's expression told him she thought this was a stupid objection. "Then why take them? People steal for profit, don't they?"

"Or for revenge, or to prove a point, or because the impulse grabbed them or to misdirect. Many reasons."

Yolanda shook her head. "This just gets weirder," she said.

CHAPTER 31

The morning started with preliminary post-mortem results on Jean Hammond and Clive Tatum. Jean had a puncture wound at the base of her skull and there were still traces of morphine in her body. Death had been caused by a massive heart attack; the pathologist was of the opinion this could have killed her before the morphine, but it was, Mac thought, a moot point. Jean Hammond was still dead.

Clive Tatum had been stunned by a single blow to the head before oral morphine had been forced into his throat. Traces remained on his lips and the post-mortem suggested that he had choked as he inhaled the rest. Morphine or asphyxia or a combination of both had killed him.

"Constance Fredericks died of cancer during the pandemic," Mac mused. "So did she receive palliative care at home before she was taken into hospital?"

"One of mum's neighbours died during lockdown," Andy said. "He didn't want to go into hospital or the hospice because his family wouldn't be able to visit so they nursed him at home. Afterwards they still had a load of meds they didn't know what to do with and no one from the GP surgery was willing to come and get them. I took everything to the local chemist for them in the end."

"So, how much is she likely to have left," Mac wondered, now certain in his own mind that the culprit had to be Sarah Fredericks. "And what's she planning next."

* * *

Later that morning Andy drove along the coast to meet Sarah Fredericks' landlady. The local officer he had been due to meet had phoned to say he had been called away on another job and wasn't sure if he could make it, could Andy cope on his own. Feeling he had done his duty by letting the local constabulary know, Andy was quick to reassure his colleague that he would be fine. If he found anything of interest it was Mac or DI Kendall who would need to be told about it after all.

Sarah Fredericks had lived in a Victorian terraced house, one of the taller, three-storey varieties with a basement. Not unlike Rina Martin's home, Andy thought. It had long since been converted into flats and having been buzzed in, Andy stood in the hallway noting the red, blue and white tiles on the floor and the separate pigeonholes for residents' mail. The place looked neat and tidy and recently painted as was the landlady who came out to meet him. Neatly dressed and wearing a goodly amount of freshly applied makeup.

She occupied the ground floor flat, she explained, no one lived in the basement anymore, this had long since been converted to house utilities like the gas and electric meters and to be used for storage. Her own flat had a little garden outside. There was a tenant in the attic rooms and four more tenants on the floors beneath. Two occupied what were glorified bedsits so far as Andy could make out and two had slightly larger units comprising, as Sarah Fredericks's did, a small bedroom subdivided from what had been a larger space that now comprised a living room, kitchen space and a tiny bathroom with a shower. It had, Andy admitted, been quite cleverly done, with a good layout and it was clean and tidy and the kitchen equipment looked modern and cared for but it was still a very small space.

"How long has she lived here?" Andy asked as they both stood on the threshold peering in.

"Almost a year. She came here after her mother died and she sold the house. She's got a job at the local bank, some kind of customer advisor specialising in mortgages. She doesn't appear to be giving herself any advice," she said echoing what Andy was thinking. "But she must have found it hard to focus on anything with her mother being ill for so long and she didn't seem to want to keep the house. This was the first time she'd lived on her own so it must have felt strange."

"And she left a few weeks ago and not been back since?"

"Three, nearly four weeks. I mean she could have come in when I was out, and then left again, but we have a CCTV camera in the hall so I think I would have noticed. We had a bit of trouble a few years ago, people buzzing to be let in who didn't belong here and one of our tenants just admitting them willy-nilly. That tenant has now left, but we kept the camera up just as a security measure. I'm not going to say I go through the recordings every day, but I have a quick glance every now and again and I've not seen her."

A quick glance, Andy thought. *I'll bet it's more than that.* He nodded and wondered if it was worth asking for the recording.

"It records over after seven days of course," she said. "But you can take it if you want. I've got a backup hard drive I can put in."

"You sound very organised," Andy said.

"I do try. I suppose I should stay while you look around, in the tenant's interest you know," she said.

In her own, Andy thought. He shrugged. "If you like," he said. "Has she had any post since she went away?"

"If she has it will be in her pigeonhole in the hall. But she gets very little post. She gets very few visitors."

"But she does get visitors?"

"From time to time."

"And do you happen to know who they are?"

"Young man, I own the house, so long as they pay their rent on time, I don't pry into my tenants' concerns. I know

243

them to say hello to, and they know they can report any problems they have and I will deal with them quickly. Ask any of them; it's a testament that most of them stay for a long time, unless they cause trouble. I won't have trouble brought to my house."

The question, *why are you here*, hung on the air.

"Very admirable," Andy said and then wondered where that had come from. "As I said on the phone, this is just a welfare check. There are people concerned about where she is, especially knowing how grief stricken she was."

This earned him a sceptical look and Andy decided that perhaps he was laying things on a bit thick. He stepped into the room and started to poke around. There were few books on the shelves, not many ornaments, everything seemed quite utilitarian and sparse. There was a small desk under the window and a space where a computer might've sat but no computer. He opened the drawers, none of them were locked, and found paper, paper clips, general stationery and then tucked beneath a stack of envelopes a small thumb drive. There were also several notebooks and he took these out and laid them on the desk, flicked through. Then spotted something that had slipped to the back of the drawer. He reached carefully for the plastic syringe, placing it with the notebooks and thumb drive on the desk.

"There are some addresses in here I could check out," he said, his back still to the door. "I can give you a receipt. And I'll leave my card just in case Miss Fredericks comes back."

He was doing his best to sound casual as though this was pure routine. It was anything but. He slipped the books and other items into evidence bags and made a show of looking around the rest of the room then wrote a receipt and handed it with his card to the landlady. Mac needed to know about this — now.

CHAPTER 32

"Ursula, it is Ursula, isn't it?"

Ursula paused in the act of locking her car and turned to look at the speaker. It was not a woman she recognised. She looked middle-aged, neatly dressed in a blue skirt and cream blouse and a pale raincoat, even though the rain had stopped. It had poured down for most of the night, battering against the window of Ursula's little flat and reminding her of the way the rain, driven in off the sea, had lashed against the panes of her bedroom at Hill House.

When she had gone out to do her early Tuesday morning cleaning job it had still been drizzling. She had returned to her flat to pick up her college books and change her clothes.

Ursula could not place the woman. "I'm sorry, do I know you?"

"My name is Sarah. Sarah Fredericks."

She must have noticed Ursula's blank expression because she said, "I was a friend of Jean Hammond's. She didn't mention me then?"

"No," Ursula shook her head. "I'm sorry, I've never heard of you. But Jean had a lot of friends, so—"

The woman's head jerked back as though, Ursula thought, she had been punched. Or at least deeply offended. Not quite

245

sure what to make of the situation, alarm bells were nevertheless starting to ring. "You obviously know who I am," she said. "So you know I just cleaned for Miss Hammond. I'm not quite sure why you're here or how you found out where I live."

"Oh, I think you did more than that."

"What gives you that idea?" Genuinely anxious now, Ursula had taken several steps back which the woman had matched in coming forward.

"You'll have to excuse me, I've got to get to college," she said.

The woman advanced a little further. She was between Ursula and the door to the apartment block where she lived. Ursula calculated how easy it was going to be to get past this woman, how to get around her. Something primal warned her that she should not get too close, that she should keep more than arm's length between them.

"Jean talked about *you*. Jean *liked* you."

"And I liked her. She was a nice lady."

"Ha. What would you know about it? She lied and she cheated. She cheated me out of my inheritance, she lied about what happened to my uncle, she lied about who my father was. She made my mother suffer all her life. She got my uncle *killed*."

She lunged at Ursula who skittered backwards and away around the rear of the car, wondering now if she could unlock the car doors and shut herself inside. She decided not, this crazy lady, whoever she was, was far too close. Desperately Ursula looked up and down the street, still quiet at this time of the morning. Would anyone respond if she screamed, would anybody open the door if she hammered on one of them? Ursula really didn't know. Both she and George and other residents of the block had been on the receiving end of unkind and downright prejudiced comments from some of the neighbours, who had the attitude that kids in care must've done something to get themselves there, and were probably little better than criminals. Their very proximity brought the house prices down.

She glanced at the door to the apartment block wondering if she could get there and input the keycode before the woman reached her, her thoughts running fast, her legs feeling slow. "What the hell do you want? Jean did nothing to you, Jean wouldn't. What's it got to do with me anyway?"

They were circling Ursula's little car, the tiny Panda giving absolutely no protection. When the woman lunged forward again, Ursula began to run. A hundred yards away was the main road, there would be people, she had begun to scream anyway she realised and she couldn't seem to stop. The woman was grabbing at her, her hand catching at the strap of Ursula's bag, the bag worn cross-body and so the perfect restraint for her pursuer. Ursula twisted, ducking her head, pulling her arm back releasing herself from the strap. She managed to grab hold of the bag and pull it away from the woman's grasp, suddenly more angry than scared. What the fuck was this woman trying to do?

She saw what she thought was a knife blade in the woman's hand and then realised it was a syringe, felt it scratch the back of her wrist before she twisted away and took to her heels again.

At the end of the road a bus had stopped for the lights and Ursula powered towards it, the woman hot on the heels. She could see passengers turning to look at her and she hammered on the door trying to get the driver to open up. She could hear voices coming from inside the bus, shouts and warnings, some angry, some sounding sympathetic. When the woman grabbed hold of her hair, twisted it in her hand and pulled Ursula towards her, the syringe raised, Ursula screamed again, the loudest sound she had ever made in her life and to her profound relief the bus doors opened and hands were grabbing her, pulling her inside. Dimly, at the periphery of her vision, she saw somebody kick out at Sarah Fredericks who fell on to the pavement. Then the doors closed and there was nothing but questions. People demanding to know what was going on, people accusing her, people shouting about drugs and violence on the streets. Ursula curled into a tight little ball, protecting the head as though the words were blows and sobbing as though she would never be able to stop.

CHAPTER 33

Sarah sat in her car somehow unable to process what had just happened. The girl had got away. How had she allowed that to happen? How had that little slut defeated her?

She pulled up her sleeves and stared at the scars on her arms. Her whole body was covered in marks like this, some old, some newer a few . . . a very few from this past year. This past year there had been less need for punishment.

But now . . . two failures in a row. The idiot farmer who had run at her with his dogs and interrupted her before she had been certain that the fire had taken proper hold and now the girl.

A setback, that was all. She was stronger than this. She could overcome it, not like her mother who would have sat and wailed and whimpered and complained and then done nothing. Not like her. No, she hadn't finished yet, Sarah promised herself. She wasn't done.

* * *

The room was silent as the recording found on Jean's phone was played. It had been discovered in one of the black rubbish bags, piled in beside paints and brushes and thinners.

Andy remembered that when they had walked from Walter Heath's office, Ursula had mentioned it being in the drawer when she had collected her things from the studio and it seemed now that this was not accidental. Jean had intended this to be found. Presumably she had had the phone in her pocket or close by and had been able to activate the recording app.

The second voice was also female.

"How much does all this stuff cost."

"My paints?" Jean's voice. "Too much but I've developed my preferences over the years. It's a shame it won't all get used. Maybe you should take it, give it away to someone who can make use of it."

There was the sound of laughter. "You'd just love that, wouldn't you. The munificent gesture, isn't that just typical."

"Actually, yes I would. I do hate waste."

"What's to stop me trashing this stuff, what's to stop me pouring thinners over that painting?"

"Nothing. But I'd ask that you don't. It's intended for someone who has nothing to do with any of this. Vengeance should be targeted, don't you think?" There was a pause. "What I don't understand is why. If you're going to kill me, I should at least understand why."

"Oh, you know. You know all of this. You must have known when you painted that filthy picture."

"The picture was intended to help you. If you sold it, you'd have made a good deal of money. I painted it because it seemed appropriate. You, William, Miles Cunningham and the house. What could have been more appropriate? I still find it hard to believe that Miles Cunningham was your father. You clearly believe it, but what if Connie was making it up. Your mother was not the most truthful of people."

"She sounds breathless," Mac said.

"She was a woman with a heart condition and God knows what else," Stella Fullhurst commented. "Someone was threatening to kill her, the stress must've been unbelievable."

"My mother never lied about anything," the woman they assumed was Sarah Fredericks said, and there was no mistaking the fury in her voice.

"Look my dear, I have absolutely no doubt that your mother told you this and that that you believed it, but what evidence have you got? I find it hard to believe that Miles would have been interested, he was deeply in love with his wife. And frankly, compared to Betty, Constance was—"

"My mother was twice what she was. Miles Cunningham had an affair with my mother, he said he loved her, then he lied to everyone and we never had a penny from him."

"She's deliberately provoking her," Yolanda whispered.

"I think she wants to be certain that the truth comes out," Mac said.

"Miles was in prison; he was hardly in a position to give you anything even if he'd wanted to." Jean's tone was sharp.

"He could have acknowledged me! We wrote to him in prison. My mother made me write to him, send him letters and pictures and gifts, just like any child would do for their father. He could have done something. He could have written back but he didn't even open my letters. And now all these lies about my Uncle William. All these *lies*."

"You mean Clive Tatum's memoir? Clive was always looking for an angle. No one took him seriously, not back then and certainly not now."

"But they are, aren't they. His so-called memoir was published and now he's written a bloody novel. He's written it as a story. He's taken people's lives and he's written it as a story."

"And do you believe any of it, do you believe that your uncle William killed the Cunningham family? I think Clive Tatum's theory is that Miles caught him in the act and took his revenge, isn't that what Clive has written? Though you and I both know there might have been a very different scenario, don't we? Did your mother kill Miles's family? Did she do that, Sarah? Did she perhaps kill William when he tried to protect them?"

"No!" More of a wail than an actual word. "It was Miles, just Miles. You could have taken care of him. William adored you, that's what my mother told me. He even sent you his writing and his pictures. I bet you didn't even look at them. You didn't give a damn."

"I never gave William or anyone else the impression that I would take him in and look after him. It was never my intention. If I was kind to him, it was because I thought he deserved kindness."

"But you took in that other kid, Cal. You looked after him."

"Calvin was practically family already and now he *is* family. I loved his parents very much and I always promised that if anything happened to them, I would take care of him, and sadly when it did I kept my promise. And now my dear, I need to sit down. Kill me or not or whatever it is you've come here to do but get on with it and stop talking nonsense."

"You have no idea what my life has been like."

"I'm sure life with Constance was abominable. She was never a pleasant woman, not in my opinion anyway. But that you have suffered does not give you a free pass to persecute others. And we both know that neither Miles nor your uncle killed Betty and the Cunningham children. Miles came to realise that when it was too late." There was a pause, a sound as though Jean was catching her breath. "Your mother went to see him, claiming what we both know is nonsense, that you were his. He told her where to go. She killed them, didn't she, Sarah. She killed them."

"Lies, lies, all lies. Nothing you could prove. Nothing!"

"No. Nothing, we could prove." There was a gasp of pain and Jean said, "And now I do need to sit down."

There was the sound of what sounded like a chair being pulled across the wooden floor and another sound as though a drawer was being closed and then the recording ended. "There were a couple of stools over by the plan chests," Yolanda remembered. "It sounds like she took the opportunity to put the phone in the drawer when she sat down on one."

Mac could hear that she was close to tears.

"She accused Constance of killing the Cunninghams?" Stella sounded disbelieving. "Do you think that's even possible?"

Mac shrugged. At this point he was willing to consider anything.

The door opened and Andy Nevins came through. "How is she?" Mac asked.

"She's in bits but Ursula is going to be OK. Her hand got scratched with the syringe but that was all. There was no injection. CCTV picked up Sarah Fredericks running back down the road and getting into a car, a red Mini Cooper. It was registered to her mother. It was picked up again on the Honiton Road."

"So heading back towards the Frantham area," Mac said. Local CCTV coverage was not that great, he thought.

"Philip Goodman and his partner have gone off to stay with friends, and Walter Heath is at Rina's place for the moment, I took Ursula and George over there like you suggested."

Mac nodded. DI Kendall had arranged a high-profile police presence in the vicinity of Peverill Lodge.

"Well, it looks as though she's heading back our way," he said. "With luck and a following wind, CCTV or the ANPR system will pick her up somewhere before she can do any more damage."

"Why dump Jean's stuff by the field?" Yolanda asked. "Why try to burn everything? She must have known what the paintings were worth at least."

This was obviously still bothering her, Mac realised. The waste and the disrespect.

"And she probably wouldn't have had the means to sell them," Stella Fullhurst reminded them. "This is no criminal mastermind, this is just a very angry, very aggressive woman. From the look of the notebooks that Andy brought back from the flat, she's been brought up to be angry, trained her entire life to hate everyone and everything her mother told her to. And after her mother died and that memoir came out, things seem to come to a head. That was the match that lit the fuse."

"Seem to have," Mac agreed.

"And you've forgotten something," Stella went on. "She might have driven the mini away after attacking Ursula but that doesn't mean she's still driving it."

"The van," Mac nodded. "We know when she was fly tipping the contents of Jean Hammond's studio she was driving a van, unless she has an accomplice with a van, which is possible of course. And she must've used the van to empty the studio in the first place."

He replayed the CCTV footage of Sarah Fredericks running down the street in pursuit of Ursula. The camera had been close to the traffic lights but it clearly showed the pursuit as they approached the end of the street. The girl looking small and frail, her blonde hair streaming out behind her. Sarah Fredericks, tall and square and, despite her bulk and size, capable of quite a turn of speed. Her movements spoke of strength and power and she would have had no trouble emptying the studio, or carrying Jean across the garden and arranging her body beneath the willow tree. And as for Clive Tatum well he probably knew her, would probably have let her in to his home not imagining that she was there to kill him. Or she could easily have forced her way in, hence the broken jar and scattered books. And Christopher Hayes was an old man in bad health, and no contest and even the much younger Graham Jackson would have given her little trouble. No one was expecting this woman to attack them, to kill them, she would have had the advantage. Ursula had been lucky.

"What about Cal Hammond and his partner," he asked. They'd had some difficulty in tracking them both down as Cal's phone had been off and they didn't have a number for Etta.

"Both safe and in a local hotel," Andy told him.

At the moment Mac's phone began to ring. He listened. "Well, we now know where she was headed," he said. "Jean Hammond's house is on fire."

CHAPTER 34

Mac arrived at Rina's house just after seven. The fire brigade had the blaze under control but just how much of Jean
Hammond's beautiful home and studio was left he could
not guess.

He smelled of smoke and his skin felt gritty. He was very
much in need of tea and cake and, more than that, reassurance that everyone was OK.

He spoke briefly to the patrol stationed across the road
from Peverill Lodge. All was quiet though he was told two
other people had arrived at Peverill Lodge in the past hour
and from the description Mac guessed at Tim and Joy.

Rina must have seen his car and now stood in the open
doorway.

"How's Ursula doing?" Mac asked.

"Very shaken. Worried about work, worried about college, scared for Philip Goodman and Walter — though he's
fine; he's fallen asleep on the sofa. She could do with some
official reassurance."

"I'd have got here sooner but . . . well you've probably
heard about the fire."

"Much damage?"

"Hard to tell. Flames higher than the roof when I arrived but the fire brigade was amazing. It's all under control and they're just damping down."

Rina led the way into the large living room and a mug of tea was placed in Mac's hand. A mug, he noted, not a cup, a sure sign that Matthew was viewing the situation with sufficient gravity.

Ursula and George were squashed together in a large easy chair. George with a protective arm around Ursula's shoulders. They were both deathly pale, freckles standing out on George's skin.

Mac pulled up a footstool and settled beside them. He reached for Ursula's hand and gripped it tight. He had known this pair since they were barely into their teens and he found he was suddenly choked and appalled by the idea that he had almost lost one of them. He could barely speak and when he did it was little more than a croak. "Ursula, I'm so sorry—"

George interrupted him. "Have you caught her yet?"

"Not yet, no. But we will."

"She nearly killed Ursula."

"I know."

George closed his eyes and Ursula laid her head against his shoulder.

"You're safe here," Mac said. "There are police outside."

"And Fitch is coming," Ursula said. She sounded as though that reassured her more.

Mac almost laughed. "Of course, he is," he said. The idea that Bridie Duggan, Joy's mother, could leave her friends unprotected was a nonstarter. Fitch, once her husband's minder and now her fiancé would make anyone with violent intent think twice, even someone as seemingly deranged as Sarah Fredericks.

He squeezed Ursula's hand again and then, knowing there was nothing more he could say, took his mug into Rina's front room. Tim and Joy were seated by the fire. An extra chair had already been brought in for him.

"Ursula tells me Fitch is coming down," he said.

"And a couple of the doormen from the clubs," Joy told him. "You know what Mum's like."

Indeed, he did. He liked Bridie Duggan. For that matter, he'd had a grudging liking for Joy's father, for all that they'd been on opposite sides of the law.

"What's the woman playing at?" Joy asked. "What's all this for?"

"We're not certain yet," Mac told her. "But it's all connected to events that happened before she was even born. Now it's hard to see how it's going to end."

* * *

So far as Sarah was concerned, there was no end. She still had a long list in her head of people who had got in her way and got in her mother's way and who had taken what should have been theirs or prevented them from getting it or just denied the truth. Connie's truth. Sarah's truth . . .

She pulled the car on to a grass verge beside a small copse and she thought about that. Sarah's truth. What was that now? It was, she realised, quite simple really. She wanted the whole damn lot of them, named and nameless, to burn in hell.

CHAPTER 35

It was approaching nine in the evening but Andy, Yolanda and Stella Fullhurst were still at their desks at one end of the stable block, studying the notebooks Andy had found in Sarah Frederick's flat. The anger and the hatred poured off the page. Constance seemed to have an aphorism for any occasion and her daughter had written most of them down.

"*There is no one underserving of your hatred and contempt,*" Constance had told her child. The lesson, it seemed had been learned too well.

Later though, after Constance was dead, Sarah had allowed her own feelings to pour out on to the page.

> "*When other kids said their mum would kill them, they just meant they'd get a telling off. I could never be sure what she meant.*"
>
> "*She consumed my life. Burnt it up until all that was left was dust and ashes.*"

"You know," Yolanda said, "I don't think she was carrying on her mother's vendetta. Or at least she was but only in terms of trying to get money. The rest of it, I think she was trying to break free of her, to exorcise her somehow.

Maybe she thought by killing these other people she could, I don't know, claim her own space in the world." She paused, looked at Andy. "But what do I know. We both have great mothers, don't we? I mean, mine's a pain in the bum sometimes, always giving me advice and that, but I know I could go home and ask for help if I needed it and she'd make it OK, even though I'm strictly speaking an adult."

Andy nodded. "But not everyone who's had a bloody awful childhood goes round killing people," he said. "Look at George and Ursula."

"Oh, sure," Yolanda gestured airily. "But they had Rina."

"I must meet the famous Mrs Martin sometime," Stella said.

Andy grinned at her. "She still scares me," he admitted.

"She writes about the painting Jean did here," Stella said. "It looks like she went to Miss Hammond, demanding money. Jean seems to have told her that she owed nothing and certainly wasn't going to give her any money. '*All that she had would be passed on to that adopted kid of hers. Like he deserves any of it. What the fuck would I do with a frigging painting?*' She seems to have missed the point that Jean Hammond was creating a unique and valuable piece that she could easily sell on."

"And without diminishing Jean Hammond's estate at all," Andy added. "Mind you, it's a pretty spooky picture. Jean Hammond wasn't exactly being subtle, was she? It's like look at how freaky we all are, standing outside this haunted house. Would it sell?"

"For a great deal of money, I would think," Stella said. "Even a freaky Jean Hammond would be bought by a serious collector and, now she's dead, it's anyone's guess what it might be worth. You've got to wonder what Sarah Fredericks did with it."

"Well, I wouldn't want it on my wall," Yolanda said.

Andy sniffed. "Do you smell smoke?"

"It's probably just my jacket." Yolanda had briefly been out to the scene of Jean's house fire. She had carried a damp, smouldering scent back with her into the incident room.

"I don't think it is. My nose has got used to that."

From down the hall came the sharp, distinctive bleeping of a smoke detector.

Andy got up and peered out of the window. A glow, orange and fierce had climbed the wall at the end of the stable block. Others in the room were also starting to react to the scent of wood smoke that drifted in through the open office door.

"There's a fire!" Andy shouted. "End of the building."

As one, everyone got up and headed for the door. No one asked if Andy was sure, the memory of Jean Hammond's house going up in flames was too new for that. The space they had turned into their office was the second to last room in the stable block, a small, unfinished space being last in line. As Andy and the others filed out, it became obvious that the fire had been set against this end wall. Brushwood and debris piled in a loose and quickly assembled heap against the bricks had been set alight and as they looked, flames caught the loose pile of leaves and timber and builders' dustsheets and the fire leapt upwards, flames licking at the edge of the roofline.

"Oh my God," Yolanda exclaimed. "There's someone there."

A woman in a raincoat stood close to the flames. It was Sarah Fredericks, Andy realised. And she was laughing as she threw more fuel on to the ravenous blaze. A stack of paint tins and dustsheets and other debris left from the ongoing building work had been assembled close at hand ready to be consigned to the fire.

For mere seconds, though they seemed to stretch on for eternities of time, no one moved. Then Sarah Fredericks, her head thrown back, howled, a sound more like that of an injured dog than a human being, as she plunged her hand into the flames.

"*Don't just cut off the hand, cast it into the flames. Fire cleanses, Fire cleanses!*"

What the fuck! Andy was already moving. Beside him he sensed others running hard. Sarah Fredericks, raincoat now ablaze, whirled towards them, screaming and laughing as though she could no longer tell what was pain and what was fury.

He caught hold of her first, but only by a fraction, his momentum knocking the woman off balance but not bringing her to the ground. Someone else had grabbed her and together they felled her. The someone else, he realised, was Yolanda. She was beating at the flames, smothering them in her jacket. He grabbed a dustsheet from the pile Sarah had assembled, wrapped it around the woman now writhing on the ground, smothering the fire.

Andy heard someone shouting for water. He helped Yolanda drag Sarah Fredericks clear of the flames. He was dimly aware of the hiss of a fire extinguisher. Of the woman howling on the ground and others kneeling around her. Of Yolanda drawing him away, her hand on his shoulder, the ruined jacket grasped in her other hand.

Other officers ordering the injured woman to stay down.

"What the hell!" Andy said. "What the hell was she trying to do?"

"Roast us all?" Yolanda sounded tense and pained. "I think I've burnt my hands," she said. "I need to sit down."

CHAPTER 36

Sarah Fredericks lay in the hospital bed, swathed in bandages, sedated, administered fluids and painkillers via a drip while machines beeped and pulsed, and the sound of trolleys moving, voices, footsteps, passed by in the corridor.

Mac and Andy sat beside the bed. Both clean and scrubbed now and in clothes that did not smell of smoke. It seemed to Mac that Sarah still carried that furnace smell with her in her hair, on her skin and in her wounds.

She would survive, Andy and Yolanda had made certain of that by their quick actions. Yolanda's burns had been treated; Andy's less severe had left him sore and shaken but Mac had seen his relief when he'd understood that Yolanda was not seriously hurt. He'd be very surprised if the two of them did not get together in the very near future.

On the bed Sarah Fredericks stirred and opened her eyes, looked straight at Mac. He pulled his chair closer to the bed noting that Andy maintained his position closer to the door, out of the woman's eyeline. Andy, Mac felt, did not want to get any closer to this woman whose motives he did not understand and whose actions had endangered two young women he cared deeply for.

"Miss Fredericks," Mac said. "I understand you're not strong enough to be interviewed at this point, but I'm here to deliver an official caution and to tell you that you'll be charged with three counts of murder and at least one of attempted murder." He paused. "Miss Fredericks, do you understand what I'm saying?"

She laughed or at least made a croaking sound that approximated to it. "I'm not stupid," she said, her voice thick and hoarse, presumably, Mac thought, from the smoke inhalation.

Mac took a deep breath and recited the caution, reiterated the charges.

"Why didn't you let me burn," she asked him. "Fire cleanses, don't you know that?"

Mac studied the scars on the woman's bare arms. The doctors had told him that she was covered in these reminders, only her face and hands and feet escaping injury.

"Fire cleanses," he said slowly. "Was your mother trying to cleanse you, Sarah? Was that what she told you when she tortured you?"

"You know nothing about it," Sarah Fredericks said. "My mother was nothing compared to me. She did nothing compared to what I achieved."

"Achieved?" Mac queried. "You mean the people you killed?"

She closed her eyes and turned her face away from him and Mac suspected he would learn nothing more that night. He wondered if they ever would.

Though perhaps . . .

As he got up to leave, he asked quietly, "Are you certain you achieved so much more, Sarah? I mean, maybe you're not keeping count but by my reckoning your mother is still ahead. Betty Cunningham, the three children, her brother. That's five dead, isn't it, and a lot more lives destroyed because of it, including yours."

He heard Andy gasp; wondered if he'd overstepped the mark. Decided that he didn't really care.

The woman in the bed turned her head. The eyes opened, and they were so full of hatred and rage that it was all Mac could do not to step away. And then she was off the bed, pulling at the drips and the cables and the machinery and hurling herself at Mac, screaming loud enough to bring the nurses running and the constable posted outside the door racing to assist.

Mac grabbed her hands and held her tight, her strength shocking him, the hatred that twisted her face something he knew he would dream about for months to come. His relief, when he surrendered her to the staff, to Andy and the constable, was profound. He made no argument when they told him he should go.

"How could someone do that to their own kid," Andy asked as they left the hospital. "Those scars. No wonder she's so screwed up."

Mac nodded. There was not, he thought, a lot more that he could add to that assessment.

EPILOGUE

The email had arrived out of the blue. It seemed that Cal had contacted the recipients of *The Wedding Coat* and told them about Rina's curiosity. They had been kind enough to email a reply. Cal had also been wise enough to apologise again for his outburst regarding Ursula and had left something with Rina in recompense.

"I did some work for Jean years ago," the email read. "She wanted a special embroidered kimono for an exhibition opening and we became friends after that. *The Wedding Coat* she depicted is my own work. I wore it, and the red dress, for my wedding. My second. My first was to a very kind and lovely man and we adopted a child. The older woman in the painting is my mother and the girl in the blue dress is my daughter and yes, you are right, she's expecting her first baby. My second marriage is to a woman I have loved all my life but back when we first met it was harder to be true to yourself. Besides, I had a happy marriage and we had a wonderful child so I have few regrets. I was so sorry to hear about Jean. She really was one of a kind."

So, Rina thought, she had been right, Jean had loved these women. They had been her friends and the painting yet another — valuable — gift.

The doorbell announced Mac's arrival and Rina let him in.

"On your own?" he asked.

"For a little while. Eliza and Bethany have gone to a tea dance and Steven and Matthew are out shopping."

"And how is everyone?"

"As you'd expect. Shaken but recovering. How's Yolanda? Were the burns very bad?"

"No, she was lucky and very brave. The jacket came off badly though and she seems quite miffed about that. Apparently, it was new. Ursula . . . will Ursula be all right, do you think?"

"With time. Apparently, her aunt got in touch and said she should go and stay for a few days. But she and George are still intent on their camping trip and I think getting away from it all will do them good."

"You can't get away from your own fears though, can you?"

"Indeed not, but she'll have help whenever she needs it. Bridie Duggan's wedding is only a few weeks away. I hope you're prepared."

"Morning suit booked, we've just a gift to buy and that's foxing me, I've got to admit. Miriam says it should be something antique."

"Something antique is a good idea," Rina said. "And if it's something she can use, so much the better."

Mac nodded, settling into his chair. He looked bone weary, Rina thought. "What will happen to Sarah Fredericks?"

"Oh, I doubt she'll stand trial. My guess is she'll end up in a secure psychiatric unit."

"And did William Tatum kill anyone? Or was it really Miles? Or was it Constance? Mac, I don't know what to hope or think about that one. Either way it was a terrible deed."

"It's likely the murderer was Constance," he told her, explaining briefly about the conversation Jean had recorded and the reaction Sarah had exhibited when he had suggested this to her. "Constance Tatum was a very angry young woman."

Rina was genuinely shocked about Jean's recording. "I wouldn't have had that kind of self-control," Rina said. "To have the presence of mind to record the person come to kill you."

"No," Mac agreed, "neither would I. Jean was an extraordinary woman and I'm sorry we never got to meet."

* * *

A little later that afternoon Mac drove along the coast to Ursula's tiny flat. He was unsurprised to find George with her. They had both been asleep, he realised, curled up on Ursula's single bed. Both looked rumpled and exhausted.

"I've brought you something," he said and laid the book he had been carrying on the breakfast bar.

"What is it?" George asked suspiciously.

"It's one of Jean's sketch books," Ursula said.

"Courtesy of Cal Hammond, by way of apology," Mac said. "He dropped it off at Rina's. I've marked one of the pages. I think you'll like it."

Cautiously, Ursula opened the book and stared at the picture.

"That's beautiful," George said.

And it was. The sketch had caught Ursula in motion, almost as though she had turned to look at the artist, her eyes laughing and a smile just beginning. A happy, confident Ursula. The girl Jean had observed.

Later, when Mac had gone, George and Ursula walked down to a local charity shop, Ursula tightening her grip on his hand as they passed the traffic lights at the end of the road, and bought a photo frame. Carefully, Ursula cut the picture from the book and placed it in the frame. Jean Hammond would not have cared that this was a secondhand frame. She set it on the chest of drawers beside the photos of herself and George and of her family at Peverill Lodge and stepped back. "Three personal touches," she said wryly. "Not bad, George. Not bad at all."

THE END

THE JOFFE BOOKS STORY

We began in 2014 when Jasper agreed to publish his mum's much-rejected romance novel and it became a bestseller.

Since then we've grown into the largest independent publisher in the UK. We're extremely proud to publish some of the very best writers in the world, including Joy Ellis, Faith Martin, Caro Ramsay, Helen Forrester, Simon Brett and Robert Goddard. Everyone at Joffe Books loves reading and we never forget that it all begins with the magic of an author telling a story.

We are proud to publish talented first-time authors, as well as established writers whose books we love introducing to a new generation of readers.

We have been shortlisted for Independent Publisher of the Year at the British Book Awards three times, in 2020, 2021 and 2022, and for the Diversity and Inclusivity Award at the Independent Publishing Awards in 2022.

We built this company with your help, and we love to hear from you, so please email us about absolutely anything bookish at feedback@joffebooks.com

If you want to receive free books every Friday and hear about all our new releases, join our mailing list: www.joffebooks.com/contact

And when you tell your friends about us, just remember: it's pronounced Joffe as in coffee or toffee!

ALSO BY JANE ADAMS

RINA MARTIN MYSTERY SERIES
Book 1: MURDER ON SEA
Book 2: MURDER ON THE CLIFF
Book 3: MURDER ON THE BOAT
Book 4: MURDER ON THE BEACH
Book 5: MURDER AT THE COUNTRY HOUSE
Book 6: MURDER AT THE PUB
Book 7: MURDER ON THE FARM
Book 8: MURDER AT THE WILLOWS

MERROW & CLARKE
Book 1: SAFE

DETECTIVE MIKE CROFT SERIES
Book 1: THE GREENWAY
Book 2: THE SECRETS
Book 3: THEIR FINAL MOMENTS
Book 4: THE LIAR

DETECTIVE RAY FLOWERS SERIES
Book 1: THE APOTHECARY'S DAUGHTER
Book 2: THE UNWILLING SON
Book 3: THE DROWNING MEN
Book 4: THE SISTER'S TWIN

DETECTIVE ROZLYN PRIEST SERIES
Book 1: BURY ME DEEP

STANDALONE
THE OTHER WOMAN
THE WOMAN IN THE PAINTING
THEN SHE WAS DEAD